MARGARET FLETCHER: GALLOP GIRL
A Fall From Grace at Forty Miles an Hour

GENEVIEVE DUTIL

Editor: Elizabeth Hackett
Cover Design: Shane Eichacker
Cover Illustration: Libby Reed
First Edition Published January 2015

FOR DAN GREENBERGER

CONTENTS

1   Margaret on the Loose   1

2   Emily Meets Her Match   29

3   Margaret Learns to Gallop   40

4   Emily Gets to Clean Up   59

5   Emily Gets a Sweet Tooth   72

6   Emily Closes a Deal   84

7   Margaret Messes Up Her Hair   96

8   Emily Takes on a Challenge   117

9   Margaret Goes on a Shopping Spree   122

10   Emily Chickens Out   128

11   Margaret Falls on Her Ass   133

12   Emily Drops the Ball   148

13   Margaret Finds Her Winning Edge   151

14   More to Margaret Fletcher Than Meets the Eye   164

15   Margaret Gets Redemption   167

16   Emily Takes the High Ground   170

17	Margaret Forgets Who She Is	177
18	Emily is Fed Up	200
19	Margaret Girds Her Loins	204
20	Emily Sees How the Other Half Lives	223
21	Margaret Finds Herself in a Sticky Situation	228
22	Emily Makes a Scene	241
23	Margaret Meets Her Father for the First Time	247
24	Emily Meets her Spirit Guide	258
25	Margaret Trades in Her Crown	267
26	Emily Chickens Out	277
27	Margaret's Plan Comes Full Circle	285
28	Emily is on Her Way	301

ACKNOWLEDGMENTS

THANKS TO:
Jen Boulden, Shane Eichacker,
Hilary Galanoy, Dan Greenberger,
Elizabeth Hackett, Michelle Meghrouni,
Andrew Paley, Box of Chocolates
and,of course, KK Matty K.

CHAPTER 1
~ *Margaret on the loose* ~

Poise, class, confidence, fantastic thighs and an even better ass. The spoils of an equestrian lifestyle, ladies. Yes, it's glamorous. No, it's not easy. You WILL fall in the dirt. Your breeches WILL get dusty. But at the end of the day, there is nothing more beautiful than the picture of a graceful equestrienne atop her trusty steed. Effortless, elegant and always striking the perfect pose. But behind the scenes, her fancy custom boots don't always hold their shine. It takes consistently applied elbow grease to maintain the glow. As I look out at this crowd, I see a lot of dull, shapeless "horseback riders". It's going to take a strong elbow to shine up each and every one of you. So if you're ready to roll up your sleeves and do the work, then I, Margaret Fletcher, am ready to apply the grease.

I understand some of you here are new to horse showing. Personally, I don't understand how one can retain a position on an intercollegiate equestrian team without any practical experience. But our dean has informed me that the Edmonton College "riding club" is about having fun and making new friends, not competition. Well, I say, *"Riding a horse is NOT a gentle hobby, to be picked up and put down like a game of Solitaire. It is a grand passion. It seizes a person whole and, once it has done so, he will have to accept that his life will be radically changed."* — Ralph Waldo Emerson, circa a really long time ago.

I, Margaret Fletcher, am here to tell you that being a member of my intercollegiate equestrian team is NOT a gentle hobby. As captain in charge, I will seize you whole and, just like Emerson, I will not let go until every last one of you is radically changed. Change can be painful and some of you look pretty terrified right now. But believe me when I say that the day will come when you will look back on this moment and be just as horrified as I am by your decision to dress in a spaghetti strap tank top and "riding tights."

Moving on! In my experience, nine out of ten people will claim they know how to ride a horse. Most of these so-called equestrians have ridden once, perhaps twice in their lives. Five years ago, some gentle, half-blind rental animal nursing a hangover from a mild cocktail of tranquilizers carted some woman's butt around a trail and now the poor rube considers herself an expert. I have been told that description also fits the competence level of at least three quarters of this Edmonton College Equestrian

Team. Despite that dismal statistic, the dean expects that each and every one of you be given a chance to compete over the course of the semester.

There are three VERY DIFFERENT jumping disciplines. I want you all to listen closely to my descriptions of each, and then select which one you feel your "skills" — or whatever you call them — are best suited for. Take this part seriously, girls. Nothing defines a young equestrian's character better than what ring she competes in. And due to budget constraints, you only get to pick one discipline to specialize in this semester. I know this is terribly unfair. Believe me, I begged the dean to siphon off money from the football team or Physics Department or whatever to make up for the shortfall. I explained to him that real equestrians are supposed to compete in all three jumping disciplines at once. But I suppose nobody here is really a real equestrian anyway. So just pick one discipline and let's get this show on the road.

THE JUMPER

The "Jumper" jumps brightly-colored obstacles as fast and accurately as she can with little regard for personal appearance or equitation style. Her polo shirt may be tucked into her breeches, but you can't always count on her to put her hair up in a hairnet. And if you point out that her sloppy appearance is disrespectful to her horse, the judge and the sport itself, she'll probably go on a rant about how a well-coiffed "do" won't help her keep the jumps in the cup. Not all jumper riders are this difficult. But one can find enough of these ruffians to make the jumper ring unappealing to those of us with finer tastes.

THE HUNTER

The "Hunter" rider jumps beautifully-decorated obstacles (think elaborate flower boxes and charming wooden fences). She is dressed in well-coordinated outfits because simply "getting over the jump" is not sufficient. The challenge here is to present a pleasing picture of a well-tuned horse and rider combination jumping confidently in the countryside. This is the essence of equestrian elegance. And that is why they call those of us who participate Hunter Princesses. I'm sure some people (such as free-wheeling, hair-flying-all-over-the-place jumper riders) use the term in a derogatory fashion. But I, Margaret Fletcher, am proud to say that I wear the esteemed crown on top of my well-contained locks proudly.

THE EQUITATION RIDER

My heart is in the Hunters, I prove myself with the Jumpers, but the glamour is in the Equitation ring. Here, the rounds are judged on the performance of the rider, not the horse. This is where the country's top juniors ride their hearts out and deplete their parents' retirement funds, all with an eye on one prize: the McClay National Equitation Finals.

Of course, none of you have a shot at anything like that. But you should know that, in the equestrian world, winning the McClay Finals is like marrying the Queen. No matter how rich or well-known you were before, you were never Royalty. Now, overnight you are.

For the three or four real equestrians here that might be serious competitors, let me assure you I have what it takes to bring out the best in each one of you. I may only be a freshman, but I grew up riding with some of the best trainers on the Eastern seaboard. Yes, they sometimes sounded like drill sergeants. Arguably, their criticisms bordered on abusive. No, that rumor about Gordon Schroder throwing horse feces into the mouth of a yawning girl is NOT true. Well, mostly not true.

I may have lied to my father, ridiculed my mother and ignored my teachers. But I ALWAYS listened to my trainers. And I expect nothing less from all of you, even the scruffy ones who don't really belong here.

So be prompt, pay attention and never be the idiot trying to give me "tude". Screw up a distance to a fence in front of a judge? Be prepared to have your stirrups taken away for a week. Forget your hairnet at home? Well, you can forget about your lesson, too. Skip a lesson before a big show? Don't expect your horse to make it on the trailer.

In conclusion, I would like to say that the stereotype of the spoiled equestrian strutting around the barn, acting like a conservatively-dressed twit is not totally unfounded. But while these girls exist, they haven't earned their Hunter Princess stripes. At least not in my book. A real Hunter Princess doesn't treat her groom like the dirt he brushes off her horse's butt. After all, he is the first person to see your steed in the morning and the last one to tuck him in at night. You can scrub your horse all day, but he will never look as good as he does after your groom gives him a bath.

Bottom line: he polishes your boots before you trot into the arena. Earn your groom's respect and he might even scrub your soles.

The same is true for your fellow competitors. Snide comments meant to shake a pudgy girl's confidence only make you look worse than she does. Aren't we all just competing against ourselves in this sport? The Holy Grail isn't an eighty-cent blue ribbon. It's seeing that perfect distance to every fence on course. It's knowing when to open our horse's stride and when to take back. It's riding each and every one of our animals to his or her potential and making the whole thing look effortless. So go out there, grab your lesson pony and let's do this thing!

* * *

Edmonton College. Margaret Fletcher, what were you thinking? I only studied there because of its proximity to The Winter Equestrian Festival in Wellington, Florida. Besides, it was the only "college" willing to let me take my classes online and still be

Co-Captain of the Equestrian Team. (My dad donated the football field and Erica Lewis's grandmother donated the library, so we had to share. In hindsight, I should have pulled rank on Erica. She could have been Assistant Co-Captain, or Assistant to the Captain, or better yet Co-Assistant to the Captain. Who really uses the library anyway?)

I didn't make friends on the team, least of all with my Co-Assistant to the Captain, Erica Lewis. Imagine trying to present a united front with a woman who insists on changing the barn colors every other week. One week, it's navy blue with grey and burgundy accents. Then, out of the blue, Mommy Dearest Lewis can't stand the sight of burgundy. Two weeks later, everything is hunter green. Hunter green monogramming on hunter green wool? How is anyone supposed to be able to read that?

Fortunately for the team, I was focused on more important things and under my tutelage, they thrived. By the end of my junior year, we had three blue ribbon Championships. That's right, I can ride! From the moment I zip up my field boots, I'm all business. Do I crack under pressure? NEVER! Do I cry after a bad spill? NO WAY! Do I make my competition sweat? ABSOLUTELY!

So there I was, living in my ivory tower of self-confidence, when out of the blue, my parents announce that they're broke. The details of my father's risky investments gone bad didn't interest me. What's a mortgage-backed security anyway? I certainly haven't got a clue.

7

But the impact on my life was painfully clear. No more ponies. My Hunter. My Jumper. My Equitation horse. They were all sold before you can say the word "bankruptcy".

One would think that the top rider at a crappy college like Edmonton would have no problem grabbing a catch ride here and there. This is where making a friend or two would have helped. It's not my fault that nobody at this school could live up to my standards. I'm not inflexible. But stained breeches, halter tops and poop-splattered paddock boots are not OK! You may not be able to afford two thousand dollar custom boots, but all it takes is some good old-fashioned elbow grease to put a spit shine on whatever you find off the rack. Hairnets are cheap; belts are required; and brightly colored saddle pads are NOT appreciated. Wood shavings in your pony's tail? Not in my arena. Synthetic tack? That can't be comfortable. Is requiring matching tack trunk covers really that big a deal?

I wasn't surprised when the entire Edmonton Equestrian Team shunned me after my family lost their fortune. But did they have to kick me off the team?! Most of my "teammates" couldn't even afford custom boots, let alone ride a horse properly. So I don't understand why I had to go.

I remember it like it was yesterday. I was busy inspecting bridles in the tack room, trying to forget the look on Mother's face as the I.R.S hauled away her entire collection of rare Mediterranean skin creams. Before I had a chance to yell at Lisa Smith for

ONCE AGAIN neglecting to polish her bit properly, Erica Lewis barged in, bellowing, "FLETCHER, you've got five minutes to dust your butt with that anti-chafing powder crap you like so much before I BOOT your ASS out the door!"

I should have put up a fight. But Erica had a team of cronies by her side, backing her up. It seems turning a blind-eye when a sloppy teammate wants to wear full-seat breeches in the Hunter ring is an effective way to buy the loyalty of the easily corrupted.

So no, I wasn't surprised when the team gave me the boot. But I'll admit that I was a little rattled when Jeff, the Edmonton Equestrian Team's one and only heterosexual hottie (a rarity on the Circuit), dumped me for Erica Lewis. Jeff and I had been together since freshman year. I really thought we were in love. But I was just young, naive, and willing to let a cute guy in tight breeches take advantage of my good nature. I still cringe when I think of all the times I stroked his ego with my insincere praise. The guy really had no idea what he was doing on a horse. But time and time again, I made excuses for his sloppy equitation and let him ride my priceless ponies anyway.

When confronted with the fact that Jeff only wanted me for my horseflesh, I lost it. I'm talking bigger temper tantrum than the time I dumped an entire bottle of Show Sheen on my mother after she suggested that my new horse made me look fat. Margaret Fletcher has never been one to raise her voice in public. So you can imagine the shockwave

9

that rippled through the Edmonton Riders' Lounge when I caught Jeff seductively applying MY "Monkey Butt" anti-chafing powder to Erica's pointy little derriere. Decorum be damned. I screamed at the top of my lungs for everyone to hear, "GO AHEAD, ERICA! HE'S ALL YOURS! MY JUNIOR JUMPER PONY IS TWICE THE MAN THAT JEFF SLOANE WILL EVER BE ANYWAY!"

Erica didn't even have the decency to pull up her pants. She just smirked and reminded me, "I know, sweetie. That's why I bought him, your junior hunter, your equitation horse and everything else in your barn that I could get my hands on. Isn't that right, Jeff?" Jeff just looked at me like the slow, dumb animal he has always been. Margaret Fletcher is out and Erica Lewis is in. And there is nothing that my broke, chafed and scratchy ass can do about that now.

After Erica humiliated me in front of the very minds I was in charge of molding, I had no choice but to retreat from the team in shame. Erica celebrated my departure with brand new pink and chocolate brown wool coolers. Pink and chocolate brown? What is this? Barbie's Malibu Dream House?

* * *

Have you ever defined yourself entirely by one thing, only to have it yanked away? Graduating with a C average from a school nobody has ever heard of doesn't give one a whole lot of options in life. All it took was one look at Edmonton College's lackluster Alumni Association to know that I was screwed.

I never imagined I'd work for minimum wage. I was supposed to be on my way to glory. Instead, here I am, answering phones and greeting "patients" at a large animal clinic just outside of town. I live in a tiny one-room apartment just big enough to fit me and all my riding equipment from the old days. I don't have any friends, except for Sam, a cranky trainer's assistant from the two-bit thoroughbred farm down the road. Sam stops by every Tuesday morning to pick up meds for his Boss's horses. The process should only take about five minutes. But he always manages to sneak in at least one long-winded story about his good old days galloping for hire. My boss says that Sam suffered one too many concussions. Just ignore him. The old guy probably won't even notice.

It's advice I wish I had taken last Tuesday when Sam spent twenty minutes waxing nostalgic about the health benefits of a long afternoon spent sweating in some gross DIY sauna. "Just find the biggest pile of manure on the farm, dig a hole and climb on in. Those fancy European saunas can't touch the kinda heat a good mountain of fermenting horse shit can generate." He can't be serious. But the strong odor filling reception suggests otherwise.

Every once in a while, though, Sam comes up with a gem and I'm grateful that I have nothing better to do all day than sit and listen. "I was a jockey by the time I turned eighteen and a cripple by twenty one. And I'll tell you something, kid, I don't regret a thing. I spent three magnificent years on the backs of thoroughbreds and they taught me every life lesson worth learning. Number one: speak softly, but carry a big stick. Number two: a champion needs to have a heart bigger than the size of his brain. Number three: horses don't know what you paid for them. A horse only knows whether or not he's got what it takes. Believe me, kid, the ones that got it? They know. If you look real deep into their eyes, they'll tell you themselves. I got my best one that way. He ran like crap his first year on the track and was one bad race away from being sold as dog chow. But when I looked at him, I could hear him say, "Boss, I'm a champion. I've got it in my veins and it's beating in my heart. You've just got to let me run the way I want to run." So I got out of that colt's way and took him all the way to The Breeders' Cup. I never had to go to my crop once. He was an amazing creature. Not because of how fast he could run: because he did something no man or woman on God's great earth could do. He taught a young, cocky kid to shut up and listen. I thank him and every thoroughbred I ever sat on for making me the man I am today. Even the bastard that flipped on me."

I usually don't pay too close attention to Sam's stories. But I did this time. His words resonated like a thunderbolt. I AM capable of a lot more than just answering phones and booking appointments. A girl with my kind of organizational skills and joie de vivre should be running this place! I've got it in my veins; it's beating in my heart. I've got to make my boss understand that I have to run this place the way I want to run this place.

Not an easy task. He's a real control freak. You know the kind that insists everything be done his way and ONLY his way, so help you God. I suppose that would be all right if his way wasn't so sloppy and wasteful. Take a look at our file cabinets. Nothing inside them is from this decade. They're totally overgrown with yellowed fax paper circa 1995 and handwritten notes that should be donated to the poor penmanship Hall of Shame. And what's up with the unsightly pamphlets cluttering the reception area? I KNOW our clients would much rather peruse a fine coffee table book featuring photographs of fantasy farms from around the world than slog through Ten Signs Your Horse Has Laminites by Dr. Boring Who Carezzzes.

If Margaret Fletcher is anything, she is a woman of action. I have the blood of a Captain running through my veins, even if it's the blood of a disgraced former Co-Captain.

So, I formulate a plan. I'll need the office all to myself for at least three days. (Thank you, North Eastern Large Animal Vet Conference. Have a great time, everyone. Don't worry about a thing. You can count on me to hold down the fort.)

I've got the dumpster parked out back in less than an hour and the whole place cleaned out before you can say, "Wow, that's some ugly furniture." It's a lot of hard work. I recommend thinking twice before attempting to hoist ten metal filing cabinets filled with twenty-five years of paperwork into a dumpster. But it's worth it. The place looks clean and classy. I especially like the way my old Championship wool coolers hang behind the receptionist desk like plush, custom-made symbols of success. Dr. Boring Who Carezzzes might be a little taken aback at first. But when the dusts settles, I think he'll realize that he's finally got an office that any girl would be proud to bring her six-figure horse to for medical care.

I spend Wednesday evening celebrating the big promotion in my future. It's not every night I pop open a fresh bottle of lederbalsam and recondition my favorite saddle. Margaret Fletcher, Director of Operations. Has a nice ring to it, right?

So one can imagine my surprise when Dr. No Imagination calls me Monday morning to tell me to NEVER SET FOOT IN HIS OFFICE AGAIN!

I guess Sam feels bad about his role in this debacle (none of which would have happened if he hadn't insisted on prattling on about his old glory days galloping) and he drops by my apartment to return my wool coolers. He smells the lederbalsam fumes, takes one good look around and says, "Kid, you sure got a lot of plastic horses crammed into this tiny apartment. And what's that smell? Saddle soap and boot polish?"

I open a window and gently fan the fumes while Sam runs off at the mouth. "I don't know how you cleared ten metal filing cabinets filled with twenty five years of paperwork out of that office in three days. That was a dumb move. But it took a lot of strength and determination. I may have underestimated you."

The blast of fresh air pouring in from the window slaps me across the face like a cold, hard dose of reality. I'm broke, unemployed and I live in a tiny apartment filled with at least five hundred Breyer Horses. Twenty-two years of poise flies out the window and I turn into a blubbering puddle of pathetic. For the first time since this whole mess with Daddy's money started, Margaret Fletcher has a good cry.

Sam is not exactly the "touchy-feely" type. But he sits down beside me, swings his arm around my shoulder and gives me exactly the kind of advice a girl in my situation needs to hear. "I can see just by looking around this apartment that you have a passion for horses. So, if you want to be happy, you're going to have to find a way to be around them."

Ya think? Of course being around horses makes me happy. But I remind Sam that horses cost money and Margaret Fletcher doesn't have any.

"No, they don't cost money. Not if you're willing to put your life in their hands at forty miles an hour," Sam says with a twinkle in his eye. He tells me his boss is always looking for gutsy kids to gallop the young racehorses on the farm. Gallop Girls. The job doesn't pay much. But as Sam says, "Beggars can't be choosers. Take the opportunity and quit your whining."

Galloping racehorses is not something that I ever imagined would be a part of my equestrian story. But in the arms of a cranky old man and lost in a puddle of tears, the idea doesn't sound so crazy. It actually sounds perfect. Who cares what the job pays? I would be on a horse again, with the wind on my cheeks and a hairnet wrapped around my head. I thank Sam profusely and promise I won't let him down.

Margaret Fletcher is going to gallop racehorses and show the world that there's a lot more to this dethroned Hunter Princess than meets the eye!

* * *

The next morning I wake up, hung over from the polish fumes, the details of last night still fuzzy in my head. Did I really agree to gallop racehorses?

Suddenly, it all comes flooding back: losing my job, crying on the couch to Sam, agreeing to have lunch with my mother!

In the old days, having lunch with mother meant shrimp salad at the club. If I was lucky, Daddy would be playing golf with clients and I might get a glimpse of him for dessert. Nowadays? Mom makes gluten-free cucumber sandwiches in the kitchenette of my parent's two-bedroom condo, while Dad practices yoga in the living room.

Today, Daddy is nowhere to be seen. He's out with a client. I'm momentarily excited by the prospect of him returning to work and making us rich again. But Mother explains that Daddy's client is an elderly woman at the local nursing home who lacks the presence of mind to turn down a free yoga lesson performed by a has-been investment banker with no business encouraging anyone's body into unnatural shapes. Come to think of it, Gallop Girl sounds like a much saner gig than pro bono yoga instructor. Mother may just take this news better than I am anticipating.

But before I can finish, she starts screaming, "Gallop racehorses! No, Margaret! No! No! No!" Unfazed by the over-the-top outburst I've grown to expect from Mother, I remind her that I am not asking for permission. She tells me that's a good thing, "Because there is no way in hell I would ever give it to you!" Mother and I are once again stuck at an impasse.

Sitting in our familiar cold stony silence, I can feel the frustration radiate off her stiff, unmoving, cosmetically-enhanced features as they refuse (try as she might) to form a disapproving frown. When she tells me that my father is not going to approve of this, I can't help but wonder what suddenly makes her an expert on the things Daddy will or won't approve of. That marriage of theirs has been on the rocks ever since the Fletcher clan went belly up. Honestly, I think the only reason she hasn't left him is because he's someone to split the rent with. Mother is not cut out for this lower-middle – (oh let's be honest, lower) — class lifestyle that Daddy's forced her into. And I can feel the resentment percolating in her boney body every time they share a room.

I'm not exactly thrilled with our financial status, either. But I am beginning to see one positive in this otherwise completely crummy situation. For the first time in my entire adult life, I've got a Daddy that's available. Available to give me advice, encouragement and love whenever the mood strikes me. After years of being parented by a crazy woman with a cocktail, I look forward to developing a deeper relationship with the more stable side of my genetic make-up. It feels good to know that even though my new Zen Daddy can't support my love of horses financially, he might be up for supporting me spiritually.

I tell Mother that Daddy says I need to go out and grab life by the horns before the man has a chance to snatch it away from me. She snorts in derision and says, "Your father traded custom Italian suits for sweatpants made of marijuana. Maybe he's not a good candidate for career advice right now." (She does have a point there. That doesn't mean he can't be there for me emotionally. Give me a pep talk when I'm feeling insecure or a hug after a hard day at work.) But the second I suggest that Daddy might take an interest in my new profession, Mother squares her jaw tightly and looks at me with the kind of determination she usually reserves for a really good sample sale. A cold chill runs down my spine as she issues the warning, "Margaret, I forbid you from even mentioning this ridiculous idea of yours to your father. EVER!"

Try as she might, Mother doesn't always have the power to terrify. Growing up, I endured all kinds of grave warnings about what a youth spent riding in the sun will do to my skin or how my chances of finding a good man would be over if, God forbid, I end up bowlegged. Usually, Mother's warnings fail to register a blip on my radar. But there is something about the look in her eyes just now that gives me pause. The longer I stay quiet, the deeper the panic appears to grow on her otherwise-frozen face.

Before I have a chance to light one of Daddy's hemp sweatshirts on fire in hopes that the medicinal fumes might calm Mother down, she screams, "Margaret, you CANNOT tell your father that you are hanging out at racetracks like some kind of degenerate! He is under a lot of stress right now. He's fragile and I'm not sure our lives can handle ONE MORE CRACK!"

Before Mother has a chance to lay on any more guilt, Daddy walks in the front door, skin radiating with tranquility and spiritual enlightenment.

"Namaste, Cookie," he says, as if "Cookie" is a totally reasonable thing to call one's adult daughter or "Namaste" is a normal greeting for someone who used to handle the finances of millionaires. "Cookie, you seem a little stressed."

I assure him that I'm fine. But he insists that I'm not, and then starts talking a whole lot of garbage about the color of my aura. Learning how to interact with the new and improved Zen Daddy has had its fair share of awkward moments. This is a new one and I have no idea how to proceed.

Mother takes one look at my perplexed face and springs into action. "Oh, don't worry about Margaret, Snuffles. Why don't I make you one of those kale smoothies you like so much?"

I can't help but notice that Mother lowers her voice a few octaves and takes care not to make any sudden movements around Daddy. Seeing him in the harsh fluorescent kitchenette lighting and witnessing the preadolescent-like glee with which he accepts his new nickname "Snuffles", I realize that she's right. He's fragile now. I do my best to mimic my mother's calm demeanor before grabbing a couple gluten-free cucumber sandwiches and quietly slipping out. Maybe I will keep my unconventional news to myself. At least for a little while.

To be honest, the thought of galloping young thoroughbreds crushes my Zen, too. Am I really ready to fly around a track at a hundred miles an hour, dirt pelting me in the face, while a nervous trickle of urine soils my breeches? I KNOW I'm a good rider. But am I good enough to pilot a two year old heat-seeking missile that nobody bothered to install brakes on? The sad truth is, being the first girl to wear a hot pink jacket lining is the closest thing to real bravery one might encounter in the Hunter Princess world. But it has been years since I could claim that safe haven of high-end riding apparel as my own.

Bottom line: I can spend my life stuck in the past like my delusional mother or I can stop complaining and start doing.

Who knows, my aura might appreciate the face-lift.

* * *

20

From a distance, Winning Edge Farms looks like a reputable establishment. I see riders galloping on a well-groomed training track and nobody appears to be in immediate danger.

I have always believed that there is nothing more elegant than the sight of horse and rider moving together as one. But elegant isn't an adjective I would use to describe the riders at Winning Edge. I can't tell if these ruffians are men or women. What is up with all the boxy jeans and unflattering T-shirts? I have NEVER felt out of place in my Tailored Sportsmen breeches. But if one more androgynous humanoid gives me the stink-eye, I might regret ironing that crease down the center of my pant legs.

Oh dear. This one appears to be headed straight for me. I suppose I have some spare change on me somewhere. I fumble in my pockets. Nope.

S/he calls out, "You must be Margaret."

And you must be… a boy? A girl? A character from a community theater production of Oliver Twist?

Undeterred by my quizzical expression, she (I'm going to go with girl for now; I'm pretty sure those are breasts under that baggy T-shirt) gestures wildly and says, "Follow me."

Before I know what has hit me, I'm standing in the cramped living quarters of a dingy horse trailer with my Tailored Sportsmans down around my ankles. I'm hoping I got my gender identification right. I get one more sample of her voice as she informs me that, "People around here don't wear breeches. It's not a show barn." Yep, that's definitely feminine. Good thing. Getting molested by a male stranger in a substandard horse trailer is not how I want to start my Gallop Girl career.

I notice an inflatable mattress and rusted hotplate on the floor. Wait. Somebody actually lives here? The philanthropist in me wants to investigate this human tragedy further. But I'm suddenly distracted by the sensation of… maxi pads being taped to the inside of my shins? Maxi pads with wings and little butterflies embossed on the squishy part?!!! My shapeless little companion tells me, "The Boss has six horses for you to work today. Believe me, there's nothing worse than rubbing yourself raw with three more horses to go. On the off chance you decide to stick around, you'll want to buy a pair of leggings."

I reluctantly accept a baggy pair of jeans, a stained shirt and something resembling a Kevlar vest. Can you believe this woman has the nerve to toss my freshly polished field boots aside without inquiring if I have boot trees? She tells me that they're pretty, but fine leather like French baby calf won't last a week in these parts. She offers me a crusty, cracked, smelly pair of paddock boots, as if that's an acceptable solution to the problem of excessive wear and tear on one's boots. I feel totally violated.

But it's not until she has the nerve to reach for my hairnet that I lose my cool. I don't know what comes over me. Without warning, I haul off and clock that grabby little trailer hermit square in the jaw before she has a chance to misplace a hair on my well-coiffed head.

Margaret Fletcher has never before put fist to flesh. I am not the kind of girl who gets tangled up in a bar fight. My knuckles sting and my opponent doesn't appear weakened by my effort. In retrospect, I regret the outburst. Now I can only hope that Oliver Twist doesn't try to hit me back. But she just stands there and quietly mutters, "Wow."

I retrieve the belt from my Tailoreds, tuck my T-shirt into the waistband and break the stunned silence with a politely extended hand, "I apologize. I'm Margaret Fletcher. It's nice to meet you."

The startled look remains frozen on her face. She refuses to take my hand. "Did you just punch me in the face?" There is no avoiding the truth. We both know what I did. I do my best to look submissively apologetic as I regretfully nod my head.

My host takes another pause to digest the last three minutes of her life before cautiously extending her hand. "Emily Morris. I'll be honest. I was kind of expecting you to be an over-privileged joke with no hope of making it past your first ten minutes of trying to be a Gallop Girl. But anyone willing to defend herself like that, no matter how crappy the punch, has a slim chance of fitting in here."

I appreciate Emily's honesty, so I forgive her for covering me in tacky clothes. I even strike up a conversation on the way to the barns. She tells me about her big plans to become an Olympian in the rough and tumble equestrian sport of Three Day Eventing. She just needs to find that cheap off-the-track thoroughbred with a heart of gold to train up into an Olympic mount. It's all very sweet, so I kindly decide against crushing her dreams with realities gleaned from years of competing against those with an actual shot of making it to the Olympics. Where I come from, girls with those sorts of aspirations have competition budgets that require their wealthy families to take out second mortgages on their third and fourth homes. They don't ride horses that almost ended up in their Jack Russell's dinner bowl. They certainly don't call a horse trailer "home". Hell, I doubt they would even call Emily's horse trailer a horse trailer.

I've never been good at biting my tongue, so I'm grateful when we finally arrive at our destination. Two identical bay colts wait for us in the crossties. They both look pleasant enough. I've already survived the most terrifying wardrobe change of my life. I can handle this, right?

Emily goes over each horse with a fine-tooth comb, checking to make sure the bridles are properly buckled and the girths tightened just right before handing me the plain bay that will be my charge. I appreciate the efficient manner with which she completes these tasks. No muss, no fuss, I always say. "The Boss isn't around. He told me to tell you that if you survive today without getting dumped, you've got the job. I'm going to give you a leg up. When you get on, grab the yoke with one hand. Put your feet out in front of you and get your shoulders back. Be assertive and ready for anything. Remember, this isn't the hunters."

And with that, she shoves a crop in the back pocket of my jeans and throws me up on the horse. I'll admit it. I'm a little nervous. I have a feeling this young colt has a more exuberant definition of gallop than the overweight warmbloods I grew up riding. So when Emily says "All we're doing is jogging today," I'm relieved.

Emily ground mounts her horse with the grace of a ballet dancer. I dare say she looks elegant floating through the air in her early model Levi's and rough suede off-the-rack chaps with fringe on the side. Like a discount bin cowgirl doll that doesn't look cheap until you get up close and see the "Made in China" label.

Now properly mounted, we head in the direction of a large field just beyond the training track. Emily explains that the track tends to rile the horses up. Apparently, the anticipation of galloping their little hearts out is too exciting to take. "We're going to take it nice and easy today. Just a slow jog in the field," she says before instructing me to plant my knuckles in my horse's withers, get off his back and let him work.

The adrenaline from my little "mixed martial arts" moment is long gone, and worry starts to creep into the pit of my stomach. Am I really ready to die with heavy-flow butterfly embroidered maxi-pads glued to my shins? I remind myself that I've jumped five-foot fences. I've won national championships. Hell, I was the first girl in my barn to dare to wear rust breeches to a show! I can do this, right?

25

I'm still weighing the pros and cons of my situation when, without warning, Emily picks up the trot, prompting my horse to do the same. This leaves me no choice but to plant my knuckles in his withers, get off his back and let him work.

Ten minutes later, I'm starting to enjoy myself. Sure, endlessly trotting around a field like a carousel horse isn't exactly the thrill of nailing eight perfect fences in front of a tough judge. But I'm back on a horse. I've got the wind in my hair and a smile on my face.

Five horses later, my maxi pads are worn thin. So much for "all day protection". I'm exhausted. I'm not sure I've got enough energy to collect my Tailored Sportsmans from Emily's "apartment". But who am I kidding? I can't abandon my favorite pants in the trailer of unlikely dreams.

I have to say I'm surprised when Emily offers me a glass of tea. I had gotten the impression that she was hoping I wouldn't stick around. She pours the steaming refreshment from an electric kettle into a small glass jar with an old tomato sauce wrapper stuck to the side and says, "I read all about your junior career in back issues of The Chronicle. It was pretty impressive. But you're in for some culture shock here. Nobody is going to pamper you at Winning Edge. If you get hurt, you'll be expected to bandage yourself the best you can and get back on another horse."

Still awkwardly staring at the strange "cup" of tea in my hand, I assure Emily that I'm much tougher than I look. She snorts and tells me that I would barely knock out a butterfly with that crappy punch of mine. I see what's going on here. A rough-and-tumble eventer chick thinks she has me pegged a lightweight, simply because I have impeccable taste in clothes, polite manners and I don't drink tea served in repurposed marinara jars.

I reach into my polo shirt, exposing the pendant at the end of my eighteen carat gold necklace. I dangle it in front of Emily Morris's face and say, "Do you know what this is? This is my tooth. I lost it ten minutes before entering the ring at the biggest competition of my life. According to witnesses, someone's mother snapped a photo just as I was about to jump my last warm-up fence. As "luck" would have it, the flash hit the buckle on her own daughter's belt just right, temporarily blinding my mare and causing her to rear, just as I inclined my body forward in preparation for take-off. I lost my front tooth and blood splattered all over the jacket I had just imported from France."

I can tell by the dismissive look on Emily's face that she thinks this is a silly story about overpriced custom jackets. I suppose I can't blame her. She is just getting to know me. It's not always immediately apparent that there is more to Margaret Fletcher than meets the eye.

So I persist. "Everyone expected me to scratch. But one look at that "innocent" competitor's smug, self-satisfied face was all the encouragement I needed. I spit that tooth out into my trainer's palm and laid down the trip of a lifetime. Technically, I didn't win.

Nobody is going to give a national championship to the rider covered in blood. But everyone who was there knows I gave the best performance."

The dismissive look melts away. Clearly, Emily is impressed by my story, and a little grossed out by my necklace. I'm a little grossed out by her idea of proper tea-serving china, so I guess we're even. She smiles, "OK, you are officially forgiven for wearing a hairnet to the track. You can keep the jeans. I'll even give you my three most important Gallop Girl rules."

Emily has my attention at *rules*. There is nothing Margaret Fletcher respects more than strict adherence to rules, especially when it concerns one's conduct around horses. I listen closely as she continues, "Number one: don't attempt to stop a runaway horse by skiing on his face. He's bigger than you, stronger than you, and more determined than you. Your arms will turn to Jell-O long before he's through. Number two: don't be too proud to call for help when you're in trouble. Nobody likes a hero and you're a danger to others if you're out of control. Number three: you can't do this job safely if you're scared. The second you feel fear creeping in, it's time to quit."

With that, I am officially hired as a Gallop Girl at Winning Edge farms. I have no idea what I'm in for, but judging by my surroundings, I am pretty sure that my life is about to radically change. I stiffen my upper lip. Change doesn't always mean the dismantling of everything one holds dear. It's not like I'm in danger of living in a horse trailer. Right?

CHAPTER 2
~ *Emily meets her match* ~

There was no way for me to know just how completely Margaret Fletcher would disrupt my life when she first set foot on Winning Edge Farms. All Uncle Sam told me was to look out for a nice girl dressed in a pastel polo shirt and an Hermes belt. One look at the hairnet tightly wrapped around Princess's head and I knew that she did not belong here. To be honest, I strongly considered leaving her to wander around the barn aimlessly until the smell of hard work sent her packing.

But I had made a promise to Uncle Sam. So I did exactly as requested and threw her up on the kindest colt in the barn, fully expecting her to cry uncle before her foot hit the stirrup. Instead, Margaret Fletcher jogged that young horses like a pro. I had no choice but to welcome her to the Winning Edge family.

When I asked Sam where Margaret Fletcher came from, he said, "Where does anyone really come from? I found you a kindred spirit. Don't question your good fortune. Just open your heart to all the possibilities."

I know Uncle Sam has lost a lot of his marbles. But the idea that someone like Margaret Fletcher could be a kindred spirit is just plain crazy. I get that she's now poor and struggling to find a way to throw a leg over a horse like the rest of us plebs. Even so, qualities like guts, grit and determination don't just appear because Daddy's bank account disappeared. And nobody that wears a pair of fifteen hundred dollar custom field boots to her first day on the job has any idea what hard work looks, smells or feels like.

On the other hand, sacrifice and disappointment have pretty much been the defining characteristics of my formative years. For as long as I can remember, I have been obsessed with a sport that my single mother had no hope of helping me afford. I had to beg, borrow and steal my way onto the playing field. It wasn't easy and it wasn't always fun. But it's my passion and always has been. I haven't cared what brand of breeches I was wearing or how perfect my hair looked under my helmet. For me, it has always been about the horse and that amazing feeling that fills up your heart when they allow you to borrow their strength. By the looks of Margaret Fletcher and her flair for pageantry, that is not something we share.

I don't understand why she even wants this job in the first place. A quick search on the internet confirmed all my suspicions about her. Spoiled, pampered and over-privileged. It's written all over every glossy photo of Margaret winning National Championship after National Championship. Does she actually think that galloping at Winning Edge Farms is going be anything like competing on the A-Circuit? Sure, she can jog a young horse in a field. But thoroughbreds don't run on autopilot like those fancy horses she's used to riding. Sooner or later, that's going to catch up to her. I predict that Margaret Fletcher is in for a rude awaking. Because all those National Championships have her convinced that she is a really good rider. And I am willing to bet my favorite Crock-Pot that she's not. I don't mean to sound like I am itching for her to fail. I just know what it's like to have your entire world-view rearranged just when you're the most vulnerable. I can't help but feel that is exactly what is about to happen here.

I haven't always been so cynical. I remember when I thought that the world was at my feet and an Olympic gold medal in my future. On my eighteenth birthday, Uncle Sam gave me an off-the-track thoroughbred he bought for a dollar. He said, "Horses can be a real pain in the ass. They'll make you broke, they'll make you cry and bust you up until you can hardly walk on your own. Congratulations, you're a woman now."

For the first time in my life, I felt like I finally had what I needed to succeed in the sport that has always been my destiny. I emailed every superstar trainer I had ever heard of, asking for an opportunity to work in exchange for the kind of riding education a girl like me could never afford.

When Kim Sullivan — three-time Olympian and owner of one of the most successful sales barns on the East Coast — agreed to take me in, it was a dream come true. I finally had everything worked out. A plum position at a top Three Day Eventing barn, a promising prospect of my own and four thousand dollars earned braiding horses for rich kids in my pocket. Never in my life was I more prepared to drink in every bit of wisdom that this situation was sure to offer me.

And then I met Kim Sullivan, the tiny blonde drill sergeant who was about to change everything. Little did I know, I would have been better off joining the Army.

* * *

My day starts at six AM sharp. You are expected to muck all thirty-five of my stalls before feeding my horses breakfast. You need to know which one of my horses gets grain and what meds, if any. Careful attention to my horses' nutrition is the cornerstone of my program. I also need you to groom my horses, tack my horses, and cool my horses in the morning. I ride between six and eight a day, so this process needs to run smoothly. My working students are the key to making sure my day runs smoothly. Next, I'll need you to feed my horses lunch and prepare the nighttime grain. You must also go over every one of my horses that I worked in the morning with a fine-tooth comb. Wrap my horses' legs, bandage my horses' boo boos, and rub each of my horses until I can see my reflection in my horses' coats. Can you handle it?

It's three hours into my first day at Sullivan Farms and Kim has not stopped talking once. Not even a brief pause long enough to take a breath. How is she not turning blue? A forty-minute lecture on how to property clean tack is followed by a half-hour presentation about various weather conditions and their corresponding blanketing schedules. Forget the notebook and pen. Tacking up, un-tacking, warming up, cooling down, setting up fences, taking down fences, blanketing, un-blanketing, re-blanketing, it's all covered in twelve volumes of how-to books titled <u>My Working Students, My life</u> by Kim Sullivan. Seriously, the Encyclopedia Britannica would be impressed.

Did I mention that this job of endless chores, half of which I've already forgotten, doesn't actually pay? Because it doesn't. Not a dime. In exchange for a bottomless pit of slave labor, I get one stall for my horse and a cot in the hayloft. I was told that I would also get lessons from Her Majesty, Queen of Over-Blanketing. But how could I possibly fit a lesson into the schedule? Or a part time job, for that matter. Careful attention to my nutrition is the cornerstone of my program. Last I checked, a girl can't feed herself with a stall and a cot in the hayloft. Oh, God. Can this woman actually read my mind? Probably. Because seconds after I have that thought, she says, "A lot of my working students come here expecting to get a part time job to cover expenses. Those that actually manage to find one don't end up staying very long."

The pit in my stomach tells me to walk away. Kim Sullivan is scary and the job sounds impossible.

But I don't walk away. I want to be a top international competitor like her. I want it so badly it hurts. So I move myself, my project horse and every penny of my savings into Sullivan Farm. The plan is to take that young thoroughbred from green bean to respectable amateur-friendly event horse. Re-sell said thoroughbred for a tidy profit at the end of the season, and use the money to buy myself a nice prospect to take up the levels all the way to the Olympics. I've got the skills to give a young horse a solid foundation, and working at Sullivan Farm will give me connections to wealthy amateurs willing to drop five figures for that reliable novice packer. I feel that even though this sounds crazy, it's going to work.

Unfortunately, I am wrong.

I knew Kim was tough. I expected the hours to be long and the process of retraining an ex-racehorse to be a little bumpy. I did NOT expect to waste three months of MY life and every penny of MY savings slaving for a crazy woman while patiently waiting for an abscess to pop on the four year old hay burner who has yet to leave the farm for one competition!

In short, I ran out of money.

Of course, Kim did not want to see me go. At the mere suggestion she squealed, "My tack has never been so clean and my barn so organized. You can't leave my operation now. I need you!" But no amount of whining was going to change the fact that I had forty dollars to my name, no source of income and an animal that insisted on getting new shoes every six weeks.

I should have known Kim Sullivan would see my misfortune as an opportunity to feather her own nest. When she "graciously" offered to take the horse I could no longer afford off my hands for a thousand bucks, I should have been suspicious. But I was broke, cold and hungry. An easy target. So I said yes, and then cried like a baby when she sold that horse five days later for fifteen grand.

Needless to say, the experience left me shattered. All of my illusions about the nobility of equestrian Olympians gone. For good.

Good old Uncle Sam said, "That woman sounds like a fruit loop. You need to spend some time with people fortified with actual nutritional value. Don't worry, I know a guy."

And that's how I got my job at Winning Edge Farms.

Sam, the assistant trainer at the farm, convinced his boss to take a chance on a kid with more guts than sense. He also wasn't about to let me give up on my dreams so easily. So he swung a deal to let me live out of my trailer on the property so I could save money for future Olympic prospects. Sounds great, right? Well, it's three years later. I've bought and sold six young horses. None of them have taken me any closer to my dreams. I'm about to give up.

And then, out-of-the-blue, I get an email that throws a wrench into my whole situation.

From: Turtle Cumberbund (Turtle@CBFarms.com)
To: Emily Morris (eventer4life@ghostmail.com)
Re: Working Student Position

Dear Mrs. Morris;

Thank you for your interest in obtaining a working student position at my yard. I realize your inquiry is three years old. But honestly, I didn't think much of you as an applicant when you first inquired. I have recently found myself competing on your side of the pond and made the acquaintance of your former employer, Kim Sullivan. She seems like a wretched woman. But she caught my attention one particularly drunken night at the pub. She was screeching to no one in particular, "Why is it that in my entire career I have only been able to find one idiot competent enough to know how to properly oil a bridle? Emily Morris! Emily! I'm sorry. Come back."

Somewhere in the midst of my horror at her crude behavior, I felt a pang of recognition. Emily Morris? I believe that girl sent me an earnest little query letter some time back. Reminded me of myself, that poor girl: plucky, precocious and far too poor to have any shot of making it in the event world. Well, look at me now. So, if you've got it in you to scrape together enough money get yourself to England, I suppose I can offer you a cot in exchange for your servitude. I figure about twenty thousand U.S. dollars should cover your expenses for the year properly, maybe more if you would like to eat and whatnot. So start saving up!

I am prepared to offer you five lessons a week in exchange for a six-day workweek. Mondays will be your own to do what you wish, regardless of whatever havoc might be taking place around the barn. My well-rested working students are the secret to the success of my program. Your duties will be restricted to exercising horses and feeding them four square meals a day. If you prove yourself to be a competent-enough rider, I may provide you with opportunities to compete a few sale horses at my expense. Either way, it's a smashing opportunity. I've been told I know my way around a horse. And I'm sure I can teach you a thing or two.

* * *

My pupils are dilated, my heart is racing. My dreams of Olympic glory are coming rushing back to me like a long lost lover. I know I said that I no longer believe in the nobility of the equestrian Olympian. But Turtle Cumberbund is a completely different breed than all those other wannabes.

As the story goes, one day, when Turtle was still just a young girl riding feral ponies up and down the English countryside, her father gave her a crazy off-the-track thoroughbred that he'd won in a bet. Before long, Turtle was making waves at all the top Three Day Events in England. The people who saw her ride that horse cross country described it as "brilliance on the edge of disaster" — terrifying and exciting all at the same time. Soon, well-funded owners flocked to Turtle, desperate to buy her horses so they too could become part of the magic.

Turtle's story is the only reason a poor daughter of a single waitress (i.e. me) ever thought she had a real chance at the Olympics. Moving to England to ride with her would be nothing short of total fulfillment of my destiny. The only problem? I have no money, a five hundred dollar tab at the feed store and only one Pony Club prospect that could net me a cool three thousand dollars — if I could miraculously somehow sell him. That twenty thousand dollars might as well be twenty million dollars. There is no way I have any hope of cobbling together the funds I need to make this lifelong dream come true.

It's a bitter pill to swallow. Fortunately, I've gotten used to the taste of bitter pills in this life of mine.

But that doesn't mean I appreciate the timing of this latest heartbreak. Why does the universe wait until the exact moment when the grim consequences of my lack of available cash are at their most apparent to hand me a spoiled brat like Margaret Fletcher?

Please excuse me if I don't agree that she's some kind of kindred spirit. That's impossible. I'll help her at Winning Edge the best that I can. But I can't be responsible for whatever downfall is waiting for her at the gates of her new employer. Right now, I've got enough problems of my own.

CHAPTER 3
~ *Margret learns to gallop* ~

DAY ONE

Speaking of rules, Margaret Fletcher has never ridden in jeans and she's not going to start now. I'll do my best to fit in at Winning Edge Farms. But I am not going to lose myself in the process. So you can forget the maxi-pads, too. "Monkey Butt" powder has always done a bang-up job of solving my chafing problems. No need to start strapping overstuffed feminine hygiene products to body parts they were never designed for in the first place.

That's right. I'm riding in breeches and I'm putting my hair up in a hairnet. I don't care what the cool kids think!

Emily gives me six horses to jog. I'm still sore from yesterday, but I get the job done.

DAY TWO

I've got the jogging thing down. Word around Winning Edge is Princess Fancy Breeches can ride. Sometime around lap number sixty five, I catch my first glimpse of the Boss. I was expecting someone older, beer-bellied, with a lifetime of regret on his face. Not the Boss. He's young, energetic and has nothing short of flawless conformation. I catch myself feeling a pleasant tingle in my saddle area as he gallops past me at breakneck speed.

Oh my, it feels good to be back on a horse.

DAY THREE

Jogging, jogging, jogging and more jogging. I pass the time watching the Boss work horses out of the corner of my eye. I've always believed one should wear breeches when seated on a horse. But I can't help but notice the bulging thigh muscles straining against the worn denim of the Boss's pants as he jogs past me on the track. My position on the whole "jeans" issue is softening. Worn leather aside, that is one lucky saddle.

DAY FOUR

I slowly post up and down in my saddle as I causally jog past Mr. Hot Pants, trying to seduce him with the consistent rhythm of my motion. His horse crow-hops with frustration. But the Boss manages to keep the impatient colt in check the entire workout, staying just a few paces behind me and my spectacular beast. I can't help but feel that my well-toned derriere provided the motivation. Well done, Margaret. Well-done.

DAY FIVE

OK, Jogging Girl just does not sound as cool as Gallop Girl! When is Emily going to let me show her what I can do? Never, apparently. She only tells that me that I have to improve my upper body strength and asks if I have been doing my pull ups.

It all sounds like hogwash to me. Pull ups? I've ridden horses my entire life. I've trained with the best coaches this sport has to offer. Not once has anyone suggested I need to perform a single pull up.

I'm beginning to think Emily is holding me back. And don't think I haven't noticed that she has yet to introduce me to the Boss, who, by the way, is wearing a pair of perfectly molded lambskin chaps today. Swoon.

DAY SIX

Guess what? Emily has seven horses for me to jooooogggggg. Of course SHE gets to zip around the track at a full gallop, waving her fanny in front of the Boss like a baboon in heat searching for a mate. Not that the Boss is any kind of baboon. He's wearing a very smart polo shirt tucked into those tight little jeans he loves so much. A good old-fashioned Kentucky work-belt highlights his strong tree trunk of a waist, confirming my suspicions. The Boss does NOT have the squishy love handles that always made Jeff so hard to take seriously. Go ahead, Erica. He's all yours. Have a blast.

And then it hits me like a crappy punch delivered in a two-bit horse trailer: Emily is never going to let me gallop because she can't stand the competition. It looks like it's time to take matters into my own hands.

DAY SEVEN

One thing thirteen years on the A-Circuit will teach you is the importance of fitting in. Don't trot into the ring dressed like a Pony Clubber and expect to be a champion at Harrisburg. Conversely, don't show up at a scruffy racetrack barn dressed in quality breeches and expect to be taken seriously as a Gallop Girl. Determined to finally put the "gallop" in Gallop Girl, I strut into Winning Edge dressed in jeans, full chaps and a collarless T-shirt that says "Fearless Female". I walk right up to the Boss like I've known him my whole life, extend my hand and announce, "Margaret Fletcher. I don't know if you're aware, but you hired me to gallop your horses last week. Except that I have yet to be given an opportunity to actually gallop."

Clearly impressed by my pluck, an amused smile spreads across the Boss's handsome face. I can't believe I ever found a squishy, love handle-afflicted wimp like Jeff attractive. "Alright Margaret Fletcher, let's see what you can do. Hey, Liz, tack up Pruney."

Pruney? That doesn't sound like the kind of horse that will test the depths of one's skills. Pruney sounds like the kind of broken-down nag one keeps around so an idiot cousin who thinks she can ride doesn't kill herself on family visits.

The Boss flashes another smile and says, "I'll be right back, Princess." Princess? Clearly, this guy thinks he's dealing with a rube. But I can handle this. You have to know this happens to me all time. People take one look at my perfectly polished appearance and assume I'm some fancy boulangerie puff pastry. Well, I didn't appreciate it back in my days on the A-Circuit and I certainly don't appreciate it now. I can't wait to show the Boss what I'm made of. Except I have a feeling I might have trouble convincing good old Pruney into any kind gait resembling a gallop.

Fifteen minutes into my internal monologue, the Boss emerges from the barn with two large, athletic prancing animals. Pruney? The Boss hands me an agitated colt and asks, "Did Emily show you how to bridge your reins?" No, Emily showed me how to dress like a Dickensian orphan and tape maxi pads to my shins, that's it! The Boss gently cradles my calf in what has to be the most seductive leg-up I have ever received in my entire life. He takes care not to let his hand travel too far up my thigh as he pushes me into the saddle. But by the time he's finished, I feel a delicious, warm glow spread across my body and I'm pretty sure it has nothing to do with the extra layer of leggings I've got on underneath my jeans.

I try to give the Boss my full attention as he explains the finer points of galloping racehorses. He mounts a beast of his own and says, "See how I'm crossing my reins? Now you want to make a short, tight cross and push down on his neck. If you get in trouble, move the cross down lower to tighten up, then push down with your upper body weight to keep the cross in place. That way, you're using the strength of your whole body to hold the horse." I'm too distracted by the Boss's bulging biceps to absorb whatever it is he's trying to teach me. So when he turns to me and asks, "Ready to show me what you've got, Princess?" I actually have the guts to say, "I was born ready."

Unfortunately, it turns out that was just the T-shirt talking. I am NOT ready. The next few minutes are a blur. I'm bolting around the track at what must be eight hundred miles an hour while the Boss, who somehow manages to keep pace with me, screams, "Relax! You're doing fine! Stop pulling so hard. You'll wear yourself out." I'm water skiing on this horse's face like it's the Fourth of July at some middle class waterpark. Sloppy equitation aside, it's the only thing preventing this fire-breathing dragon from taking me all the way to Texas. The Boss is doing his best to talk me through this terrifying situation. He screams at the top of his lungs, "Bury your hands in his neck and let him pull against himself!" But nothing he says makes any sense at forty miles an hour.

Emily, you were right. I haven't been doing my pull ups. My arms are turning into Jell-O and I'm pretty sure I'm going to die wearing this ridiculous T-shirt! "There you go, Princess. One more lap then we'll pull up." I want to scream, "How the hell do I pull this thing up?!" But I stopped breathing ten minutes ago and I need to conserve whatever oxygen is left in my body.

The Boss reads the panic on my face and bellows, "Use your whole body for leverage and hope the sucker stops. Otherwise, you're going to have to keep going until he gets tired."

I eventually pull that sucker up. I'll never forget the mixture of exhaustion and exhilaration coursing through my veins. My arms are throbbing; my heart is pounding; my mind is racing. The Boss and I hop off our mounts in tandem and hand them to a hot walker to cool out. It takes me a moment to catch my breath. My cheeks are flushed and my heart is pounding in my chest. When the Boss asks, "Well, Princess, what do you think?" all I can say is, "Wow."

The Boss laughs. I'm charmed by the crinkles gently forming at the corners of his eyes. Still bathing in the excitement of galloping my first racehorse, I could probably be seduced by a three hundred pound hairless monkey right now. So you can only imagine how a handsome man like the Boss is looking to my over-stimulated senses. Take a deep breath, Margaret. Getting involved in a romantic relationship with your boss is not appropriate.

With a mischievous look in his eye, the Boss asks if I want to do it again. So soon? I'm impressed. Should we try with you in front this time?

Ten minutes later, I find myself on the back of another young colt with the Boss once again mounted beside me. His sweaty polo shirt clings deliciously to his chest. I am still trying to catch my breath as he leans in to say, "This one is a little stronger than the last. But don't worry. You'll be fine. You just have to trust him. Let him go a little and believe that he won't take advantage of you and run away."

I look the Boss squarely in those beautiful blue eyes and say, "Isn't that what young studs do? Take advantage of you and then run away?"

He smiles. Crinkles spread around his baby blues and that's when I know I'm really in over my head here.

* * *

My workday at Winning Edge starts at five AM. I'm finished by noon and down for a little catnap two seconds after I walk through the front door.

Three hours later, I wake up screaming in agony. Did I break every bone in my body? I can't move. I'm not even sure I can breathe. Thank God my phone is within reach. Time to call Mother, the only person with keys to my apartment.

Twenty minutes later, she's at the door with a masseuse and five gallons of seaweed for him to rub onto my sore, unfortunately tanned body. "Margaret, you look absolutely terrible. What did they do to you? Sven, is there anything you can do about those tan lines on her arms?!"

Sven is strong enough to pick me up and put me on his massage table, while also being gay enough to take off my clothes without making me feel cheap. And then it begins. Mother starts criticizing, "Why are your hands so white and your forearms so brown? You look ridiculous!" As Sven begins the agonizing process of massaging my petrified muscles, my screams briefly drown Mother out. I come up for air in time to hear, "I can't imagine this new job of yours has anything in common with what you grew up with. Quite frankly, the whole thing sounds dangerous and unsavory." Yep, when it comes to criticizing my life choices, Mother is nothing if not persistent. "You're not going to meet anyone worth socializing with. Honestly, I doubt you'll meet anyone who isn't fresh out prison."

Trying to describe my love of horses to her has always has been a waste of a perfectly good attempt at conversation. We have a script. Mother criticizes, complains and emotionally terrorizes me. I quietly endure it, because she has something I want. Years of experience have taught me that just when you think you've spent all the money on horses one could possibly spend, a good A-Circuit trainer will come up with something ELSE you need. A new competition horse to replace the one you just outgrew, a new practice horse to make sure you don't wear out the competition horse, another new competition horse because your last competition horse just isn't getting you into the ribbons as often as you should be. It goes on and on. And all of it is expensive. Growing up, I always needed my mother and her access to my father's money.

Mother attempts to raise an eyebrow for effect (no luck) and says, "You know I never understood your horse habit. But I let you persist because the outfits were cute and social connections worthwhile. But, Honey, I don't know if I can support this anymore."

And this is when it hits me like a two-by-four. My new horse habit isn't something that REQUIRES her support anymore. Back in the good old days, the prospect of being benched for even one weekend of horse showing had me jumping through hoops like a well-trained pup. But, racehorses give me something that show horses only took away from me:

Independence.

I don't know how I'm ever going to walk again, much less gallop racehorses. But deep in my heart (the only fully functioning muscle left in my body), I know that I have found my niche. For the first time since Daddy went broke, I'm looking forward to what life has to offer me.

I am just barely able to walk the morning after my Gallop Girl debut. I'm sure everyone is expecting Princess Fancy Breeches to call in sick today. (That's what everyone calls me, by the way. Princess Fancy Breeches. Liz, groom/hot-walker/pain in the ass extraordinaire, came up with the nickname after I explained that, no, I would not like to have lunch in the middle of a field when I have access to a perfectly clean picnic table that won't stain my breeches green. Had I known in advance the consequences of my actions, I might have sacrificed my Tailoreds for the cause of fitting in. But there is no point in living in the past.)

Liz and everyone else on the farm who calls me Princess Fancy Breeches watch me hobble to the Boss's office with a look of shock and awe. I overhear a couple of whispers. Wow, I had no idea that so many people were betting against my return. I'm a little hurt when Emily joins in on the chorus of naysayers. "Margaret, are you sure it's a good idea for you to ride today? You look like you're having a hard time carrying your own body weight."

What's the matter, Emily? Have you already run out of horses for me to JOG? You girls think you're so tough in your ugly jeans and sloppy ponytails. Well, let me tell you something. Until you have survived thirty minutes in an enclosed arena with sixty very determined Hunter Princesses strategically navigating their thirteen hundred pound German Warmbloods in front of the judge's box and emerged victorious, you don't know what the word "tough" means.

Here comes the Boss striding towards me like a well-muscled racehorse. All right, Margaret, shoulders back, tits up, look elegant. Ouch, on second thought, that hurts.

"Princess, I've got a really important job for you today. Find my saddle stretcher." That doesn't sound important. "I've got ten saddles to stretch and I can't put you up on a horse until that gets done." Maybe I'm underestimating the severity of the situation.

I don't realize just how important a job it is until Emily pulls me aside and tries to convince me that I'm not up for the task. "Margaret, you're not going to be able to find the saddle stretcher." Just like I'm not going to be able to gallop a baby? I like Emily. I really do. But don't think I haven't noticed her tendency to underestimate my abilities. I don't appreciate it. Not one bit. And I'm not afraid to put Little Miss Crusty Boots in her place.

"You know Emily," I say, "I thought poor girls were supposed to be different. But you're acting like a jealous little Hunter Princess stuck with last year's Hermes saddle." That came out a little harsher than I intended. But it has the desired effect and Emily backs off.

To be honest, I have no idea what a saddle stretcher looks like. I'm sure it's something I should be familiar with. I bet Emily would just love it if I confessed my ignorance. One more opportunity to make fun of the girl who grew up with a silver spoon in her mouth. I'm not falling into that trap. I'm sure I'll know what it is when I see it.

Three hours later, I'm still looking. A few of the exercise riders and grooms have taken pity on me. One of them even drew me a picture of what a saddle stretcher looks like. Maybe everyone at Winning Edge isn't so bad, even if they call me Princess Fancy Breeches and make fun of my hairnet.

Oh, there's Sam! I'm sure he'd be happy to help me find the Boss's saddle stretcher. One look at Sam's expression and I know I'm an idiot.

"Kid, you need to find the Boss and kick his ass for jerking your chain," Sam grunts, amused. That's right, there is no such thing as a saddle stretcher! I've been hobbling around Winning Edge like a cripple for the past three hours looking for a fictional piece of equipment and NOBODY took pity on the girl with a serious sunburn and giant bloody WELTS on the inside of her thighs.

There's the creep. Hey, Boss. I found your saddle stretcher. Now come over here so I can hit you over the head with it!

The sexy little bastard doesn't even have the decency to look remorseful. No, he looks amazing in the crisp navy blue windbreaker that is zipped down low enough to tickle a girl's imagination. He smiles. His eyes crinkle. And he says, "Princess, don't be mad. Everyone's got to put up with a little hazing around here." Hazing! Putting my underwear in the freezer is hazing. Making me wander aimlessly around the track for three hours when every bone in my body feels like it's broken is just plain cruel.

But when the Boss points out that it would have been much crueler to give me horses to gallop, I have to admit he has a point.

Then he offers to buy me a drink at some local jockey hangout called Shorty's. It's not exactly a date. But it's a start. Maybe this day wasn't a big waste, after all.

* * *

I should have been prepared for the broken peanut shells on the floor, the bad lighting and colorful characters. But I wasn't and once again I feel out of place for taking a shower. The Boss, Emily and a few other recognizables from the track are at the bar, eager to buy me a drink. So it's less a private meeting of two young able-bodied people interested in seeing where things might go and more of an after-work gathering. Fine, I'll have a Grand Marnier. Neat.

But the Boss has other plans. "Sorry, Princess, no old lady drinks. You're having a saddle stretcher. One part tequila in a shot glass." He slides some sort of pale brown liquid down the bar.

I take a breath and quaff it. Done. Swallowed. That was disgusting. Although, minutes later, I am enjoying a warm glow brewing inside my belly and everybody is starting to look a LOT more attractive.

The Boss raises his shot glass, commanding the attention of everyone in Shorty's, and says, "Princess, I know we gave you a hard time today. But tonight, we raise our glasses to you — or for you — because you're probably in too much pain to do it yourself." And to that, everyone gives a good "Here, here."

Maybe it's the tequila, but for the first time since I left the Circuit, I feel like I'm a part of something special. Riders are sharing war stories of their first time galloping. Grooms are patting me on the back for doing such a good job with their favorite filly. Country music is playing and Emily is dancing with a handsome older man in cowboy boots. I gather I'm not the only one with tomorrow off, and the prospect of sleeping in past four AM has my coworkers cutting loose. I've been to my fair share of year-end banquets, competitors' barbecues and post clinic luncheons. I've been surrounded by my peers in the spirit of celebration. But I've never actually been comfortable in those situations.

Tonight is different. I accomplished something big this week by venturing outside of my perfectly polished box and into a strange new world. I've always had poise. But this feels different. This feels like real self-confidence. The kind your trainer doesn't just import for you from Germany. And it isn't so easily taken away with a snide comment about money buying ribbons.

No, self-confidence like this doesn't require a six-figure budget to keep up with and right now I am positively swimming in the cheap buzz of it all.

The Boss slaps me on the back like a football buddy and asks, "So, Princess, are you coming back?" Nothing about that felt anything like a seductive come on. But I'm determined to shift the mood. Emboldened by my new friend Tequila, I rest my hand on his thigh, take a moment to appreciate the delicious firmness and say, "What do I have to do to get you to stop calling me Princess?"

The Boss smiles. He's finally starting to warm-up. I feel the heat as he says, "You asked for it when you showed up for work wearing an Hermes belt and a hairnet."

I bite the bottom of my lip suggestively and let the tip of my knee embrace the strong denim encasing the well-defined area just above his bulging calf muscle. "What if I go au natural? Would you stop calling me Princess then?"

I don't have a lot of experience seducing men and I'm not 100% confident that I'm doing it right. His awkward silence can't be a good sign. Just when I'm about to dive right in with another double entendre, he says, "You remind me of my girlfriend, Erica. I think you guys knew each other in college. You were her assistant on the Edmonton Equestrian Team or something?"

What did he just say?

Then it hits me like trunk filled with pink and chocolate brown wool coolers. "YOU'RE DATING ERICA LEWIS?" I scream as loud as my lungs will allow me. "AND THE STUPID COW TOLD YOU I WAS HER ASSISTANT?!!!" The Boss looks at me like I just grew three heads. I should be embarrassed by my inappropriate behavior, right? But I'm too busy not-so-quietly panicking about this nightmarish turn of events to care. "YOU'RE DATING ERICA LEWIS? ERICA LEWIS!" I bellow one last time into the dark, smoky air of this two-bit watering hole.

This can't be happening. Erica Lewis CANNOT re-enter my life right now. Sure, I've got all this newfound confidence and crap. But that doesn't change the fact that the best I can do now is a cheap polo shirt and a pair of outdated breeches! Seriously, Universe, I know I don't have a whole lot. OK, I know I don't have ANYTHING. But if you let Erica Lewis back into my life, she will find a way to take it all away from me.

I am in a state of total despair. But the Boss just keeps on piling it on. "Erica's family owns most of the horses you galloped this week," he says. That news is like a hot poker in the open wound that is this whole evening. I knew Erica Lewis's father owns thoroughbreds. But I had NO IDEA that they are Winning Edge thoroughbreds!

I can't help myself. I have to ask, "Do you call her Princess, too?"

The response breaks my heart. "Sometimes," he says. A word I have never until now associated with such disappointment.

That's it. I'm getting drunk. I have never gotten drunk in my entire life. But I'm already two saddle stretchers into this nightmare and there's no point in holding back now. Let me tell you, when Margaret

Fletcher decides to do something, she goes full force. I don't even wait for the bartender to return to order another drink. I reach over the bar, grab a half-full bottle of tequila and tell the Boss to take it out of next week's paycheck. I get three good swigs out of that bottle before the Bartender catches wind of the situation and starts screaming at me for "messin up his set-up."

In hindsight, I should be grateful that the shouting caught Emily's attention, alerting her to my need of rescue. Specifically, rescue from myself. She drags me into the bathroom, splashes water on my face and puts the last five minutes of my life into perspective for me. "Margaret, I don't know you that well. But I know that you're not the girl who gets drunk at a crappy bar then demeans herself in public for the sake of some boy."

I assure Emily that I'm not drunk. She grabs my face to refocus my gaze back onto her and insists that I am. OK, fine, maybe I'm slightly drunk. But I'm not demeaning myself.

Emily snorts in derision, "You're pretty close. I recognize the signs from across the room. The shouting and the slurring of your words. The inability to stabilize yourself on the barstool. Have you ever been drunk before?"

Of course not! Who does she think I am? My mother? I inform Emily that getting drunk in public is unbecoming. The look on her face suggests that she agrees. When she asks me if I can control myself for the rest of the evening, we both know the answer is no. So, like a good horseman, Emily promises to stick by my side and kick me when I need to get back in line. Sounds like a good deal to me.

CHAPTER 4
~ *Emily gets to clean up* ~

I guess they didn't teach Margaret how to hold her liquor in debutante school. "Emilyth, I didn't go to debutantaith school. I don't even know what that is. Where's the Boss?" And off she goes, stumbling haphazardly towards the last man she should be drunk and ridiculous in front of.

Margaret is blissfully unaware of any negative consequences to grabbing the Boss's biceps and squeezing them inappropriately before demanding, "I want you to X-splain to ME why someonth like you is with something like Erica Lewish!" I'm speechless. And the Boss looks like he's trying to plan an escape route out of this situation. Margaret continues with an incoherent monologue about stolen ponies, ugly monograms and some guy named Jeff.

The Boss looks at me and laughs, "It's a good thing she can ride, right?" (Oh, please, you must be kidding!) He sees my dubious expression. "I'm serious, Em. Have you ever watched her gallop? She has the kind of natural balance that gives everything she sits on confidence. It's kind of remarkable."

I'm stunned by the Boss's outburst of admiration for Margaret's riding skills. I haven't really been paying much attention to the Princess since she started galloping. I've got my own horses to worry about. Sure, she did a good job jogging in the beginning and I'll admit I'm impressed that she hasn't gotten herself dumped yet. But "the kind of natural balance that gives everything she sits on confidence"? Could that really be true? A loud crashing sound interrupts my thoughts and a fraction of a second later we are treated to the sight of Margaret's pink paisley cotton underwear and legs in the air. "Ohhhth, Crapth... I fell off my stool."

This is exactly the sort of situation that I'm supposed to be looking out for. Oops.

Seemingly unaware of the irony of the situation, the Boss gingerly helps Margaret to her feet, discreetly encouraging her to cover herself with the skirt that has migrated up around her waist. I point out that I don't think Margaret is giving that stool a whole lot of confidence. He laughs at my lame joke. But the Boss can't take his eyes off Margaret, totally mesmerized by her messy patrician charm. It's a good thing that he has always been too "Captain America", chiseled jaw and prominent forehead for my taste. Because judging by the way he's handling our tipsy Princess, if I was attracted to him like every other single female in striking distance of Winning Edge Farms, I would have one more reason to envy the little tart.

Crash! And down she goes again. Gravity is not on this girl's side tonight. Maybe if we put her up on a nice young thoroughbred, she'll manage to hold her balance for longer than fifteen seconds. Watching Margaret's glassy eyes as she steadies herself with the help of the Boss's awaiting pectoral muscle, I begin to think this is all a carefully-choreographed joke. But then spittle flies off her lips as she insists, "That STOOLTH isHHH BROKEN!" and I immediately dismiss the thought. I watch her struggle with the lime green and salmon pink skirt that we now know matches her underwear. It's not the perfect, poised picture she usually presents.

When Margaret says, "Emilish, I think I need to go home," I couldn't agree more.

* * *

Nobody asks me if I'm in the mood to deal with a Hunter Princess in the midst of her first experience with inebriation. The Boss just pours Margaret into the passenger seat of my truck and coaxes an address out of her in her last bit of consciousness.

If I was smart, I would drive Sloppy Drunk Equestrian Barbie home and call it a night. But I can't get what the Boss said about Margaret's riding out of my head. So before he has a chance to close my door, I lean in and ask, "Do you think she's a better rider than me?" He pretends not to understand the question. So I ask again, pointed, "Do you think Margaret Fletcher is a better rider than me?"

He does. It's written all over his face. But instead of stabbing me in the heart with the cold hard truth, he asks, "Since when are you so insecure?" Since you made that stupid comment about the superhuman, confidence-inspiring balance thing!

Clearly, I'm in no condition to withstand hearing the Boss confirm my worst nightmare. I'm sure he's wrong anyway. Rich girls don't really know how to ride. The only thing standing in the way of me surpassing their every accomplishment is that one nice horse I can't afford. Right?

"Just tell me, Boss. Is Margaret Fletcher a better rider than me? I promise, I can take it."

Of course I can't. So when the Boss slowly nods his head, tears immediately roll down my cheeks. I want to say something to restore my tough girl image. But I'm pretty sure if I so much as open my mouth, I'll start blubbering like an idiot. Despite my best efforts, I give myself away. And it's obvious that the Boss is regretting his role in my trembling chin. He gives me a sympathetic look and says, "You know, you could be just as good as her, Em. But you question yourself too much. The horses feel that."

I nod my head and roll up my window before I really let the waterworks come out.

I can't believe I thought Margaret was the one getting a bitch slap from reality. Nope, she's doing just fine, galloping racehorses like she's been doing it her whole life. It took me six months to progress from jogging to galloping! I sit in the truck immobile for the next twenty minutes, trying to convince myself that this is all just a horrible nightmare. Eventually, my quiet moment is shattered by the elephant roar of Margaret's persistent snoring in my passenger seat. Fine, Princess. I'll drive you home.

Ten minutes later, I arrive at Margaret's palace. I jostle her awake and make a silent prayer that she can find her keys. Good news. She appears to at least recognize her surroundings, "Come on, Emilythhh. I want to make you hot coco coco."

Even with all the natural balance in the world, Margaret is not going to make it to her apartment on her own. Together we stumble through the halls of her building, neither of us with the slightest clue of where we are going. Fortunately, the scent of boot polish and well-conditioned bridle leather leads me to Margaret's front door.

The musky odor quadruples once we are inside. Wow. It's like an overstocked, overpriced, fancy tack store in here. Countless bridles, bits and breastplates adorn the walls. All of it handcrafted from soft French leather and fine German silver — glowing from meticulous care and conditioning. Several pairs of custom baby calf field boots stand at perfect attention beside a closet that can only be filled with more overpriced breeches and hunt coats. I can't help but try to calculate of the street value of Margaret's stash. I bet I could get twenty grand selling it all online without even trying.

Margaret interrupts my reverie with a barely intelligible, "Emilith, you should stay here. It's a lot nicer than sleepith in your truck." She opens a cedar-lined oak tack trunk filled with Italian wool horse blankets, prizes from numerous championships. She lovingly fashions me an itchy little nest. "Emilith, you can spend the night sheeeping on my success."

That's it. I'm out of here. I am NOT spending the night SHEEEPING on Margaret's success. This place is creepy and sad. And I decide that no amount of superhuman riding talent is going to change that. But then Margaret opens a closet revealing twelve Hermes saddles lined up in a neat little row and makes a gesture encouraging me to select one for myself. I have never been one to covet overpriced tack. But any one of those TWELVE Hermes saddles is worth more than anything I've ever owned, and I'm getting the distinct feeling that Margaret is about to give me one in a drunken display of poor judgment.

"Go ahead. Pick one," she says like a French leather fairy godmother. The few thousand dollars I could get for an Hermes saddle isn't going to get me to England. But it's a start. I know I shouldn't take advantage of Margaret's inebriated state. But I point my unremarkably bred finger at a dark Havana model. Margaret scoops up that saddle along with the nearly identical Hermes beside it and places each one on an arm of her sickeningly sweet floral Laura Ashley couch.

Margaret gestures towards her freshly-saddled furniture and says, "Sit downTHH." This is getting weird. I should leave right now, saddle or no saddle. But before I have a chance to move a muscle, Margaret straddles her couch and closes her eyes. A look of complete happiness spreads across her face as she says, "There's nothing like an Hermes. You have to try one."

So we're playing My Little Pony. The twelve-hundred Breyer horses displayed on Margaret's bookshelves should have clued me in that this one enjoys a rich fantasy life. Free Hermes saddle? What was I thinking? Margaret Fletcher isn't giving up one square inch of her stash of baby calf. And then I notice that Margaret has lulled herself into some kind of creepy little trance. It's a sight more disturbing than her behavior back at the bar. Even though there is only so much personal damage she can do locked in her own apartment, I feel compelled to stay.

"EmilyTH, imagine that you are sitting on the most elegant horse you've ever seen. You canter into the Dixon Oval. The crowd is hushed as you lay down the trip of a lifetime. Your pace is perfect, your distances are shhhpot on, and your horse is jumping the snot out of everything for you." (Instead, I am imagining how I could transport all this equipment out of Margaret's apartment in the time it takes her to sleep off one too many saddle stretchers. I'm not a thief. It's a morally complicated fantasy. It's just that this crap could solve a whole lot of my problems.)

The sound of Margaret crashing to the floor puts an end to my impure thoughts. Natural balance, my ass. "Uhhh ohh. I got bucked offfth the couch," she giggles. With no regard for the six thousand dollar saddle that just came crashing down on top of her, Margaret crawls on all fours in the direction of the Championship blankets littering the floor. "Don't worry about me. I do thishh all the time. Ever since I went broke."

I can't take this anymore. I know Margaret is too drunk to realize what she is saying and I should probably just leave her here to sleep it off, but I can't help myself. I scream at the top of my lungs, "You've got five figures worth of tack locked up in this crackhead pony princess shrine of yours, just so you can pet it and cover it in oil! You are not BROKE!!!!!"

Margaret responds by throwing up all over her Devon Horse Show Working Hunter Championship Cooler from 2012. "Woopthhh," she burps loudly.

Woopthhh indeed. I'm pretty sure that nothing I am saying is registering. But that doesn't stop me from pointing out that if Margaret sold even HALF this stuff (the part she hasn't barfed on), she could buy a nice new show horse.

Predictably, my logic is lost on the Princess. "You can't buy a horse with a couple of used saddlethhh," she offers up another burp, "Besides, if I sold all my saddlethh, what would I ride the horse in?"

Why am I wasting my time arguing with a crazy person? But I can't help myself. "Margaret, none of this stuff you're hanging onto has anything to do with being a horseman. You realize that, right?" She gives me a look that is equal parts hurt and confused. It would be better for both of us if she would just pass out right now. Instead, she asks, "What's your problem?"

What's my problem? "You know what, Margaret? No matter how hard I work or how much I try, I can't get anywhere. Meanwhile, girls like you have everything handed to them and half the time you're too worried about something stupid like a hairnet to appreciate the good fortune."

The corners of Margaret's glassy eyes suddenly fill with real tears. Something about the drunken puppy dog look on her face pulls at my heartstrings as she cries, "Eth Toooth, Emilith? Eth Tooothhh?"

OK, I don't know what "Eth Tooothh" means. But Margaret is on a roll and I don't dare stop her. "All my life I've been told that the only person responsible for my successthh was my father's money. I was told that I would be NOTHINGTHHHH without Daddyth's money! Now look at me. I'm broke. I can't even affordth a horse and you're still SAYING IT ABOUTH ME!" She bursts into big, sloppy, uncontrollable tears.

Oh dear. Maybe I was too hard on her. I've really painted myself into a corner here. Now I've got to pray that Margaret stops crying or passes out from dehydration. I apologize and explain that I'm just a little touchy about money right now. Margaret responds that she liketh tooth touchy the moneythhh too. Her tears turn into giggles. Maybe I can get out of here before the stench of vomit makes me sick.

But Margaret isn't finished. She grabs my arms, looks me straight in the eye and says, "Let me tell you a secret. Having money isnith so great. Everybody just shits around and waits for you to fail. It suckth. The only thing good about ith you get to have a lot of horses."

"Or you get to travel to England, train with your idol and become an international champion," I bitterly mutter.

"What are youth talking about," she asks. Margaret is the last person I feel like discussing the limitations of my poverty with. How could she possibly understand?

Oh, what the hell. I'm sure she's too drunk to remember anything that I tell her anyway. So I slump down on the sweet cabbage rose print Laura Ashley couch and explain everything about Turtle, her offer and the twenty thousand dollars standing between me and my destiny. I'm surprised by how closely Margaret is listening to my tale of woe, nodding her head with sympathy at all the right moments and developing an unmistakable look of concern in her eyes.

"Emilith, I will fix this problem for you," she promises. Oh please, the girl can't even keep her paisley panties under cover in mixed company. How on earth is she going to solve a real problem? "Let me tell you a secret, Emilith. There is nothing I love more than figuring out how to solve a good problem. I was the firsthh Hunter Princeth in my barn to figure out that spraying Show Sheen on your calves helpthhh sticky boots slide on. That didn't matter so much when everyone started putting zippers on their booths. But that trick helped a lot people that couldn't afford zippers. And I always felt really good about that. I like helping friends. You are my friend. I give you my solemn oaththhh that I will help you." Then, as if soothed by the prospect of becoming my savior, Margaret curls up in a ball in the center of her itchy success. She's asleep in seconds.

I lock the door behind me when I leave. We wouldn't want anyone to lift any of that precious tack. Because that would be wrong. No matter how many of my real world problems it would solve and how few of Margaret Fletcher's fantasy fairy princess problems a theft would complicate…

***

To: Turtle Cumberbund (Turtle@CBFarms.com)
From: Emily Morris (eventer4life@ghostmail.com)
Re: Working Student Position

I apologize for taking so long to respond to your generous offer. For the past seven days, I have been carefully weighing the pros and cons. So far, I've come up with six hundred and seventy seven pros and only one con. The con being the small matter of that twenty thousand US dollars that I don't possess or have plans to accumulate anytime soon. So it is with a heavy heart that I decline this amazing opportunity of a lifetime. Please know that I have printed out your email, placed in a frame and hung it over the space heater in my trailer for those times when I need to be reminded of what could have been.

Best of luck at your next Olympics.

***

To: Emily Morris (eventer4life@ghostmail.com)
From: Turtle Cumberbund (Turtle@CBFarms.com)

Re: Working Student Position

I'll hold your spot for three months. I figure that should be enough time for a plucky girl like you to figure out how to get her mitts on twenty thousand US dollars. Best of luck and try not to get yourself into too much trouble or light your horse box on fire.

* * *

As if anything could possibly happen in three months to change my financial situation. I'll admit part of me is hoping for some magical solution to my twenty thousand dollar problem. But I'm not some rich kid masquerading as the working poor while twenty thousand dollars of fine equestrian equipment is locked up in my creepy apartment full of little plastic horsey figurines. It's time to start living in reality.

And the reality is: Margaret Fletcher is poetry in motion on a horse. I finally stopped what I was doing long enough to watch her gallop. The Boss is right. Her hands are soft; her position is strong; and the horses just go better for her.

Once again, my understanding of the horse world — and my place in it — is completely turned upside down.

CHAPTER 5
~ *Margaret gets a sweet tooth* ~

We're not going to talk about my behavior the other night. It was unseemly and uncharacteristic. "Oh, Margaret, honey, have a gin and tonic. I didn't raise you to be such a stick in the mud!" Since when is encouraging one's daughter to develop a recreational drinking problem considered good parenting? Not that I could ever rely on Mother to be much of a role model. What kind of woman voluntarily shortens her hamstrings for the sake of high fashion? No wonder I lost all control at my first whiff of tequila. I was raised by grain alcohol's number one fan.

But I'm not too worried about the slow and steady destruction of my character. Because the past two weeks at Winning Edge have been a whirlwind of personal growth. With experience, comes confidence. I got run away with and survived and I rarely throw up before galloping anymore. I've mastered the art of wrapping an ace bandage around whatever bruised appendage is bothering me at the moment, and I've got a kitchen cabinet full of over the counter pain medication to make me feel like new again. Being surrounded by tiny jockeys in tight pants should spell disaster for a young woman raised in the body-conscious Equitation world. But my waistline is shrinking, my thighs are hardening and my concept of feminine beauty is changing with each new layer of muscle. My mother would insist that I'm starting to look like a boy. Even if she's right, I feel like a goddess.

Speaking of heavenly creatures, the Boss is striding towards me with a spring in his step and a smile on his face. Gorgeous. It's been a few days since the fateful night he revealed his relationship with Erica Lewis. I can't help but notice that he hasn't mentioned her name since the last time I fell off my barstool. Maybe the Boss broke up with his "lady" love. It happens. Something better comes along and suddenly the boney little demonic harpy you used to find attractive no longer seems appealing. Sure, one doesn't want to cross the boundaries of the employee /employer relationship contract. But feelings are feelings.

The Boss reaches his destination by my side, but no invitation for any kind of extracurricular activity is extended. Instead, he starts babbling on about a horse he bought with money he doesn't have. His name is Box of Chocolates and his daddy was a big deal back in his day. Chocolates, on the other hand, is turning out to be a real dud. All the ingredients are there:

impeccable breeding, beautiful conformation and legs that can run for days. But Chocolates isn't having any of this tawdry racetrack lifestyle. And for reasons that aren't completely clear, the Boss decided to buy the little prima donna in hopes that he can somehow turn his attitude around.

I don't really care about anything the Boss is saying. I'm simply watching his soft, welcoming lips as they form words like "beautiful hindquarters" and "sloping shoulder." But when he says, "Chocolates seems kind of horrified by the size of his stall and the quality of grain the staff serves. I figure if anyone can help him transition to life on the wrong side of the tracks, Princess can," I'm not amused. It is one thing for me to call myself Princess. But it is a totally different situation when the Boss mocks me with my royal title.

Sure, there will always be a part of Margaret Fletcher that feels more comfortable in a hairnet. But when I look at the overpriced filly trotting towards me in an impossibly shiny Hermes belt and custom crocodile paddock boots, I know that I am no longer a Princess. And for the first time in three years, I am happy to give up the title.

Erica Lewis. There she is in all her glory. Skinny, beautiful and rotten to the core.

The last time I saw Erica, her pants were wrapped around her ankles and her naked bottom was covered in far too much "Monkey Butt" powder. Compromising pose aside, I was the one who was in the vulnerable position then.

Three years later, the dynamic between us still has not shifted. We both know I'm the wounded animal here and Erica wastes no time going in for the easy kill. "Oh, Margaret, I hope things aren't as bad as you look. I mean, THEY look. I can't believe I just said that!"

I'm willing to admit that Erica Lewis had the power to make the old Margaret Fletcher feel insecure. I've always been jealous of her thigh to calf ratio and flexible ankle. The Equitation judges just loved her. All she had to do was sit in a saddle with that perfectly proportioned leg of hers and they handed out blue ribbons like they were going out of style.

"I can't believe you're working for my family now. How weird is that? I just had to come down and see you toiling away in the trenches."

I remind myself that I am not the girl I used to be. I've grown. I've matured. I am a Goddess now. I gather up all my newfound Gallop Girl strength, unclench my jaw and say, "It's good to see you, Erica." But despite my effort to appear cool, the sweat trickling down my forehead gives me away.

Savoring my discomfort, Erica tosses her hair back and looks at me like a hungry lion about to devour something small and fuzzy. "You know galloping is going to ruin your equitation. I've seen it happen. Perfectly decent riders start looking like the Hunchback of Notre Dame. I guess it doesn't matter. You're never going back on the Circuit."

Bitch.

I'll admit that last comment stung. I take a moment to gather myself. Determined not to let Erica see me sweat (who am I kidding? I'm spritzing like an oversized Italian marble fountain), I casually say, "Oh, I don't know about that, Erica. Now that I'm back in the game, I have every intention of returning to the Circuit."

Erica raises a perfectly plucked eyebrow in disbelief. But I'm not backing down. I stuff my sweaty palms into my pockets and defiantly insist, "Who knows? Maybe I'll make my debut at the New London Classic later this summer."

I should know better than to tangle with an unrepentant sociopath on her own turf. And as much as I hate to admit it, Winning Edge is Erica Lewis's turf. Like that fuzzy little bird of prey, I never had a chance.

"Margaret, I know what you gallop girls make. My father pays your salary, remember? I think it's cute that you're trying. But we both know that you can't possibly afford anything more than the occasional coin operated pony ride at the grocery store."

I don't think the Boss has ever seen his beautiful little Princess (I'm referring to Erica, NOT ME!) behave so ugly. And when Erica catches sight of the disapproving expression on his face, she immediately softens her tone. "Don't worry, Margaret. You're not missing a thing. Now that I ride in the Grand Prix, I'm too focused on making the U.S. Equestrian team. It's bye-bye, fun and games. Hello, prize money and

Olympic glory. You would probably hate it. You know, if things are as bad as I know they are, I can probably get you a job on my new reality T.V. show. I'M GOING TO BE A REALITY T.V. STAR! Can you believe it? I guess my life is pretty glamorous. You know how America loves seeing how the other half lives! But seriously, it's a lot of hard work. Sometimes I don't know how I do it all!"

I give the Boss a desperate look, begging him to make his creature crawl back into her shell. But I don't think he fully appreciates just how wretched Erica is behaving until she says, "But I guess all that hard work is worth it. Because there is no better feeling than riding the perfect jump off and knowing you haven't left room for anyone to catch you. Listen to me going on about all the amazing horses I'm riding now while you're trapped in your new "pony girl for hire" lifestyle. I'm terrible!"

The Boss opens his mouth for the first time since this whole nightmare of a conversation started and says, "Oh, I don't think you have to feel too sorry for Margaret. She galloped your father's new prized colt yesterday."

I'm not really sure what he is talking about. I don't remember any talk of a prized colt. But Erica has a look of envy on her face that I haven't seen since my custom hand-woven hairnets shipped in from France before hers. She squeaks, "The one Daddy paid five million dollars for?"

I feel the tectonic shift of this situation moving in my favor. I can see the wheels turning in Erica's head as she says, "Daddy never bought me a five million dollar horse," then deflates into a harmless little child too consumed by her own insecurity to hurt anyone anymore.

The Boss flashes me a private smile, and it hits me. Erica Lewis and I have one last thing in common: daddy issues. I suppose a better person would be overcome by empathy in this situation. Instead, I pick up the baton and pile on, "Right, Erica? I had no idea that a horse could even cost five million dollars! I'm sure you can imagine how silly I felt remembering how special I used to feel when MY Daddy bought me one of those six figure imports from Germany. As if six figures is a lot of money for a horse."

On cue, Erica bursts into tears and runs off as fast as her crocodile paddock boots can carry her. I look at the Boss with the perfect innocent shrug, "Was it something I said?"

A look of regret washes over the Boss's face. "Princess, I have a feeling I'm going to pay for that later. I just hate when she plays that bratty little rich girl routine." Routine? I don't know. That just looked like Erica Lewis being Erica Lewis to me. But I hold my tongue. Instead of pointing out the obvious, I say, "You know she's on the phone with her trainer right now demanding he find her a six million dollar jumper for Daddy to buy."

The Boss laughs. His eye crinkle. I swoon. Then he pats me on the back like we're old drinking buddies and walks off in the direction of his woman.

Emily is right. Life just isn't fair.

BOX OF CHOCOLATES

Box of Chocolates sold for twenty million dollars as a yearling. The combined value of every horse I have ever sat on in my entire life does not come close to twenty million dollars. I can only imagine what it's going to feel like to ride that all of that pedigree at once.

I arrive at the barn exactly on time and ready to gallop my heart out with my new royal charge. I find a horse that I assume to be Chocolates all tacked up and standing in the barn aisle. He looks a lot more relaxed than your average young colt. Must be the quiet confidence that comes when one is the product of perfect breeding. I can't help but admire the dapples on his glossy coat and his long wavy tail. His soft bedroom eyes seem to carry a wisdom... Oh dear, he just backed into a fresh pile of poop. And he's just standing there, ankle deep in another horse's excrement like it's not even a problem. That doesn't seem like a very royal way to behave. This can't be right.

There's the Boss, appearing just in time to redirect me to the proper horse. But he takes one look at the soiled equine standing across from me and says, "Hang on, Princess, I'm going to get you a heavier whip." I'm getting the sinking feeling that Mr. Pooper over here is my ride.

The Boss returns with the biggest, heaviest whip I've ever seen. He slaps it in my left hand and warns me that Chocolates can be a little lazy. Oh, please. Try riding an overweight warmblood in the dead of summer after your trainer insisted that he needed to be lunged for an hour before his class. Chocolates may not look like much of a firecracker, but I highly doubt this well-bred racehorse is lazy. I hop on the beast and sternly remind myself to not judge a book by its cover, as I prepare to discover what riding twenty million dollars of horseflesh feels like.

"A little lazy" turns out to be the understatement of the decade. Who the hell paid twenty million dollars for this horse? It barely moves! But Margaret Fletcher is not one to give up easily. I deliver a strong whack to Sir Highness's butt with that five hundred pound whip. Nothing. I get the feeling that he's happy to canter all day long. A real racehorse gallop is not something that Box of Chocolates ever plans to achieve. I feel like a failure. It's like getting kicked off the Edmonton College Equestrian Team all over again.

But then, something magical happens. My frustration melts into a feeling of sheer bliss and I'm reminded of the simple joy of riding a hunter. A nice, quiet, pleasant hunter. The kind of horse that's happy to spend a long, lazy day cantering out in the countryside chasing foxes. I've never had any interest in fox hunting. It's my understanding that those who do spend most of their time in the saddle a little tipsy and covered in mud. But showing a hunter is a whole other ball of wax. The outfits are gorgeous, the horses are gentlemanly and the company is downright civilized. No one expects you to chase a wild animal around a muddy field. One simply has to canter around a manicured arena in a manner that convinces the judge that you and your horse would look fabulous chasing a fox with a flask of hot port strapped to your side. The longer I enjoy Box of Chocolate's smooth, effortless canter, the more I'm convinced that is where he belongs.

I've heard the urban legend about people buying thoroughbreds on the track for cheap and turning them into something special in the show ring. My trainers used to assure me those stories are fantasies poor girls tell themselves around the Pony Club campfire. But riding Chocolate's canter is like finding the pot of gold at the end of the rainbow and suddenly realizing leprechauns are real.

The Boss shatters my reverie at the top of his lungs with, "Do what I'm paying you to do and gallop my horse!" I've never been one to argue with authority figures. Unless one considers my mother an authority figure. But this horse is not a racehorse and I'm not going to pretend I have any hope of convincing him to become one. So I hop off Chocolates, hand the reins to the Boss and apologize for failing to follow orders.

Defeated, he suppresses his initial impulse to rip my head off for dereliction of duty and says, "Do yourself a favor, Princess. Ignore anyone who tries to convince you to invest your money in a proven loser. Unless you want to make a habit out of filling up your stable with a bunch of well-bred, no talent hay burners."

"Well-bred, no talent hay burner"? Yeah, I've heard that term of endearment before. If memory serves me correctly, that's exactly what Erica Lewis called me when she kicked me off the Edmonton Equestrian team. Maybe I'm still high off my trip down Hunter Princess memory lane. Maybe it's the way Box of Chocolates uses my sweaty brow as his own personal salt lick, inadvertently removing my hairnet and revealing a sexy unkempt 'do that is definitely catching the Boss's attention. Or maybe I just feel sorry for the colt. So much untapped talent going to waste just because he happened to be born into the wrong situation. Who knows? But something totally unexpected is prompting cautious, predictable, pragmatic Margaret Fletcher to throw caution to the wind.

I put my hand on Chocolates' shoulder, do my best impression of a savvy negotiator appraising the value of a used car she is not even sure she wants to buy, and I cautiously offer to take Chocolates off the Boss's hands. He reminds me that he claimed the horse for ten thousand dollars. I don't have ten thousand dollars. Or any amount of cash resembling ten thousand dollars.

My attempt to purchase Box of Chocolates appears to be dead in the water. Until later that afternoon when Sam finds some heat in Chocolate's tendon. And the only thing worse than a no-talent hay burner is a no-talent hay burner with a minor soundness issue that isn't going to hold up to the demands of racehorse training.

So the Boss gives me Chocolates for a dollar.

I'm pretty sure most of the hairnets in my collection cost more than a dollar. OK, Chocolates. You may only be worth that right now and I might be the girl who has to buy her polo shirts out of the discount bin, but I have a feeling that together we're going to do something really special.

CHAPTER 6
~ *Emily closes a deal* ~

I'm not sure what Margaret expected when I told her about Green Acres. I know she's used to high-end barns. (rich wood paneling, old world cobblestone paving and polished brass.) But did she honestly think that she was going to find anything even closely resembling that for under five hundred dollars a month?

Against my better judgment, I show her the communal tack room. Her face just crinkles up into a prune of disappointment. It's a look she usually saves for when she catches me scrubbing my paddock boots with saddle soap. "Oh, Emily, that's not meant for fine leather. You'll never be able to get those boots to shine up now!" I swear every time that girl puts on a "proper pair of breeches and a Hermes belt" she starts talking like Jackie Kennedy doing her best Scarlett O'Hara impression. I detect a slight Southern drawl as she declares, "Oh dear, it appears nobody bothers to monogram anything around here.

It must be a nightmare for the barn manager to keep the laundry in order." Is she kidding? The only laundry the barn manager is doing is her own and those washing machines you see at the end of the barn are not for public use.

I'm still not sure I understand why Margaret Fletcher bought this horse. I hope she doesn't think she can use it to return to the A-Circuit. Don't get me wrong. Chocolates is nice. I probably would have bought him myself if I had known the Boss needed him gone. But that horse is a long way away from becoming anything anyone would look good riding in a show ring. He's young. He's green. And the only thing he knows how to do is run "fast" in a straight line. Margaret is a good rider and all, but she has NO idea what she's in for. The better part of me wants to fill her in. But when she says, "Emily, I'm getting the distinct vibe that the barn colors here at Green Acres are whatever colors are on sale at the local tackle and feed store," I hold my tongue.

But Margaret is on a roll. "I suppose you think that keeping barn colors is silly. Just like requiring identical tack trunks so the barn aisles look neat and tidy is silly. Just like I, Margaret Fletcher, am silly!" My patience is wearing thin. I want to tell Princess Fancy Breeches to take her business down the road where everyone's crap matches and board is three times as expensive.

But I don't. Instead, I spread my thin lips into a pained smile and try not to sound too condescending as I explain, "Green Acres is a boarding facility. Most of the riders that board here don't have trainers, let alone matching tack trunks."

Margaret refuses to understand. "Emily, they might not have trainers, but someone has to be in charge, right? It would be great if the horses all kept themselves trimmed and tidy on their own. But we all know that's not going to happen. I would really like to talk to whoever is in charge of the body-clipping schedule. I hate it when they clip too late in the winter. I find that that the sheen of the spring coat suffers if one makes that mistake."

Like I said, I've seen glimpses of the pristine world Margaret Fletcher comes from. I'm sure Green Acres looks like a developing third world nation compared to the barns grew up in. She's not trying to be obnoxious. She just doesn't know any better. I should be patient, right?

"MARGARET," I scream, "Have you ever wrapped a horse's leg? Or pulled a mane. Or driven a trailer. Or loaded a resistant horse into a trailer. Forget resistant; have you ever loaded a horse into a trailer EVER?" Judging by the look on Margaret's face, I've hit a nerve. Good. Someone has to knock her off her high horse.

Margaret doesn't actually answer any of my (totally valid) questions. She just turns her nose up at my "inappropriate temper tantrum" and says, "I know what's happening here, Emily. You're just putting me down because you're upset that I don't like your frumpy barn." She's not entirely wrong. But there are bigger fish to fry here.

"FRUMPY? It's a barn, Margaret, not a prom dress!" I take a deep breath, gather my composure and ask, "Have you bothered to check the quality of bedding in the stalls or footing in the arena? Forget that the barn aisles don't have matching tack trunks. Are they safe? Is there an adequate area for lunging and bathing? These are the questions a real horseman would be asking. Not crap about color schemes and matching tack trunks!"

Margaret storms off in a huff. She probably would have kept going right off the property and never spoken to me again if she didn't need a ride back into town. Poor Princess is stuck waiting in my truck while I show my resale project to a perspective buyer. I say good riddance for now.

* * *

Winston isn't the most talented horse I've ever sat on. But he never puts a foot wrong, even when the rider screws up royally. He is the perfect first horse for a fourteen-year-old girl just starting out in the sport, and I can't help but envy the kid standing before me in brand new breeches and boots.

That is, until her mother opens her mouth. Apparently, little Suzie is our next great Olympian. Her biggest accomplishment may only be a sixth place finish in the Beginner Novice division at a local unrated horse trial. But Mom is convinced that the only ingredient missing in Suzie's success is the right horse.

I put Winston through his paces so Mom can assess his talents and determine if Suzie should waste her time. Of course, he's perfect. But Mom doesn't look convinced. I try my hardest to conceal the fact that I think this woman is an idiot as she screams across the arena, "I'm not sure this horse has what it takes. He doesn't seem to have that "it" factor we're looking for. You know what I'm talking about? The IT factor? It's that thing in a horse that tells you that IT will take you to the Olympics."

I really need to sell this horse if I am going to make it to England. Not that I have any hope of actually putting together enough money to make the trip. But Turtle's last email convinced me that if I want to be an international competitor as much as I claim to, I need to at least try. The only immediate problem is that I'm not sure I have what IT takes to deal with this woman's bullshit factor.

Fortunately, Winston starts doing my job for me, selling himself to little Suzie with a kind eye and gentle nicker. Even Mom starts to soften. She reluctantly concedes that Suzie should go ahead and try poor Winston out. Mom throws little Suzie up onto Winston's back with the grace of a forklift and the wisdom of a master horseman who learned everything she knows about horses from an online forum. Without the slightest bit of irony in her voice, she instructs Suzie to "Try to get him to look fancy like that German horse we saw on Youtube." Instead, Suzie trots around the arena with a death grip on the reins and a look of sheer terror on her face while Mom screams, "Fancier! Fancier!"

Unfazed by the commotion, Winston never gives Suzie more than she can handle. Twenty minutes later, the kid agrees to pick up a canter. When she loses her balance, Winston slows down until she has a chance to adjust herself in the saddle. Ten strides later, and Suzie's got a giant grin on her face. By the end of the ride, Winston gives her enough confidence to jump over a two-foot vertical. I am surprisingly moved. Watching Winston encourage a timid girl to exceed her expectations almost makes dealing with her mother bearable.

When Mom asks, "Do you think he's got what it takes to take my daughter all the way to the Olympics?" I resist the urge to tell the awful person standing across from me to pick another sport with which to live vicariously through her daughter.

"I don't know about the Olympics, but that's an A-Circuit canter if I've ever seen one." The voice behind me makes me cringe. Margaret? Who let her out of the truck?

Sure enough, there she is, waltzing up. "Emily, I'm so sorry to interrupt. But this little girl caught my eye and I just HAD to ask about this magnificent animal she's riding. He's not still intact by chance?"

One look at Margaret's Hermes belt and Mom's expression perks up. She takes Margaret's cue and insists that she has been meaning to ask if dear Winston is intact. I can't decide what is more absurd. Asking a question filled with words you clearly don't understand or believing that the gentle giant who just babysat little Suzie over there might actually be a stallion.

I don't know how to best handle the situation, so I tell the crazy person standing across from me that poor Winston lost his balls in an unfortunate pasture accident. Margaret almost breaks character with a laugh. But I've got to hand it to Princess: she holds it together and proceeds to charm the pants off Suzie's mom. Margaret pretends to be genuinely disappointed by Winston's dislocated balls and makes a big show of insisting that she would have made me an offer right on the spot otherwise. "He is exactly the type I need to fill a hole in my breeding program."

I'm pretty sure Suzie's mom has no idea what fancy expressions like "breeding program" and "A-Circuit canter" mean. But she can smell the allure of prestige from a mile away. In less than five minutes, Margaret has her convinced that my sweet but unspectacular horse has IT in spades. The checkbook comes out and arrangements are made for a hauler to take dear Winston to his new home. If I wasn't so sure that he is indeed the perfect horse to teach Suzie the ropes, I might feel guilty about the whole thing.

After Suzie and her monster leave, I brace for Margaret's derogatory comments about my inability to sell my own horse without her help. But she just stands there, looking inexplicably lost and a little scared. I've never seen the bold, brash Margaret Fletcher look so helpless. I give in and break the ice. "Thank you, Margaret, for convincing that crazy lady to buy my horse."

With a look of genuine remorse on her face, she says, "I was pretty angry sitting in that dirty, smelly truck of yours thinking about all that stuff you said." I choose to ignore the "dirty" and "smelly" comment and let the Princess continue uninterrupted. "Just when I thought I couldn't possibly get more upset, I noticed a glop of yellow goop on my breeches. Surprise, surprise. Emily didn't bother to properly close that jar of yellow stuff she's got stored in the front seat of her truck. How sloppy! Then I thought, what the hell is this stuff and why is my thigh suddenly ten degrees warmer? Or for that matter, what are all these other strange ointments with pictures of horses on the bottles she's got scattered about the cab? I started reading the labels. That's when I discovered that there is a whole world of smelly products out there, fashioned to treat all kinds of equine ailments that I've never even heard of! You're right, Emily. I have no idea what I'm doing!"

And with that, perfectly poised Margaret Fletcher bursts into sloppy tears.

I'm stunned. I can only understand every other word that is pouring out of her mouth. Something about how she can pick out the perfect hunt coat to complement any shade of horse. But when it comes to the really important stuff, she's just as clueless as that woman who actually believed my horse might be a stallion.

She's right. When it comes to real horsemanship, she is clueless. But I have to admit I find the news that you're supposed to color coordinate your jacket with your horse's coat astonishing. So I ask Margaret to clarify, hoping my genuine interest in her area of expertise might help her feel better. But she just sobs louder, "You don't need to be making FUN of me right now, Emilth!"

I better nip this in the bud before the mucus gets out of control. I put both my hands on Margaret's shoulders and bark, "MARGARET! COMPOSE YOURSELF!" At the sound of my authoritative tone, Margaret sets her jaw and puts those tears back where they belong. "So you're a little out of your depth here," I say, "Big deal. You're hardly the first person to find herself in a situation where she's bitten off more than she can chew. I've got news for you, Margaret Fletcher. Life is tough. You've just got to be tougher."

A strange look of recognition spreads across Margaret's face. She whispers, "That's exactly what Bunny used to say." I have no idea who this Bunny person is, and I'm not sure I care. But that doesn't stop Margaret from telling her story. "Emily, Bunny Beale was my old trainer. She's the one that broke the news about Daddy losing all his money. And when I collapsed on the floor, irreversibly staining my favorite pair of white breeches, she said "Life is tough, honey. You just have to get tougher." I miss that woman. We used to stay up all night at horse shows playing "Guess who bought my old breeches at the consignment shop". Bunny would really hate this place. We're talking about a woman with a "no domestically-bred horses allowed" barn policy. Can you imagine what she would have to say about this crap? Or what she would think about me galloping racehorses for a living?"

Margaret starts laughing and crying even harder at the same time. I'm not sure how to respond. So I just let the storm run its course. She eventually settles down, dries her eyes and says, "You know, Emily, I think we make a really good team."

Team? Really? I'm not a hundred percent sure we even qualify as friends.

So imagine my surprise when the next words out of Margaret Fletcher's mouth are, "I just had the most brilliant idea! Why don't we train Chocolates up to become a winning show Hunter? We'll show him at The New London Classic and then sell him for more money than you could possibly need to go to England. It's the perfect solution for all of our problems. You get to live the dream you can't afford; I return to the show ring; and Chocolates doesn't die under my completely incompetent care!"

I know Princess Fancy Breeches has spent most of her life sheltered from reality. But even she couldn't possibly be naïve enough to believe that ridiculous fairytale. As if we could sell that horse of hers for enough money to get me to England. I'd be lucky if I made five hundred dollars off Winston after six months of really hard work! Once again, I put on my "adult talking to a child" voice and explain, "I would have to sell at least forty horses like Winston to make enough money to get to England."

Margaret just looks at me like I'm an idiot. "Emily, my last hunter cost three hundred thousand dollars. I'm not saying that I think Chocolates will sell for that much, but I'm pretty sure we can do better than a five hundred dollar profit."

Three hundred thousand dollars for one horse? No wonder this woman is appalled by my trailer. Part of me wants to believe this ridiculous fantasy of Margaret's. Chocolates would only have to sell for a little more than forty thousand dollars to net me enough money to get to England. But my pragmatic side takes over. "Come on, Margaret. You mean to tell me that when push comes to shove and it's time to sell your nice winning hunter, you're really going to be on board with that?"

Offended, Margaret puffs up her chest and lets the superior Southern accent come out for the second time this afternoon. "How dare you imply that my integrity is anything less than impeccable! You have never seen the philanthropic side of me. But I can assure you, it's quite spectacular. I once donated all of my mildly stained breeches to a therapeutic riding center and I didn't even ask for a receipt. I told you, I like helping people. It makes me feel good."

I'm not impressed by Margaret's pathetic idea of philanthropy. I'm also not entirely sure that she has any idea how to retrain an off-the-track thoroughbred for a new career. Of course, she does have the kind of natural balance that gives horses confidence. I bet she could have Chocolates jumping hunter courses like an old pro in no time. Ugh, even thinking that gives me a pain in my chest. Yeah, this isn't going to work.

"Margaret, I'm an eventer. You know, galloping solid fences the size of houses at breakneck speed on cross-country? I don't know anything about how to make a horse into a hunter."

"That's why you're broke, Emily." Once again, Princess Fancy Breeches is right. The hunter ring is where all the money is and I would be a fool to not take this deal.

I have never partnered on a horse before. And a partnership with a spoiled brat like Margaret Fletcher sounds like a nightmare. But I want to get to England, and I have a feeling that she might be the only person in my life right now that can help me make that happen. Then I remember that promise I made to myself when I was just twelve years old, long before I learned that Olympians are assholes and rich kids are actually really good riders. That promise was to do whatever it takes to make my dreams happen. Even if it means throwing my fortune in with the last person I ever expected to lean on.

All right, Margaret Fletcher, I'll let you be my savior. Just don't tell anyone from my old Pony Club. We don't want them to think I've gone soft.

CHAPTER 7
~ *Margaret messes* *up her hair* ~

Word from Mother is that my stressed-out aura left a negative impression on Daddy. Nothing but promising to submit to weekly meditation sessions will satisfy his concerned soul. Meditation has never been my thing, but I look forward to finally spending more time with the man I am just getting to know.

I arrive at the family condo on time, wearing my most relaxed disposition and an open mind. Mother answers the door draped in an elaborately patterned silk muumuu, afternoon cocktail in hand. Daddy is nowhere in sight. Great, she's going to make me spend time with her before she gives up his location. Clearly, Mother is irritated by my new arrangement with Daddy. I'm sure it bothers her to know we are on the verge of a deeper relationship. All I can say is, sorry you don't get to have me all to yourself anymore.

Mother crinkles her face into a sour expression and informs me that Daddy is still taking his nap. Nap? The old Daddy used to say that sleep was for sissies. Besides, I'm here ON TIME. Shouldn't somebody wake him? Punctuality is the key to success, remember? It's the reason he never made it to any of my horse shows. The classes never start on time and the ring steward rarely adheres to the pre-published order of go. Without a reliable ride time, Daddy was concerned he would either be too early or too late, but never perfectly punctual. Anything less is unacceptable.

Mother looks me up and down and says, "Oh dear, Margaret, you've become tan. You look like a migrant worker." She hasn't changed one bit. She may be broke and living in an unflatteringly-lit condo. But that imperialistic country club attitude is just as sharp as ever, particularly when she finds something or someone to criticize. "You know, Margaret, you can't possibly hope to find a nice boy from a good family if you're going to insist on looking like you make your living with your hands."

I roll my eyes and tell her that I don't care. But she isn't giving up that easily. With the sternest voice she can muster on two and half cocktails, she bellows, "LIFE discriminates against those who insist on parading around with patchy sunburnt skin! I didn't make the rules, honey. I just play by them." She is doing her best to sound like an evil witch casting an ominous spell. But I'm not concerned. I have years of experience dealing with her when she's in one of her emotionally destructive moods. It's child's play, really.

I dangle a gin-soaked cocktail olive in front of Mother's pointy nose, "Well, Mother, it just so happens I have met a nice boy from a good family and his dad is worth millions." Mother's face lights up like it's Christmas morning and the gluten-free ice cream comes out of the fridge. I can tell that she is hunkering down for a long afternoon chat about boys. "Oh, honey, it's like you're Cinderella and he's Prince Charming. Only you weren't always so poor and dirty."

Should I burst her bubble now? This is too cruel, right? It's not like she just called me poor and dirty. "Maybe we can swing by his place after my meditation, Mother. Do you happen to have a more sensible pair of shoes?"

She assumes that "sensible" means something smaller, shinier and fresh from an overpriced designer's spring collection. "Oh, Margaret, darling, it has been sooo long since I've allowed myself the luxury of buying a new pair of sensible shoes. We don't want your new beau to think he's marrying into a family that buys their couture on eBay. Let's swing by Saks and splurge!"

"Don't worry, Mother. That new man of mine doesn't particularly care where you buy your shoes. Being a horse and all." With that, Mother deflates harder and faster than she did the day she realized her plastic surgeon stopped taking her calls.

Mother throws her hands up in frustration and loudly proclaims, "Oh, Margaret, I'm absolutely not buying you a horse right now. I can't even afford a sensible pair of shoes, let alone a horse!"

With great pleasure, I explain the situation with Chocolates, my partnership with Emily and my complete lack of need for any of her help.

Mother simply looks at me with a raised eyebrow and asks me how many concussions I've suffered at my new job. "Margaret," she says, "I haven't a clue what they are paying you. But there is no way you can swing horse show bills. I don't care how many little friends you've got splitting the tab."

I knew she was going to say that. I'm sure Mother thinks I'm still the same clueless Princess she raised. But I've changed. I'm growing into the kind of young woman who understands the hard work and sacrifice that happens behind the scenes of real life. "Don't worry. Emily put together a spreadsheet with all our expenses laid out, including shows. So thank you for your concern, but we've got it covered."

Why does my mother suddenly have a twinkle in her eye? They're still glossy from her inappropriate afternoon buzz, but I can recognize the watery glint of mischief when I see it. She takes another sip of her cocktail and puckers her lips like she just finished sucking on a lemon. "Margaret, darling, make sure this Emily person hasn't forgotten to budget for tips, meals and hotels for your grooms, in addition to their day rate."

Crap. Something tells me Little Miss Purple Plastic Schooling Helmet neglected to add tips, meals and hotels for our grooms. I do my best to look cool as a gluten-free cucumber sandwich, even though I am panicking inside.

But it's too late. Mother smells blood in the water and she's ready to attack.

"I'm sure the price of braiding has gone up, so be sure that's on the spreadsheet," she says, "Oh, and don't let this girl you call Emily try and save pennies on food for the weekend. I always insisted that your trainers provide you with fresh salads and fruit from the best local restaurants. If you ate the salt and fat they serve on the show grounds, you would have been busting out of your breeches by the third day. Let's not forget last minute expenses covered, as well. Leave a whole column open in the spreadsheet for that one! Because let's face it, no matter how organized you thought you were, there was always something you needed to pick up at the show. Saddle pad, gloves, spurs. Whatever it was, it was always ten times more expensive when we had to buy it last minute."

My aura is totally stressed. I came here today to humor my confused, financially-stricken father. But by the time Daddy wakes up, I am in full need of his services. Mother can hardly stand the sight of Daddy in his hemp pajamas, so it doesn't take much effort to clear her out of the room. Candles are lit and curtains are drawn. The place is starting to take on the appearance of a cheap salon where one might have her fortune read.

Daddy gestures for me to join him on the floor. He closes his eyes, puts his hands on his temples and says, "Cookie, I want you to think about all the things that are important to you. Now take a deep breath and expel them things from your universe. BE GONE UNIMPORTANT THINGS! BE GONE!"

Right now, all I can think about is braiders, grooms and last-minute expenses. And my new financial reality has already taken care of expelling all of it from my universe. So I'm not exactly sure what we're doing here.

Daddy tells me that the things I think matter actually don't matter. That doesn't make any sense. Because I'm pretty sure one can't make it through a real A-Circuit horse show without a proper braider and at least one groom. Believe me, it matters.

"Cookie, the only thing that is important is what is in front of you right now, in this moment," he says.

I don't believe him. But he slips into some kind of yogic trance before I have a chance to argue. Completely oblivious to the puddle of panic sitting across from him, Daddy hums a melodic chant. It's like butter knives stabbing into my brain repeatedly. Twenty painfully "silent" minutes later, Daddy opens his eyes and takes a deep breath. "May you always let the peace be with you."

Is he serious? Do I look like someone in any kind of proximity to peace? Still, I got more attention from Daddy during that completely-ineffective meditation session then I've experienced in the past twenty-two years combined. Growing up, he always told me that pigs get slaughtered. So I should probably just smile, nod and go off on my merry little way. But I am determined to cultivate a meaningful relationship with this man now that he has time for me. Because as far as I can see, that is the only potential upside to being poor. I cut to the chase and ask, "Daddy, do you ever have trouble adjusting to this new life of poverty?"

"I'm not poor. I have a rich life of peace and tranquility and fulfillment and beauty and yoga and my senior friends," he insists.

DADDY! It's the middle of the afternoon and you're wearing pajamas made out of the discarded stash of some enterprising hippie. YOU'RE POOR.

Of course, I don't actually say any of that. He's fragile, remember? Still, I know that behind all the sandalwood fumes there is a cunning businessman. The kind of man who could help a girl figure out how to come up with the cash she needs to show on the A-Circuit in style.

Then I remember my promise to Mother. I'm not supposed to tell Daddy that I've got anything to do with racehorses. I have no idea why the subject is taboo. But it is, and I can't be honest with Daddy about what is really going on with my life unless I break that promise to Mother. I should go ahead anyway, right? The woman did just take way too much pleasure in putting me through the emotional wringer. So why can't I bring myself to betray her? Did all those years of master manipulation leave me permanently subject to that woman's will?

Daddy tells me that my aura is now clean, confirming my suspicion that he is a complete charlatan. Maybe that means that one day he'll give up all this new age crap, return his old ways and start making this family a whole bunch of money again. As great as that would be, my window of opportunity to get to know him might be closing. I should open up and tell him everything. Then we can finally be close.

But for reasons I don't entirely understand, I can't go back on my word to Mother. It must be some kind of voodoo. I wouldn't put it past her to find some online course that teaches Witchcraft 101. I give Daddy a hug, make an appointment for next week, and then slip out before Mother has a chance to cast another spell.

* * *

I probably don't have to tell you that there is no mention of grooms, grooms' expenses or last minute purchases in Emily's spreadsheet. When I point out the holes in her financial planning, she loans me a copy of Horse Showing on a Shoe String Budget by Camile Watson.

I was expecting Camile's book to wax poetic about the benefits of forgoing fashion in favor of outdated secondhand show clothes. I totally get that I can't afford to show in quite the same manner that I'm used to. I had already committed to choosing chicken over shrimp on my lunch salad. But avoiding big hotel bills by throwing an inflatable mattress into a stall and calling that a bedchamber? Does this woman really expect her readers to live on a steady diet of string cheese & mixed nuts to avoid *"getting gouged at the food stands?"* Camile, honey, I just don't believe that you enjoy *"staying up all night braiding horses by the light of your pick-up truck for extra cash."*

Don't get me wrong. Margaret Fletcher is not afraid to get her hands dirty. I fully expect to help Emily tack up for me in the morning. But a serious competitor needs to be focused on the actual competition. Growing up, my trainers wouldn't even let me do homework for a week prior to a big competition. Let alone *"earn an extra few bucks throwing morning hay while the well-heeled are still getting their beauty sleep."*

I'm sure these penny-pinching techniques are great for your average unfortunate Pony Clubber hoping to bring home a ribbon from her local unrated horse trial. But we're talking about the A-Circuit here. We're talking real competition! Clearly, Emily doesn't fully grasp what's at stake and it's my job to set her straight.

I invite Emily out for a drink (no tequila this time) at Shorty's and bring along a couple horse show photo albums to illustrate my point. Elegance. Poise. Grace under pressure. I forgot how beautiful I look in my old show photos.

"Emily," I ask, "Do I look like I stayed up all night braiding or woke up early to throw hay at the crack of dawn? Does the girl in these photos look like she subsists solely on a diet of string cheese and mixed nuts?"

I think I'm making a pretty compelling argument, but Emily loses her cool. "You look like a spoiled brat sitting on a fancy horse. A horse that you never bathed, groomed, fed or cared for in any kind of meaningful way in your entire life," she says.

It's never pretty when jealously rears her ugly head. I'm ready to cut this meeting short, but Emily is not finished giving me the business. "I've got a news flash for you, Margaret Fletcher. You are not that girl anymore. Chocolates is a nice horse. But I can promise you that he won't be carting you around the arena in the same style as that lovely, well-schooled beast in those pictures. In fact, I can pretty much guarantee that he's going to make an ass out of you at least once before the weekend is over. Not because you're not a good rider. Because that's what green racetrack rejects do. By the end of it, you're going to be covered in more dirt than you have ever been in your entire life. Muscles having nothing to do with riding are going to be sore and you won't even remember the last time you got a good night's sleep. If you're lucky, you might get a ribbon out of the whole deal. But you won't get a fancy picture like this. You know why? Because show photographers are expensive and you CAN'T AFFORD IT! So are you up for this, Margaret? If not, please tell me now so we can dissolve this partnership and I can move onto something worth my time."

Emily storms out, leaving me alone with two untouched Grand Marniers. Ten minutes later, I'm still at the bar trying to gather my composure when the Boss walks in, unaccompanied. He takes a seat, sizes me (and the two drinks sitting in front of me) up and then says, "Princess, what's a nice girl like you doing in a place like this before sunset?"

I'm won over by his fake cowboy pick-up line. I slide Emily's untouched Grand Marnier across the bar and say, "Late afternoon meeting with my business partner gone bad. Care for her drink?" He ignores my offer, eyeballing my photo-album instead, gesturing for permission to peruse it. And I'm pleased to say, "Go ahead, Boss. Knock yourself out."

As the Boss starts flipping through the pages of the best years of my life, I can't help but notice him pause at a photo depicting the rear view of my jumping effort. Without taking his eye off that photo, he says, "Let me guess: you showed Emily this photo album in an innocent attempt to educate her on the requirements of competing on the A-Circuit." (Well, it sounds like someone has a history of overreacting in the face of helpful advice.)

I feel vindicated by the Boss's characterization of Emily's hair-trigger temper and immediately start to imagine how I will address the situation with her in the near future. "Do you think she would listen to reason if you had a talk with her, Boss? Maybe just explain that she can't just fly off the handle every time someone tries to help her?"

The Boss finds another photo of my backside arched in preparation for take-off and chuckles to himself. Normally I'd be pleased, but right now I'm beginning to think that he's too distracted to provide any more meaningful insight. But then he says, "Princess, I know Emily looks a little rough and ready. But she's not clueless. So try not to be so uptight."

Uptight? I think someone here is quite fond of how "uptight" Margaret Fletcher looks in a pair of show breeches. "Hey, Boss, just because I don't allow fly-a-ways to have a party outside of my helmet doesn't mean that I'm uptight!" I finish my Grand Marnier in one gulp, untie the bun in my hair and shake my locks wildly about my shoulders and say, "I know how to have fun."

The Boss chuckles, "I don't believe you," before slamming back his own Grand Marnier in similar fashion and treating me to a playful wink.

I imagine a normal girl would probably take the opportunity to act all adorably indignant or something like that. But back-to-back weekends of horse showing as a teenager prevented me from ever learning, much less mastering the art of flirtation. So naturally, I demur. I assume our little tit-for-tat is over.

But then the Boss leans in and I catch a delicious whiff of his fresh and manly aftershave as he challenges me, "Prove it."

Prove it? I have absolutely no idea how to prove it. So I sit there, frozen, waiting for him to let me off the hook with a flirtatious joke or intimate display of physical familiarity.

Instead, he says, "Let's take a couple of the horses galloping on the beach tonight, just for fun."

I snort in derision, inadvertently filling my nostrils with the orange cough syrupy sensation of Grand Marnier. I can't imagine he is serious. "Galloping on the beach isn't on anybody's work schedule." Strict adherence to a predetermined work schedule is something I have always admired about the Boss. Nothing turns me on more than personal discipline.

"Don't worry, Princess," he responds *innocently* combing his fingers through the untamed locks of my recently untethered mane, "Galloping on the beach is a great way to clear a young horse's mind and build muscle. I've got two colts that would benefit from a little unscheduled adventure. So are you ready to prove that you can let your hair down or not?"

I'm not. Not at all. Galloping young horses on the beach sounds terrifying. I really wish the Boss would just pinch me on the cheeks and let me go home to my depressing apartment. But I have a feeling that if I want to give the impression that I can be fun, I'm going to have to step outside of my comfort zone. So I look him square in those big, beautiful, blue eyes of his and say, "Let's go."

Hey, Emily, guess what? I'm loading TWO resistant horses onto a trailer all by myself. Do I get to be part of the cool kids now?

Something tells me the two three-year-old colts chosen for the dubious task of proving that Margaret Fletcher is fun know something I don't. Neither seems particularly thrilled to be marching towards a trailer at this late hour. I'm willing to bet that "Jumpy" and "Hoppy" over here will only get LESS cooperative once they get their first glimpse of the great big ocean. I keep looking at the Boss, waiting for him to burst into laughter and admit the whole thing is one big joke. But no. He just tells me it's time to stop fussing with my hairnet and hit the road.

Once again, I find myself at an equestrian crossroads. I can either do exactly what everyone expects an uptight Hunter Princess to do and bail on this ridiculous idea, or I can get in the truck and hope that the Boss is bluffing. I get in.

Ten minutes into the drive, I accept my fate. The sun has set. The air has a chill. And in a matter of mere moments, Margaret Fletcher is going to be galloping on the beach. The Boss parks the truck in an empty parking lot by the lifeguard station. The ocean spreads out before us. The sun is setting and there isn't another soul around to bother us. It's so peaceful, someone should light a meditation candle and look for my aura. But as I get out of the truck, the sound of the ocean crashing on the shore is deafening. At least the sand will provide an adequate cushion should (oh, sorry, WHEN) I get dumped.

The Boss takes one look at my panicked expression and says, "Lose one of my horses out here and you're fired." Good thing I didn't just do something stupid like buy a horse I can't really afford or anything.

The Boss tacks up Hoppy while Jumpy waits in the trailer. Ground mounting this equine firecracker is not an option. So he cradles my leg for one of those leg-ups I've grown to appreciate, then instructs me to wait while he tacks up his mount.

I don't wait for the Boss so much as immediately get run away with at full speed. Crap. Luckily, I'm a pretty seasoned Gallop Girl now and I manage to bring Hoppy to a screeching halt in relatively short order.

While I'm busy congratulating myself, Hoppy figures out that he's all alone on an alien planet surrounded by a giant, roaring, horse-eating ocean. His entire body shudders as he screams at the top of his lungs, desperate to be rescued. I hear you, Hoppy. I know what it's like to suddenly be all alone and not recognize your surroundings. But you've got to trust that nobody is going to ask you for more than you can handle.

Seconds later, I hear the pounding footfalls of a horse galloping towards me, followed by the Boss's faint cry of "Hang on, Princesses. I'm coming."

I don't know what comes over me, but it's like a giant gust of wind slaps me awake and I scream at the top of my lungs, "DON'T CALL ME PRINCESS!!!" Margaret Fletcher may be a little lost right now. But she is not waiting around to be rescued by some Knight in shining armor. I gallop ahead, confident that I know where I am going. By the time the Boss catches up, I'm cheering "WHOO HOO" and "YEE HAW" like some kind of possessed cowgirl.

The Boss and I gallop side by side. The whole scene feels like a romantic fairytale. I know that when the evening is over, I'll turn back into a pumpkin — a poor and dirty pumpkin. But right now, I can't imagine anything worth having more than this moment.

Before I know what hits me, I'm back at the trailer reluctantly dismounting my tired mount. The moment my feet hit the sand, I'm struck by the reality of my situation. My un-hairnet-ed hair is fashioned in a giant tangle. My skin is burnt from the wind and my jeans are completely soaked through with saltwater. I'm sure that I'm going to get sick and I'll probably have to shave my head in the morning, but all I can say is, "Wow! That was so much FUN!"

The Boss laughs, looking straight at me with the most intense gorgeous crinkly eyes I have ever seen. I think I just may have had the best night of my entire life.

* * *

Back at the barn, I've got both horses unloaded and drying under their wool coolers. Next it's time to unload the tack, unhook the trailer and sweep out the poop from the back. I think the Boss is taken aback by the enthusiasm with which I complete these menial tasks. But the hard work feels good and the leftover adrenaline from our beach ride is helping me get the job done in record time. Next, the Boss tells me to rub the horses down with liniment, wrap their legs and tuck them in good night. I'm not sure I know how to do any of those things. In all my years of riding, I've never tucked a horse in good night, wrapped one leg or rubbed down a single tired muscle that wasn't my own. Don't get me wrong, my horses always received the best care money could buy, and I took great pride in the bloom of health glowing on their coats. But until now, it didn't occur to me that I might be taking pride in the fruits of someone else's labor.

I tell the Boss that I want to become a better horseman. He bursts into uncontrollable laughter at the sound of the word "horseman". "Princess, you're a decent rider, but you're light years away from being anything resembling a horseman." Ninety seconds into this nightmare and the Boss is still laughing. But it's not until he calls Sam to include him in the joke that I become seriously offended.

OK, fine. I get it. Let me tell you something, Johnny Racetrack: I may not be a horseman, but do you have any idea how difficult it is to juggle five horses on the winter circuit while completing your senior year of high school online? Of course, I don't actually say that out loud. Because deep down, I know he's right. The idea that someone who has never tacked up her own horse could even think to call herself a horseman is ridiculous.

"Sorry, Princess. It's just sometimes you say the funniest things and I can't control myself." Can't control himself? Sounds like someone is preparing to spice things up with his favorite Gallop Girl... strict adherence to the boundaries of the employer/employee relationship be damned. I need to let the Boss know I'm ready to behave inappropriately in return. So I dip my toe in these deliciously warm waters and coyly say, "Why don't you show me how to rub the horses down with all that other fancy stuff you keep talking about?"

I think the Boss is a little taken aback by how quickly the cool and cautious Margaret Fletcher is willing to tread into such dangerous territory. How's that for uptight, Boss? He cracks a sly smile and I can feel the situation heating up as he leans in to say, "OK, Princess, the first thing to remember is that a thoroughbred is a lot like a man. Sure, we look big and strong on the outside. But inside we are delicate creatures who appreciate a sensitive touch." I've got to say, watching Johnny Racetrack gently rub liniment onto the hindquarters of an appreciative animal has completely changed my attitude towards the man. Sure, he can be a bit of a jerk. But, man, "That's one lucky horse."

I can't believe I just said that out loud. Watch out, Margaret Fletcher is feeling bold. The Boss looks me up and down like he is appraising a fine antique and says, "Princess, are you flirting with me?" I don't know what I'm doing. But whatever it is has him involuntarily flexing pectoral muscles and speaking in a soft husky tone. So I'm not going to stop. I should probably say something sexy. But my lack of flirtation skills are starting to show.

On my silence, the Boss pulls out the Biegle Oil and my entire body begins to warm up as he pours the liquid into my hand. I know in my heart that I have to acknowledge the romance of this situation. So I put on my best come hither look and say, "You're not supposed to call me Princess anymore, remember?" I can hear the reasoned voice of Emily discouraging me from upping the ante. But something about the smell of Biegle Oil and horse sweat is making me feel reckless. So when the Boss responds, "Well, you're not supposed to flirt with your boss," I act all sultry and say, "I'm not the one rubbing that horse down like it just bought me dinner."

I think the kitchen is getting a little too hot for the Boss. His cheeks are flushed, but husky accent is gone and he stubbornly refuses to meet my glance. I'm desperate to rekindle that spark. Do I dare offer him a massage? The Boss breaks my concentration and says, "Alright, Tiger, let's wrap these horses' legs and put them to bed before I get myself in any more trouble."

Wait, where did "Princess" go? "Tiger"? Isn't that what one calls one's favorite nephew before ruffling their hair? I'm sure when I look back on this moment I'll realize that "Tiger" was the Boss's signal to take things down a notch. But right now, I'm still high on adrenaline from the greatest night ever, so I respond to his attempt to rebrand me with an asexual nickname by asking a bunch of really inappropriate questions about his relationship with Erica. "Is she really good in bed? Because I can't imagine you're with her for the conversation. And I bet cuddling with her at night feels like trying to warm up next to a stainless steel champagne bucket filled with ice and no champagne."

The Boss looks at me like I've lost my mind. As we stand together in uncomfortable silence, I can feel the sparkle of sexual tension grind to a complete halt. Like I said, no one ever taught Margaret Fletcher how to flirt. Instead of addressing my inappropriately familiar comments, the Boss hands me a bandage and delivers a dry demonstration on the proper technique with which to apply a standing wrap. The moment has passed and there is no getting it back.

We wrap the next four legs together in silence. Stony silence. The kind of silence that gives a girl the chance to come down off the Biegle Oil fumes and reflect on her behavior. What am I doing? The Boss is a taken man. Besides, how great can he possibly be? He has already chosen to mate with Erica Lewis. That shows some serious lack of judgment. I'm probably just flirting with him in some misguided attempt to get back at my childhood nemesis anyway. I bet the second he breaks up with Erica, he turns into a troll.

I take a moment to remind myself that I am in the midst of a transformative stage in my life. I have significant goals ahead of me just waiting to be achieved. Goals more important than trying to land a boyfriend. Goals like getting back into the Hunter ring and showing all my old detractors that Margaret Fletcher may be down, but she is not out!

So I go home and spend the rest of the evening combing my hair and reflecting on my role in that argument with Emily. If I can gallop a feral horse on the beach, I can learn how to braid a mane, muck a stall and sleep on an inflatable mattress in the back of a pick-up truck. It may not be glamorous. But if that is what is required of my new budget equestrian lifestyle, I am ready for the challenge!

CHAPTER 8
~ *Emily takes on*
a challenge ~

To: Emily Morris (eventer4life@ghostmail.com)
From: Margaret Fletcher (BabyCalf@ghostmail.com)
Re: Sorry

It has been brought to my attention that my behavior the other day was out of line. And I am sorry. I know sometimes I come across as a little judgmental and maybe even a smidge pompous. But please be assured that my admiration for you and all that you have accomplished despite the unfortunate circumstances of your upbringing is sincere. You are a remarkable person, an amazing rider and an even better friend. I would be absolutely gutted if I ever did anything to offend you again.

Now that we've got all that messy groveling out of the way, I would like to propose that we set aside an afternoon in the near future for you to teach me how to braid a mane, muck a stall and sleep on an inflatable mattress. I feel confident that I already know how to eat string cheese and nuts. But I guess I have to learn how to do all that other stuff, now that I'm a scruffy "pick herself up by her bootstraps" kind of equestrian. And there is nobody I would rather have teach me than you, Emily Morris.

* * *

She can't be serious. Nobody needs someone to teach them how to sleep on an inflatable mattress. I don't care how rich they were growing up. Blow it up, put on your pajamas and lie down. It's not a mystery. I've already forgiven Margaret for her display of equestrian excess yesterday. But I'm not sure I've got it in me to teach her something that should be pretty intuitive by this stage in her life. Uncle Sam accuses me of giving Margaret a hard time out of jealousy. Jealousy? Please! Yes, of course I wish I had had more opportunities in my life. But I never wanted to be the kind of person who makes it all the way to adulthood without learning how to muck a stall.

But I guess when I agreed to take on the job of retraining Chocolates, I also accepted the challenge of retraining Margaret Fletcher. So I tell her to meet me at Green Acres dressed to get dirty. Margaret shows up in tan breeches and perfectly polished Italian field boots. Yeah, that's appropriate for getting dirty.

"Of course this is an appropriate way for me to dress for the barn, Emily," Margaret preemptively announces, "Don't worry. I'm not afraid to get these breeches dirty. This is my schooling attire." Schooling attire? I'm counting at least five hundred dollars of overpriced riding gear. And that's not counting the boots.

As annoyed as I am by Margaret's outfit, I don't want to scare her away. So I start with the genteel task of equine hairstyling. First, we must pull Chocolate's mane so it is the proper length and thickness for braiding. But Margaret is too squeamish to "rip Chocolate's hair out from the follicle like some kind of barbarian". I get the sense that Margaret is prepared to dig her heels in on this one, so I do my best to ignore her dramatic flinching as I take care of the job of pulling Chocolate's mane all by myself. All right, Princess, if you can't pull a mane, you can at least learn how to braid one. But as it turns out, no, she can't. After forty five minutes of watching her tie poor Chocolate's mane into messy knots, I'm left wondering if she even has opposable thumbs.

Screw genteel. We're mucking stalls.

"Emily," Margaret replies, "These are my favorite Italian schooling boots. Horse urine is going to burn a hole right through this fine leather. I know you said that we'd get dirty, but I really think this is over the top."

I throw a pair of rubber wellies in Margaret's direction. Her face scrunches up like a prune. She makes the tough decision to sacrifice her fancy boots instead of "wearing something that was purchased at a tractor supply store". Margaret dedicates a whole two minutes to the job of mucking Chocolate's stall. Finished, it looks as bad as when she started. But I guess I should be happy that I got her to pick out one whole pile of manure. The only thing left is teaching Princess how to sleep on an inflatable mattress. And I'm just not doing that.

Forty-five minutes into this training session, and Margaret is as spoiled and ridiculous as ever. It's a disaster and I'm faced with the humiliating reality that I've bitten off more than I can chew. I've never been good at dealing with failure. It all started twelve years ago when I got eliminated in the dressage phase of my first Pony Club rally because my horse wandered outside of the arena for a graze. Uncle Sam convinced the organizers to let me continue on to cross-country anyway. "It will be a good experience kid." But I refused to leave the start box. No matter what Uncle Sam said, I couldn't get past the humiliation of my earlier failure. So I packed up my things and didn't try again for another year. He never let me live it down. "Let me tell you something, Emily, the only surefire way to fail in life is to never try."

Just remembering those words puts a pit in my stomach that lasts all day. The only surefire way to fail in life is to never try. I eat a box of saltine crackers for lunch and drink a six pack of ginger ale. But the queasiness doesn't go away until I find the courage to send Turtle Cumberbund an email asking her to save my spot. I might have no hope of teaching Margaret Fletcher any new tricks. But I'm going to make that Box of Chocolates of ours into a world-class hunter and we're going to sell him for all the cash I need to make my dreams come true. Trying is succeeding and nobody is ever going to accuse me of giving up too soon again.

CHAPTER 9
~ *Margaret Goes on a Shopping Spree* ~

I feel good after my afternoon learning how to behave like a farmhand. Yep, it turns out Margaret Fletcher can shed her pampered ways and find it in herself to slum it with the worst of them. But that doesn't mean that Chocolates should. He is the product of royal breeding. He deserves the very best. I have just the bridle to show off his noble head. I bet if I have the cheek pieces shortened, it will be a perfect fit.

* * *

I haven't visited Mary's Tack Shop since my halcyon days of spending sprees and leather hording. Oh, how I have missed that smell. It pains me to know that I can't afford to purchase anything while I'm here. Not even a fresh tub of lederbalsam. No, I am here on a mission. Get my cheek pieces shortened and get out before siren smell of French baby calf leather becomes impossible to resist.

It figures I would show up the one day Erica Lewis is getting fitted for a new pair of custom boots. I turn and make a beeline for the door, praying I can make it out before she sees me.

But when I hear her screech, "Oh my God, look at that bridle! Talk about a blast from the past. I hope you're not hoping to sell that old thing, Margaret. Because NOBODY would be caught dead showing in a wide noseband anymore," I know I'm screwed. Erica takes one look at my old bridle and seizes on the opportunity to point out that everything I own is now hopelessly outdated. "Wow. Can you believe fancy stitching like that was ever in style?"

I would love to prove to myself that I'm above exchanging barbs with Erica. But I just can't stand the smug look on her face. So I take advantage of the knowledge that she has been fixated on the width of her calves ever since she measured a medium on an Italian boot-maker's size chart. "New boots, Erica? Are your calves swelling up again?"

But Erica is in rare form today. "No, Margaret, I'm still a perfect thirteen and a half inches. No bigger than those new biceps of yours." I do my best to ignore the insult until Erica insists Mary hand over the tape measure so she can measure my biceps. Just for fun.

Mary knows where her bread is buttered. Before I know what hits me, Erica is molesting me with the tape measure, giggling, "Look how bulky you are!

123

You look like some kind of heavyweight boxer now!" Little does she know, I'm proud of my brand new 100 percent Grade-A muscles. And I use them to fling Erica's scrawny little body back into the overpriced custom boot section of the store.

Disoriented, Erica mutters, "Did you just push me, Fletcher?" I put my hand on my hip and give her a look warning her that if she doesn't back off, I can do it again. Easily. A look of shock washes over Erica's angular features. I detect a hint of genuine fear in her voice as she blubbers, "This isn't the streets, Margaret! It's a tack shop. In case you have forgotten, which you clearly have, you're expected to behave like a lady in nice places like this!"

Erica is flustered and I'm feeling victorious. There are benefits to becoming a more rough-and-tumble person and I have Winning Edge to thank. Then I notice her breeches. Who makes those beautiful works of art and where can I get a pair?

Off my drooling expression, Erica knows she's found HER weapon in this battle. She gives me an evil smile, "Aren't these breeches great? I got them in Germany. The fabric is specially engineered to reflect the sun keeping you — oh, sorry, ME — at least 4 degrees cooler. You've got to love the Germans. They never miss an opportunity to find a competitive advantage. Remember when we refused to be seen in anything but Tailored Sportsman? It was such a quaint time. What are you doing here anyway? I hope you don't expect to find a new pair of goggles here! Mary, do you carry goggles? You know those hideous things that grooms wear at the racetrack?"

"I am not a groom, Erica. I'm an exercise rider," I say through gritted teeth.

Erica apologizes to Mary for my outburst and explains that my new work schedule requires me to get up at an ungodly hour every morning to muck stalls. If looks could kill, I would be peeling those breeches off Erica's cold dead body.

Right on cue, Erica gives me an innocent look and says, "Oh dear. I know what's going on. You came here to try and sell that bridle so you can pay your rent and here I am cracking jokes. Sometimes I can be such a ninny."

I know I should stop feeding the troll and walk out that door. But I just can't bring myself to let Erica Lewis have the last word. So I say, "It just so happens, I've got a new hunter prospect that I plan on showing at The Classic. Word on the street is everyone is going retro in the hunter ring this year. A discriminating equine with a refined head wouldn't be caught dead in anything BUT a wide noseband with fancy stitching."

I hand the bridle over to Mary and ask her to make the necessary adjustments. But I can tell from the expression on Erica's face that she's not buying what I'm selling.

"Well, knock me over with a feather," she says with an evil glint of mischief in her eye. I want to hit her over the head with a baseball bat. Instead, I smile and order a custom wool cooler from Mary. All the bells and whistles, please. I know I can't afford a custom cooler. But I need to make a statement here.

The gesture isn't lost on Erica. While Mary rings up a bill I have no business signing my name to, Erica fires off the backhanded compliments designed to make me feel small. "Wow, Margaret. That horse of yours must be something special if you're willing to sacrifice an ENTIRE month's salary on a new wool cooler in the middle of summer."

I am not a hundred percent sure who is winning right now. But I feel confident enough that I can leave with my head held high.

But Erica Lewis is a malevolent genius and she's not going to let me get out of this situation with nothing but a wool cooler I have no use for and can't afford. "Hey, Margaret, why don't you bring that horse of yours to the Geoff Maurice clinic I'm hosting at my farm? It's two weeks from Saturday. I won't even charge you."

It's an insanely generous offer. Generous because a weekend clinic with Geoff Maurice can easily run upward of a couple thousand dollars. Insane because I haven't even jumped a cross rail in over a year. Notorious for his exacting standards and hair-trigger temper, one does not take signing up for a Geoff Maurice clinic lightly. I'm well aware that Erica Lewis is setting me up to be the laughingstock of her clinic. I politely decline, reminding the little witch that some of us work for a living.

Erica cackles like a hyena and says, "I'm sleeping with your Boss, remember? I'm sure I can convince him to give you the time off."

Oh, Erica, gross me out all you want. I'm not falling for your trap. So when she continues, "Oh, silly me. I hope I'm not being too pushy. Sometimes I forget that we're just not in the same league anymore. You probably haven't even jumped a fence in over a year," I can't help myself and say, "Sign me up."

Crap.

CHAPTER 10
~ *Emily chickens out* ~

I've been retraining ex-racers for three years. Not once has Uncle Sam taken an interest in one of my projects. But Chocolates is different. Every morning he calls, asking for an update on "Money Bags". I'm pretty sure Sam has him confused with another horse from his distant past. But I humor him and admit that "Money Bags" is still enjoying his mini-vacation while I finish my research on how to make a nice hunter.

At the sound of the word *vacation*, Sam screams into the phone, "Emily, if you want make cookies, you've got to spill some flour on the kitchen floor."

Sam is clearly confused. I don't expect him to understand. I should stop listening to his incoherent ramblings the moment the unsolicited baking tips start. I'm about to hang up the phone when suddenly I hear clarity in Uncle Sam's voice that hasn't been there in years. I stop and hold my breath, eager for a glimpse of the man I remember before Sam's brain got all fuzzy.

"When your mother was your age, she used to always talk about starting her own business," he says, "But for every example she had of how it was going to change her life, she had three reasons why that business might fail. Instead of risking failure, she sat on her hands and did nothing. Let me tell you something, the only surefire way to fail in life is —"

— to never try. I get it. That's what I'm doing. I'm trying to not screw up. I am trying to get myself to England to train with the best. I'm trying to become an international event rider on a shoestring budget. I realize that my mother never had the guts to try. But that's not my problem anymore. My problem is I don't have the money it takes to make my dreams come true, and if I don't do a stellar job of retraining Chocolates, I never will."

I hang up feeling inexplicably defeated. I know taking my time to give Chocolates a slow, confidence-building start is the right thing to do. So why am I afraid to tell Margaret about Chocolates' vacation when she storms onto the farm, demanding to see evidence of our progress? For the past two weeks, all she has cared about is fancy stitched bridles and herringbone versus windowpane plaid wool jackets. But now she's barging onto Green Acres with a look of purpose on her face, announcing at the top of her lungs, "Emily, I'm riding Chocolates in the Geoff Maurice clinic in two weeks. So whatever you're working on, it's time to speed things up!"

My mouth is agape in disbelief as Margaret describes her little game of tit for tat with Erica. It sounds ridiculously juvenile to me. Sure, we get two free lessons with the best horse trainer in the country. But it's not like Chocolates and Margaret have any hope of performing well at a clinic like that. He's too green and she's too rusty. Geoff Maurice will eat them alive.

I have no choice but to tell Margaret the truth. I take a deep breath and confess everything: the mini-vacation, Uncle Sam's accusations and my firm belief that Chocolates just isn't ready for something as complicated as a fancy clinic.

Surprise, surprise, Margaret is not taking the news very well. "You have had him for THREE WEEKS! What the hell have you been doing?" she screeches.

When she says it like that, it sounds like I haven't been doing my job. I immediately start to get hot under my collar. But then I take a deep breath and remind myself that, like a green horse learning a new job, Margaret Fletcher doesn't mean to be so difficult, she just doesn't know better. "Margaret, Chocolates isn't some made packer that was just imported from Germany. He needs time to learn his new job. You're just going to have to cool your heels and turn down Erica's generous offer. I'm sorry. Sending Chocolates to this clinic before he is ready is literally putting the cart before the horse!"

Aside from that sucker punch in my trailer the first day we met, Margaret Fletcher has always struck me as someone with a firm grasp on her emotions. So I'm a little taken aback when she screams at the top of her lungs, "PUTTING THE CART BEFORE THE HORSE? HOW ABOUT YOU JUST TRY PUTTING A SADDLE ON IT AND RIDING IT AROUND LIKE YOU SAID YOU WOULD!" Now Margaret is the one taking a deep breath, trying to cool her heels. I don't say a word, strangely terrified to speak unless spoken to. "I know I'm new to this whole DIY horse-training thing, Emily. So please tell me how is Chocolates is supposed to get trained sitting in a field eating grass?! That horse is going to be a hunter, and hunters jump over fences with a RIDER ON THEIR BACK. We have to start him under saddle NOW. If you're too chicken to do it, I will."

Chicken? The little tart is calling me chicken? Margaret Fletcher may be a good rider, but she is not braver than I am. I could get on that horse right now and jump a course of fences if I wanted to. I bet even Margaret would be impressed with my skills in the jumper ring. Sure, I don't have years of top-notch training under my belt or a lower leg that never shifts out of place. But jumping horses is about more than just having the kind of feel and timing with your aids that makes riding even the toughest horse look effortless. It's about getting the job done. And that might not always look pretty or "classically correct" to someone like Margaret Fletcher. I'm sure she would have all kinds of rude things to say about my heel not being deep enough or my shoulders snapping too far forward. I can already hear her equitation critique. "Emily, you need to soften your hands and give him a better release over that fence!" Ridiculous!

131

You know what? If Margaret wants to humiliate herself in a clinic that she is totally unprepared for, go for it. This could be a teachable moment. Rushing into things when you're not ready is never a good idea. I tried to protect her, but it looks like she'll have to get a little egg on her face before she is ready to listen.

"All right, Margaret," I say, "If you want to take Chocolates to the clinic, you're going to have to ride him yourself for the next two weeks. That means it's going to be your job to teach him how trot, canter and jump like a show horse. Do you think you can handle that?"

Margaret assures me that she is up for the task. I'm pretty sure she's not. But some girls just have to learn the hard way.

CHAPTER 11
~ *Margaret Falls*
on Her Ass ~

DAY ONE

Why is Emily making such a big deal about riding Chocolates? I've ridden him before. In an exercise saddle, no less. Those things are so tiny you can't even sit properly. I've been begging the Boss for weeks to let me gallop in my Hermes. Nothing like perfectly-balanced French leather to make a girl ride her best. But he just laughs at me and tells me I'm cute. So dismissive. Sometimes I don't know why I find him attractive.

Well, now I finally get to ride Chocolates in serious equipment and I can't wait. Emily is stuffing all kinds of weird towels and memory foam pads under my saddle, insisting that she's improving the fit. Ten minutes later, she's still not completely satisfied. With absolutely no regard for time, she insists I go back to my apartment and bring back every saddle from my collection. I do. Of course, she picks my oldest, least favorite model in the bunch. "It's about Chocolates' comfort, Margaret. Not yours." As if I'm trying to make Chocolates wear some kind of itchy wool sweater.

Finally, I get the go-ahead to swing a leg over Chocolates. But the second my butt hits leather, I'm struck by an unfamiliar sensation. This isn't how this saddle feels when I ride my couch. Why are my stirrups a mile long? I suppose I have gotten used to riding shorter when I gallop. I stand tall in these new stirrups, stretching my legs and deepening my ankle as I make my way down to the arena. I'm sure everything will start to feel more comfortable once I start jumping fences.

I only asked Emily to come so she could set some fences, so I don't understand why she's yelling at me from across the arena like some kind of authority figure. "Sit down in the saddle and stop bridging your reins. We're not at the track!"

I look down at Chocolates' mane and see that I've got my reins in the tight cross I've grown to rely on at Winning Edge. That's not a very classical piece of equitation, Margaret. Looks like I have some new habits that I'll have to break before I return to the Hunter ring.

I uncross my reins and prepare to start this racehorse's reeducation. But Chocolates is just as confused by my new position in the tack as I am. Every time I try to sink into the saddle, he raises his head and drops his back. When I apply gentle pressure on the reins to encourage Chocolates to give to the bit, he quickens his pace, making it impossible for me to let go. Riding Chocolates around the small, enclosed space of Green Acres' jump arena feels like trying to wrap a steel rod around a blob of Jell-O. It's just not working.

All this flatwork is making me crazy. What does it matter anyway? Hunters jump fences: they don't perform aimless patterns in the sand. I beg Emily to set up a fence so I can start jumping and get into my old groove. She reluctantly throws a pole on the ground and instructs me to approach it at a trot.

I ignore her foolishness, pick up the canter and aim Chocolates at the ridiculous "jump" in the center of the ring. He charges at the pole with the kind of motivation he never displayed on the gallop track. Ah, there is nothing like the feeling of riding a good jumper when he has locked onto a fence.

I'm still basking in that familiar glow when, without warning, Chocolates slams on the brakes in front of the pole, leaving me with no choice but to jump the fence myself, sans equine. I land with a thud — flat on my back, inch deep in unsanitary arena sand. Ouch.

I know exactly what Emily is thinking right now. Little Miss Fancy Breeches can bring home a ribbon in good company, but put her on something that cost less than six figures and she falls apart. It's a jab I've heard many times before. The petty voices of jealous railbirds always floated across the arena as I collected my ribbons. *"I would be up there too if my Daddy could afford to buy me a push-button packer."* I always knew that my well-schooled horses gave me an advantage. But I also believed my talent was never dependent on my family's money.

Emily takes her time strolling across the arena, seemingly unconcerned about my wellbeing. She arrives at my side in time to help me wipe the dirt off my helmet. "Don't worry, Margaret. You're doing fine." No, I'm not. My butt is covered in arena sand, I've got a horse poop stain on my polo shirt and my ego needs a trip to the ER. But I'm too disoriented to say any of that out loud. Instead, I brush the last bit of dirt off my breeches and say, "No, Emily. Nothing about this situation is fine."

DAY TWO

I'm up until two AM trying to manufacture a plausible excuse to drop out of the Geoff Maurice clinic. But all I can think about is Erica's smug, knowing expression if I decline her challenge.

Three hours later, I'm at Winning Edge, where I'm expected to gallop seven horses for the Boss. But my tailbone, right hip and ankle are still screaming in pain from yesterday's fall on Chocolates. The old Margaret Fletcher would have scheduled a visit to the chiropractor, a full-body massage and a Dead Sea seaweed wrap to combat the discomfort. But the new Margaret Fletcher knows that she is expected to work through the pain. So I put on my stiffest upper lip and march into the barn prepared to do my duty.

"Princess, you look like you can barely move," the Boss says.

I'm not in the mood for the whole Princess shtick. I tell the Boss that if he's got a problem with that, he should talk to his girlfriend. Because she is the one who's rattling my cage.

"I'm afraid to ask," he says with a guilty look on his face. Those dimples pop out of his luscious cheeks and he casually hooks a thumb in the front belt-loop of his jeans, effectively pulling them low enough to capture my imagination.

I'm completely disarmed. So I tell him about Erica's offer and all the nefarious reasons behind her "generosity." I don't mean to get emotional. But something about the Boss's soft blue eyes makes me want to open up. I let my voice get shaky as I describe the events of yesterday's horrific schooling session.

A look of sympathy and understanding spreads across the Boss's rugged face. "You can't keep riding Chocolates like a racehorse and expect him to go like a hunter."

"Great advice," I say, "But I already tried to ride him like a hunter and I fell on my butt!"

"Then don't do that, either," he says. "Just give him support when he needs it and take it away as soon as he starts to figure things out."

Suddenly, it occurs to me that I've never taught a horse how to do anything before. They've always been the ones teaching me. No wonder I was so lost yesterday. I had no idea what I was doing. I've always said that the hallmark of a great trainer is the ability to

137

tell his rider exactly what she needs to hear at the exact moment she needs to hear it. And that's what the Boss just did. No wonder big beautiful animals are so eager to run fast for him.

Now if only the Boss would say the magic words that would make all my aches and pains go away. Instead, he hands me a thick crop and delivers a hard slap to my backside before sending me off to battle with his horses. I'm not saying that a nice long seaweed rub wouldn't hit the spot right about now. But it does feel good to know that I'm tough enough to do this job.

I smile at the Boss and give him a wink. I'll run as fast as you want, Boss. As fast as you want.

* * *

I replay the Boss's sage advice in my head as Chocolates and I carve out sloppy serpentines in the arena sand. I'm trying to teach this horse how to bend his body softly around the turns from nose to tail like a good little hunter. We look like two drunken sailors lost at sea, and we are not likely to find dry land anytime soon. I'm trying to remain positive here, but the two chuckling Dressage Queens lurking in the corner aren't helping. Then it starts to rain. I aim Chocolates in the direction of the barn. The last thing I need right now is for the bridle I spent ten hours oiling to get drenched.

But Emily is not happy about my decision to end this training session on a dry note. "I don't care if it's raining, Margaret. We've got a clinic in less than two weeks and you both look terrible. Now get back in the arena and pick up a left lead canter."

I had no idea that someone wearing a purple plastic schooling helmet could command such immediate and unwavering respect from me. Let me make one thing clear, I HATE RIDING IN THE RAIN. It's cold, it's sloppy and any well-conditioned saddle will bleed all over your breeches. But before I know what hit me, I'm back on Chocolates, struggling to pick up a left lead canter while Emily barks orders at me through the driving rain. Chocolates is just as frustrated with his situation as I am. He reluctantly picks up the canter and waits until we reach the soggiest part of the arena to dump me and then take off in a rider-less victory lap.

I don't know who makes me angrier: Emily for making me ride in the rain, or dog meat over here for making me the butt of his jokes. Chocolates eventually lets Emily catch him. I storm over with a sense of purpose I haven't had since the last time I could afford to splurge at Mary's "Year End French Leather Blow-Out". I hop back on Chocolates without a second thought as to how long it's going to take me to get the mud out of the seams of my saddle. I will get a left lead canter out of this horse. I don't care how hard it rains or how long it takes.

A half hour later, I'm victorious. I'm not sure if that's rainwater, sweat or tears pouring down my face, but it sure tastes sweet.

DAY THREE

I wake up at four AM to the sound of driving rain. I should have the day off from Winning Edge, right? Wrong. The Boss calls first thing in the morning to inform me that the footing on the track is fine. "Get your butt in the office, Princess."

Five hours of galloping in wet jeans presents all kinds of new chafing problems that no amount of "Monkey Butt" powder can possibly solve. The lady's locker room is closed for repairs and the nearest available restroom is clear across the farm. The wet denim on my thighs feels like sandpaper on my delicate appendages. I don't think I have the fortitude to make that long walk to the bathroom and I'm already running late for my schooling session with Emily.

I quickly dart into the first empty stall I can find, peel off my jeans and apply the appropriate bandages. In my haste, I thoughtlessly deposit my wet jeans on the dirt floor of this impromptu changing room. I'm five bandages short of covering all my wounds. I can't possibly put muddy jeans back on my body without risking infection. This is quite a pickle.

Fortunately, I've got a clean pair of breeches in the trunk of my car, which I estimate to be seven hundred meters away. Streaking across a proper hunter/jumper training facility is not something the old Margaret Fletcher would ever consider doing. But life at Winning Edge is a whole lot looser. Everyone is always encouraging me to let my hair down. So why not?

I peek my head out the Dutch door of my stall and confirm that the coast is clear. After a quick mental tally of everyone that might be in danger of seeing the half-naked dash to my car, I make the hasty decision to go for it. I've never been much of a runner. But the thought of being caught in my skivvies by one of the sketchier characters of Winning Edge Farms has me striding out like a champion thoroughbred.

"Princess?" I hear, seconds into my near-naked parade across the property.

Panicked, I execute a perfect swan dive through the open widow of my awaiting vehicle, huddling for cover in the nook of my backseat. The sound of my heart beating out of my chest is interrupted by a gentle knock on the driver's side window.

"Is everything OK, Princess?"

I flip through my mental calendar, trying to recall the exact date of my last encounter with a razor. Once I determine that there is absolutely no way to turn this into a sexy situation, I meekly say, "Um, Boss would you be so kind as to retrieve the breeches from the trunk of my car and throw them through the open window."

Without a word, he obliges and moments later, I emerge from my hiding place, fully-clothed, all four cheeks flushed with embarrassment. The Boss looks pretty flushed himself. Maybe I underestimated the erotic potential here. I crack a mischievous smile and say, "Sorry, Boss I thought I was covered."

The Boss's cheeks go from red to deep crimson as he struggles with the English language. "I didn't mean to look. It's just. I thought. I thought you were in trouble or something. You were running so fast."

I enjoy watching him fumble awkwardly. "No harm, no foul, Boss," I say, "I'm just trying to stop being so uptight." With that, Margaret Fletcher drives off before he has a chance to catch his breath. No harm, no foul indeed.

* * *

I'm still tingling with excitement from my unplanned, unclothed interlude with the Boss. Nothing can bring me down. Not even Emily's suggestion that we take Chocolates out for a trail ride. The arena at Green Acres is a mud pit and Chocolates can't afford to miss a single day of training. Ugh, the trail. What kind of productive training could possibly be accomplished on the trail? It sounds so long, slow and boring. Can't we just take a day off so I can go home and think up another situation that ends with me taking my pants off in front of the Boss? As usual, Emily remains an impenetrable force of "no fun allowed".

I find Emily in the barn aisle cavorting with a colorfully-dressed character named Sara. Sara is an endurance rider. Her horses know these trails inside and out, and Emily always begs her to tag along when she takes a prospect out for the first time. My eyes are having a hard enough time adjusting to Sara's black spandex pants with hot pink accents. But then she starts extracting tack from her hot pink plastic "trunk". This isn't the first time I've been confronted by the horrors of synthetic leather. But a nylon bridle? That can't be safe. And please tell me those cotton lead ropes are not her reins. No wonder that Arab of hers looks so startled. I can feel Emily judging me as I stare at this pair with a gaping mouth. So I do my best to keep it shut and train my eyes on the task of tacking up Chocolates.

The three of us head out to the trail in silence. (That would still be stunned silence on my part.) Sara makes a stab at striking up conversation, saying, "Emily told me that you used to be a big deal on the Hunter/Jumper circuit."

I can see my reflection in Sara's "breeches" as I nod my head.

But when she tells me that she also used to do the Hunters, I involuntarily snort in disbelief. I can see Emily cringe out of the corner of my eye. I didn't mean to react so rudely. But the only thing more shocking than a nylon bridle is the idea that Little Miss Circus Pants here ever did the Hunters. And when she insists that she once brought home a ribbon at Devon, I can't help but blurt out, "Impossible!"

Emily tells Sara that she will have to excuse me, as I am just now learning how to be tolerant of people who don't wear their hair in a hairnet. Very funny.

Surprisingly, Sara comes to my defense and admits that there was a time when she too would have been startled by a nylon bridle. That's very gracious coming from a girl dressed like a Japanese cartoon. Maybe I shouldn't be so quick to judge. After all, I can only imagine what Margaret, the sixteen-year-old Hunter Princess, would think about my current incarnation. Riding in jeans, running around naked in public, drinking one too many shots of tequila and flirting with my boss? Nope, the old Margaret Fletcher wouldn't approve of pretty much everything about my new Gallop Girl lifestyle.

I'm beginning to think that maybe Sara and I have more in common than her garish appearance suggests. So, I ask if her father lost all his money, too.

It takes a good ten minutes before the laughter subsides. Apparently, Sara's father never had any money. At least not in the amount that my trainers insisted is required to bring home a ribbon at Devon. Sara goes on to describe her Hunter-on-a-budget lifestyle. The nights spent sleeping in a trailer eating string cheese and exchanging manual labor for coaching at shows. It all sounds like the perfect little Cinderella story, except...

"I'm having a hard time believing that there are enough stalls in the world to muck your way to a ribbon at Devon," I say.

Emily butts in to explain that what Sara lacked in funds, she made up for in raw talent and the ability to recognize the same in young horses. Sara gets all shy and says, "Emily is exaggerating." But then Rainbow Brite cracks a smile. "I do have to admit that there is nothing more satisfying then finding that diamond in the rough and then beating all the fancy imports with something you paid a dollar for."

In other words, Sara is the polar opposite of someone like Margaret "I wouldn't be anywhere without Daddy's money" Fletcher. All right, Emily. I get it. Message loud and clear. You brought me on this trail ride to tell me that you don't think I have what it takes to give our green prospect the mileage he needs to get sold. Let me guess: Sara here is just itching to ditch her disco breeches and get back in the Hunter ring. Maybe it would be best if I handed over the reins.

Sara and Emily are too busy making jokes about my obsessive-compulsive desire to monogram saddle pads to notice my quiet fuming. I'm not sure how to handle this situation. I do my best to ignore them and focus on the natural beauty surrounding me. Deep breath, Margaret. Let's not let the Goodwill Twins ruin a lovely afternoon on horseback.

Growing up, trail riding was not something I was encouraged to do. It was always "Get up on your horse and get your heels down! Focus on your fence!" It's kind of nice to amble along peacefully without the pressure to perform. Then it occurs to me that Chocolates and I have crossed quite a few fallen tree branches in the past twenty minutes. If I remember correctly, he stepped over each one without a second thought. Look over there. That's a pretty big puddle up ahead.

I don't know what comes over me. Margaret Fletcher is not prone to impulsive acts of daring. But I pick up a quiet canter and aim Chocolates for that puddle, knowing full well that there is a good chance he might drop me in the middle of it. Five strides out, I start to feel him question my judgment. *"I don't know, lady. That looks like a hole to China if I've ever seen one."*

Emily screams from five paces behind, "Margaret Fletcher, what do you think you're doing?"

You know what, Emily? You're right. I have no idea what I'm doing. Did you hear that railbirds? It's all true! Margaret Fletcher is nothing special without a six-figure horse between her legs.

Three strides before puddle, I make a deal with Chocolates. Dump me in the muck, I'll take the hint and quit before I make an even bigger fool of myself. But if you find it in your heart to trust me, even though I might make some mistakes along the way, I'll return the favor.

I can feel the hesitation in Chocolate's body all the way to the base of the puddle. A part of me is hoping to take a mud bath and put this whole mess behind me. But together, Chocolates and I sail over it in perfect hunter form.

I'm speechless. I've jumped five-foot fences on horses that cost well into the six figures. I've won ribbons in some of the most prestigious arenas in the equestrian world. But I have never felt anything quite as exhilarating as jumping that muddy puddle on the racetrack reject I bought for a dollar.

For the first time since my whole life started falling apart, I feel like the luckiest girl in the whole world.

CHAPTER 12
~ Emily drops
the ball ~

It's the morning of Margaret's triumphant return to the horse world for people who matter. Her words, not mine. I, of course, see things differently. And I am pretty sure that today is the day that Margaret Fletcher finally gets knocked down a peg or two. I'm not proud of myself for secretly looking forward to the moment when she realizes that she's in over her head. I suppose it's in my best interest for Margaret to do really well. It's just there's no way that will happen. The past two weeks have been a disaster. That puddle is the only "fence" they've jumped together. Hardly adequate preparation to ride in front of the most intolerant horse trainer ever known to mankind.

The clock keeps ticking and Margaret is nowhere to be seen. I'm starting to get nervous. We only have twenty minutes to wrap Chocolate's legs, load the hay, pack the tack room and hitch up the trailer. And after all that lecturing from her! *"Emily, I don't know if you've ever ridden in front of someone of Geoff Maurice's caliber. He has exacting standards! Everything has to be perfect from the shine on my boots to the sparkle on my spurs. Anything less than perfection is INSUFFICIENT!"* I may not polish my spurs or spend an hour rubbing down my boots, but I show up on time. I am pretty sure that for a man of Geoff Maurice's caliber anything less is INSUFFICIENT!

I hook up the trailer all by myself. Still no sign of Margaret. That girl is too persnickety to be anything but perfectly punctual. A sick feeling creeps into my stomach and I'm starting to feel bad for cursing her name when I dropped the trailer ramp on my foot. Maybe she's dead. Or more likely, having second thoughts about this whole clinic situation. She's probably too embarrassed to admit that she's bailing. Not that I blame her. Margaret and Chocolates are not ready to ride in front of the likes of Geoff Maurice. They can barely hold it together in an arena smaller than a gallop track. Part of me admires the guts it takes to even think about riding a green horse like Chocolates in this clinic. Yes, it would have been brave. But it also would have been reckless. The last thing Chocolates needs right now is to find out that he might not be good enough. I'm glad Margaret finally came to her senses.

My phone rings and all my good thoughts about Margaret's newfound pragmatism are shattered by the sound of her screaming, *"What do you mean you haven't left the farm yet? Emily, I have to be in the arena in thirty minutes! MOVE IT!"*

Wow. I can't believe I gave her the benefit of the doubt. Margaret Fletcher isn't absent because she suddenly feared that she was in danger of over-facing her horse in a misguided quest to satisfy her ego. No, Margaret Fletcher is absent because it never occurred to her that it might be the responsibility of someone of her caliber to get her OWN DAMN HORSE to the clinic that she has no business riding in to begin with!

I want to like Margaret. I really do. But it's times like this, when I'm forced to ignore the persistent throbbing in my foot as I race around like a demon to come to her rescue as she screams into the phone, "*THIS IS UNACCEPTABLE!!!*", that I wonder if we can ever truly be friends.

CHAPTER 13
~ *Margaret finds*
her winning edge ~

I can't believe Emily screwed this up! Why would I meet her at Green Acres? I'm already a bucket of nerves. I stayed up all night polishing my tack and ironing my breeches. I really want everything to be perfect today and now I'm in serious danger of being late to a Geoff Maurice clinic!!! Do she have any idea what a huge faux pas that is???!!!

My aura is off the charts dark. I need to settle it back down if I have any hope of riding at my best. I take a deep breath, close my eyes and think back to my last meditation session with Daddy. Not that it went well. I blame Mother and her irrational fear that Daddy is poisoning my mind. "Margaret honey, I'm not sure these brainwashing sessions are such a good idea. I know your father means well. But he is not emotionally stable enough to provide any kind of reliable guidance. Do you really want to turn into the kind of person who wears clothing made out of illegal substances? Do they even make hemp riding pants?"

Of course I don't want to turn into the kind of person who wears illegal riding pants. But I hardly think that a man who says things like, "Look around you. Everything you need is here," has the power to brainwash. Especially when that person is standing in a windowless basement room filled with nothing but cheap beeswax meditation candles.

But as I look around Erica Lewis's perfect farm, I can't help but think Daddy is right. Everything I need IS here. Lush pastures as far as the eye can see, filled with the most beautiful horseflesh that can be found on this side of "the pond." The barn is pristine, the arenas are filled with soft felt footing and everything MATCHES PERFECTLY. Drink it all in, Margaret. Erica Lewis aside, this is where you belong.

My aura is finally starting to turn all pink and fluffy. But then I hear the rhythmical footfalls of Erica Lewis's latest import headed my way. And there she is, already mounted, totally prepared and completely confident about her plan to ruin my day. Her horse is gleaming, her boots are shining and her groom, Pablo, stands at attention, eager to meet her every need. One look at this equestrian princess and sheer panic is quickly replaced by the feeling of overwhelming frumpiness.

Just when I thought I couldn't possibly feel more out of place, Emily rolls in on an old trailer fit for transporting cattle to slaughter. Where on earth did she get this relic? Not that her normal trailer is any great shakes. But this rickety thing is just plain embarrassing. Judging by the look on Chocolates' face, he's as humiliated as I am.

Oh, sorry, did I mention I can SEE the look on Chocolates' face from OUTSIDE the trailer because the walls are not even SOLID! Is this death wagon even safe? I hear the gasps and guffaws of the well-heeled Hunter Princesses as they watch Emily rattle and roll down Erica's cobblestone driveway. Even though I share their feeling about the "vehicle" barreling towards us, I keep my jaw clenched shut.

I don't know why Emily is in such a grumpy mood. She's not the one who is about to commit the biggest faux pas of her entire equestrian career. She doesn't even meet my eye as she says, "Margaret, don't give me that look. This "thing" is perfectly suitable and I'm not hauling my entire apartment fifteen minutes down the road because you don't like the look of a stock trailer."

I don't quite recognize the expression on Erica's face. I think it might be speechlessness. But she somehow finds the words to ask Emily, "You live in a trailer?"

Emily is too busy being annoyed with me to be embarrassed by the question. She just ties Chocolates to the side of her "trailer" and says, "Yes, and I sleep on a bed of straw and take baths down by the river when no one's looking. Margaret! We've got five minutes to get you in the arena. Let's get this show on the road!"

I suppose I should be happy that my groom understands the importance of swift action in this circumstance. Given Emily's behavior, however, I would rather be left to my own devices. Let me try to illustrate the severity of the situation. Pablo's appearance is smart and workmanlike: pressed khakis, a neatly tucked-in polo shirt and a proper belt. Emily is dressed in alfalfa hay, horse slobber and stall bedding. Pablo swiftly and efficiently gives Erica's already perfectly-polished boots a final wipe-down from the very tip of their Spanish tops to very bottom of their soles. Emily limps along like a wounded animal, barking orders with the delicate tact of a truck stop waitress. While Pablo carefully applies a final coat of hoof polish on all four corners of Erica's mount, Emily slaps tack on poor Chocolates like she's making a ham sandwich.

Before I have a chance to so much as wipe off the horse poop that has made its way onto my boots, Emily hoists me up on Chocolates with the grace one might use to throw a sack of potatoes into a shopping cart. The jarring action of my body tumbling into the saddle irritates my sensitive thoroughbred's back. He raises his head in the air like a periscope and trots off in the same frantic pace with which he was prepared.

Now Erica IS speechless.

And I'm screwed.

DAY ONE

A lot of people mistake Geoff Maurice for a mean old man on an ego trip. They wonder why any equestrian would subject herself to so much verbal abuse at the steep price of five hundred dollars an hour. But while Geoff may lack concern for his students' feelings, the man knows how to get the best out of any rider tough enough to endure his criticism. I'll never forget the time he called one of the country's top equitation riders an "incompetent fool" for misunderstanding the approach he asked her take to a fence. Word got out on the Internet and recreational riders from across the country demanded he be banned from ever teaching our fragile youth again.

What they didn't know was that the incompetent fool wasn't offended at all. She just had the best lesson of her life with a man who could not care less who her daddy is or what his money can buy. He didn't treat her like some kind of delicate flower too spoiled to hear the truth. By the end of the lesson, that incompetent fool rode better than she ever had in her entire life.

Five years later, she can't wait to get back into the ring to ride with him again.

Here I am, that incompetent fool, back in Geoff Maurice's arena, ready to try my heart out. Only this time, I'm sitting on a tense and confused horse that would rather canter in place than execute a nice, relaxed trot.

Mr. Maurice takes one look at us and turns the volume up on his megaphone to ten. "Girl with the muddy boots…TrrrrrrROT!!! I said TRRRROT!" It takes every ounce of determination I have to make Chocolates transition into a gait almost resembling the trot. It's horrible. And when Geoff Maurice bellows at the top of his seventy-five-year-old lungs, "NOT like that. Not like a sewing machine. That's not how you trot. This is not a home economics CLASS," I can't help but feel that he is being kind.

Margaret Fletcher has never been one to give up when the going gets tough. I sit deep into the saddle, carefully wrapping my legs around Chocolates' barrel, trying to encourage him to soften his body.

With the anger of a drill sergeant reprimanding a difficult cadet, my childhood idol screams into his megaphone, "WHY are you HUMPING your saddle like a confused eighteen-year-old boy? It's not going to buy you DINNER!"

And then I hear the Boss's familiar laugh amongst the sea of auditors. Who invited him? I didn't invite him. Did Emily invite him? Oh, I know. Erica invited him! That little scheming tramp. It's not enough for her to make sure that I embarrass myself in front of everyone in the equestrian world who actually matters. No, she has to make sure everyone at Winning Edge also has an opportunity to see me looking like a fool. I'm about to hyperventilate when Geoff Maurice interrupts the onset of my panic attack by screaming, "PAY ATTENTION! I don't have TIME for you if you don't PAY ATTENTION in my arena! Because you, my dear, are not GOOD enough to NOT pay attention! Beezie Madden doesn't have to pay attention. McClain Ward doesn't have to pay attention. You and your muddy boots MUST pay attention!"

A lightning bolt of panic courses through my body, traveling through the delicate French leather of my Hermes saddle, striking Chocolates' sensitive back and causing him to bolt across the arena like someone just lit his tail on fire.

"STOP! Girl with the muddy boots, STOP!"

I have absolutely no control of Chocolates at this point, but Geoff Maurice does. The authoritative tone of his voice could stop a runaway freight train in its tracks. On Chocolate's screeching halt, Mr. Maurice demands, "You stand there. STAND and WATCH how you trrrOT a HORSE! You watch how you cannnnTER a horse! Watch how you jumP a horse!" And with that, the riding part of my lesson comes to an end before it has a chance to officially start.

One hour later, however, I'm still praying for the ground to open up and swallow me whole. Every time Erica's horse canters by, she covers me and Chocolates with a fresh coat of arena dirt. I'm sure we blend in quite well with our surroundings by now. I should be annoyed, but I'm grateful for the camouflage. Maybe Geoff won't realize that we're still here?

But then, for the first time in an hour, he turns his attention from Erica's beautiFULLL riding to acknowledge my presence. "Now, you. Tomorrow you will prepare BETTER. You will present yourself BETTER and you will ride BETTER!!! You think I don't remember who you are. I know who you are. I reMEMBER who you are. YOU'RE the one who doesn't remember who you ARE! Dismissed!"

* * *

It takes every ounce of strength to keep my composure in the few minutes required to exit the arena. When Emily asks me if I need help, I don't dare answer her for fear that my voice will crack and a flood of tears will come out. She gets the hint. I need time alone with my pony, the pony I just let down in front of the most important man in the entire equestrian world. There's an empty box stall at the end of the barn aisle. I usher Chocolates inside, close the Dutch door, and press my face into his neck crying as hard as I did the day my last pony sold to the highest bidder.

I hear the sound of a gentle knock on the door. I highly doubt I can get away with pretending that nobody's home. Even if I could, Chocolates has already nudged the door open, revealing the Boss. He gives me a sympathetic look and says, "Tough day at the office?"

The single tear sliding down my cheek says it all, and the Boss is sensitive enough to drop the line of questioning. He asks if I can meet him back at Winning Edge in an hour. Sure. Why not? What else am I going to do with the rest of my day?

I dry my tears, drop Chocolates off at Green Acres and hustle over to Winning Edge Farms. My Tailored Sportsmans are trashed. I'm covered in dirt, sweat and tears.

But I don't even bother to shake the alfalfa from my hairnet. It's time to stop pretending that I'm someone I haven't been in years.

* * *

Back at Winning Edge, I find the Boss alone in the barn grooming a brown colt named KK Matty K. Apparently, some deadbeat owed the Boss money and gave him this horse instead. One look at the scrawny colt standing before me and I conclude that a smarter man would have written off the debt. At least Chocolates is pretty. This guy? He might be able to get a job working as a scarecrow on some poor farmer's field after he flames out on the track. Which, judging by his shaky conformation, should happen pretty soon. But if the Boss wants me to gallop this horse, I'll gallop the horse. Who am I to turn my nose up at anyone or anything at this point in my life? I hand the Boss my favorite exercise saddle and help him tack up my charge.

"So, Princess, I heard you met my old friend Sara." I'm guessing "old friend" is code for ex-girlfriend. Whatever, Boss. Your past is your past and my future sucks. Let's stick to the task at hand and keep our personal stories to ourselves today.

But for reasons I don't understand, the Boss turns into a Chatty Cathy. "Did she say anything to you about me?" (Clearly, he is still obsessed with Sara.)

The old Margaret Fletcher would have pressed for more information. But the new Margaret Fletcher doesn't show up for clinics on time, polish her boots properly or care about other people's problems. So I remain silent on the matter.

Matty is dressed to run, and the Boss gives me a leg up. Two seconds ago, I was ready to get down to business and get out of here. But there is something about the way that man grips a girl's thigh that can lighten even the most stubborn of moods. Maybe I shouldn't give up on what might be a juicy love story so quickly. I'm not exactly in a position to turn my nose up at a cheap source of entertainment.

So I cautiously dip my toe into scandalous waters. "Come to think of it, Boss, Sara did get very excited when I mentioned your name. Maybe she is still in love with you."

But I'm not getting the reaction I was looking for. Instead of pushing for more information on Sara's latent desire, the Boss just walks along in silence as Matty and I make our way to the track.

Not one to enjoy long uncomfortable silences, I make a joke about inviting Sara to the clinic tomorrow in the hopes that the useless tart he calls a girlfriend starts a catfight in front of Geoff Maurice.

The Boss warns me to tread carefully. But the playful tone in his voice confirms that he is charmed by my unabashed persistence.

So I continue. "Come on, Boss, I'm in need of a distraction right now. Throw me a bone. Tell me that you're still in love with Sara and this whole Erica thing is just one big joke."

He flashes a mischievous smile and says, "You need a distraction, huh? How about another half-naked jog around the property to clear your head?" Clearly, someone is STILL thinking about my cotton-clad bottom sprinting across the farm. I crack my first genuine smile of the day.

We arrive at the track and before I have a chance to jog off with Matty, the Boss puts his strong hand on my thigh to stop me. "Sara is not my ex-girlfriend. Back in high school, I had a bit of a reputation for going after you Hunter Princess types and she used to give me a hard time about it." Had a reputation for going after Hunter Princess types? Who does he think he's dating now? A Rodeo Queen? I snort involuntary at the Boss's hilarious lack of self-awareness.

"My sister showed on the circuit," he continues, "What can I say? I was popular with the girls. Sara said that I got passed around the Hunter/Jumper scene more times than the twenty-year-old pony every girl wants to ride at her first show."

So the Boss has a thing for us Hunter Princesses. I suppose that would be good news if he wasn't already shackled to our least attractive representative. The buzz from our back-and-forth wears off, and I remember that I'm not a Hunter Princess anymore. A Hunter Princess would have showed up to that clinic on time, clean, polished and prepared to impress. She wouldn't have made a complete fool of herself, only to be forced to suffer the humiliating fate of standing in the corner of the arena with a dunce cap on her head while the real riders got to work.

No. I'm a scruffy little Gallop Girl. Erica Lewis is the true Hunter Princess. So, Boss, I guess you picked the right girlfriend, after all. All right, let's get this sucker galloped so I can go home to my crappy apartment and cry into a nice big tub of lederbalsam.

To my delight, Matty wastes no time getting with the program. He calmly walks to the track like he's been doing this his whole life. When I ask for the jog, I'm surprised to discover a pleasant, workman-like gait that is a pleasure to ride. This fellow is all business. After an afternoon of dealing with a lunatic that refuses to comply with even the most simple of requests, I find Matty's attitude refreshing. You know what, buddy, there's more to life than just being pretty. Sure, you'll never be a show pony. But what's so great about all that crap anyway?

I think I've got a good feel for this horse. I'm ready for a fun little gallop around the track. So I turn Matty around. Before I have a chance to bridge my reins, a monster explodes. It's the most terrifying, fire-breathing gallop I have ever experienced in my entire life. Matty is propelling himself forward with the determination of a war horse charging into battle, and I'm pretty sure nothing short of a nuclear bomb would stop him. Three seconds into this ride and my biceps are already screaming for mercy. I am not strong enough to hold this horse-shaped rocket for much longer.

I should be terrified.

But for reasons I can't explain, I'm not.

I thought I knew what bravery was. I thought I knew what boldness felt like. But I have never felt anything like KK Matty K. Only three years old and he already knows he's a champion. Every muscle in his body is telling me, *I know who I am. I know what I can do. Take me wherever you want and I will always be the best one there.* This horse doesn't know that he was bought for nothing at a no-name auction somewhere far, far away from Kentucky. He doesn't know that he's small, scrawny and not much to look at. Or that a horse with his unremarkable pedigree and wonky conformation shouldn't be this good.

All he knows is that he loves to run fast, and he does it better than anyone else in the barn.

Just try to tell me different. I dare you.

CHAPTER 14
~ *More to*
Margaret Fletcher
than meets the eye ~

I show up at Green Acres half expecting to find Margaret passed out in a pile of well-conditioned strap goods. I probably shouldn't have left her alone after we unloaded Chocolates yesterday. But Uncle Sam took one look at her gently caressing that overpriced wool cooler that is of absolutely no use to anyone this time of year and said, *"She just needs some time alone with her plastic ponies."*

I have no idea what he meant by that. But it doesn't sound like something a girl should do in the company of someone she's just getting to know. Besides, pointing out that I told her so probably wouldn't be all that helpful right now and I'm pretty sure that I wouldn't be able to help myself. Not that I'm looking for Margaret to fail. I just think the whole embarrassing situation could have been avoided if she had shown a little restraint when Erica egged her on to accept this completely insurmountable challenge.

Uncle Sam refuses to acknowledge the error of Margaret Fletcher's impetuous ways. He lets me finish complaining and then says, "That girl isn't afraid to get flour all over the kitchen. You need to pay attention because you could learn something." Once again, nothing he says makes any kind of sense. And I'm beginning to regret asking him to come along today for moral support.

It's not like I actually expect Margaret to show up for a second day of emotional torture anyway. I bet she's locked up in her apartment, playing My Little Pony on her couch.

Turns out I'm wrong. Far from being tangled up in well-oiled French leather, Margaret is awake, alert and briskly sweeping out the same stock trailer she couldn't bring herself to touch the day before. Little Miss Fancy Breeches is wearing a crisp pair of jeans, a "perfectly pressed polo shirt" and a brand new pair of deerskin work gloves. I'm not sure what to make of the outfit. I can't imagine she plans to present herself in front of a man of Geoff Maurice's caliber in jeans. I hope she's not expecting me to take her place in the irons today. Because I am NOT as quick to make a fool of myself as some people.

On closer inspection, I can see that Margaret's hair is tightly wrapped in "hunter hair" with that overpriced helmet of hers perched on top of her head. I guess it looks like she's ready to return to the scene of the crime, after all.

A smile spreads across Uncle Sam's face, "See, kid, I told you this one's got spunk. She doesn't give up easily like you do."

I decide to ignore Uncle Sam's not even thinly-veiled insult. Spunk! Please, I think we both know this one probably had one too many Grand Marniers for breakfast. Mix in the toxic fumes from that over-priced lederbalsam she loves so much and I bet Margaret Fletcher doesn't even know where she is right now.

I make sure to get a whiff of Margaret's breath as she barks, "Come on Emily, let's hustle. We wouldn't want a repeat of yesterday would we?"

It smells like decaf coffee and English muffins. She's lucid. I suppose that's a good thing. But I hope Margaret isn't under the impression that the ONLY thing that went wrong yesterday is that she was a little late for her lesson. Poor Chocolates was in way over his head. There was NO WAY someone like Geoff Maurice was going to take him seriously. And he didn't.

I think the prudent thing to do right now would be to slow things down and examine the situation more closely. But Uncle Sam already has Chocolates' legs wrapped. And from the looks of Margaret's determined stride, there is no stopping her from loading that horse onto my trailer.

All right, fine. Here we go again.

CHAPTER 15
~ *Margaret Gets Redemption* ~

DAY TWO

Today is a new day. I know who I am. I know what I can do. I may be small, scrawny and not much to look at. My pedigree may have lost its stature and I work at a no-name farm for chicken scraps. But none of that matters to me anymore. Because I love to jump horses. You can take me wherever you want and I will always be the best one there. Just try to tell me different. I dare you.

* * *

I walk into the arena with my boots perfectly polished and my horse properly warmed up, ready to show the world what we can do. I'm not there five minutes when Geoff barks, "Let me see the girl who gave me so much trouble yesterday. You! Give me your horse."

With that, I am instructed to hop off Chocolates and hand over the reins to Mr. Maurice. So much for showing the world what I can do. I don't even have to look up to see Erica's smug expression as Geoff Maurice mounts my horse, preparing to show me how it's done.

"Watch me CANTerrr this HORSE. Watch me TRRROT this horse. Ohhhh, this is a hot horse. This is an intelligent horse. Not like your horse, Erica. Your horse is duller. Slowwwwer to reACT. A horse like this requires patience he needs to be ridden with TACT!"

I'll admit that getting kicked off Chocolates before my lesson even had a chance to start stung. But watching the Chef d'Equipe of the US Show Jumping team get runaway with in much the same manner I did twenty-four hours earlier eases my suffering. Geoff coos, "Ooohh this one is HOT. He needs to learn to accept my legs BETTER. He needs to learn how to accept my hands BETTER."

Five minutes later, that's exactly what Chocolates is doing. And I'm getting the distinct impression that Geoff Maurice is actually having fun riding my horse. "This is a HORSE. This is a HORSE that requires a RIDER, not a PASSENGER. Not like your horse, Erica. You are a PASSENGER on that HORSE of yours!"

I don't know which sight is more pleasing: Geoff Maurice executing a perfectly-balanced flying lead change on the horse I bought for a dollar, or the look on Erica's face suggesting that at any minute her head might explode.

"People today don't have the patience to find a horse like this. They don't have the patience to learn to RIDE a horse like this. Everything has to be easy. Oh, Margaret, what a horse. What a horse! It takes TALENT to find a horse like this. It takes TALENT to ride a horse like this. If you don't have TALENT, you have to go to Europe and spend a lot of money. Right, Erica? Oh Margaret, do I have to give him back? Don't make me give this horse back," he says as he counter-canters circles around Erica's overprice import. "If I were a younger man, I would buy this horse and win the grand prix of AACHEN on this horse!"

And then the most important man in the entire equestrian world dismounts Chocolates, hands me the reins and says, "He is different now and I expect you to ride him well today."

It's amazing what twenty minutes of schooling from a top professional can do. Chocolates is a different horse. He's supple, relaxed and confident in his work. As I approach my first jump, so am I.

"BEAUtiful!"

Let's make that an oxer and raise it three inches.

"Super, Margaret. SUPER!"

For my final trick of the day, I'll put a loop in the reins and canter on down the line like we've doing this our whole life.

"Ahhh... she's good. She's good that Margaret!"

That's right. That Margaret, she is good.

CHAPTER 16
~ *Emily Takes the High Ground* ~

I'm not sure how to process what just happened. Chocolates was nothing short of amazing today. I should be thrilled, right? So why am I filled with envy? I OWN half of that horse, remember? The better he is, the more money I pocket when he sells. I've already come to terms with Margaret's meteoric rise to Gallop Girl success. So she had an easier time learning how to gallop than I did. That doesn't prove anything. Yes, she rode well today. But I'm pretty sure that if I had been stupid enough to ride a green off-the-track thoroughbred in a Geoff Maurice clinic, I would have done just as well.

My emotions are not making any sense. I decide to take a long walk around the farm to collect my thoughts while Margaret prepares Chocolates for the drive home.

As I wander around my lush surroundings, I can't help but wonder what my life would be like if I had even half of what Erica Lewis has. I don't care about the cobblestone barn aisles or the shiny brass nameplates on the stall doors. It's the opportunities that I'm envious of. Imagine having nothing to do all day but ride a stable full of beautiful, talented horses. The bottomless competition budget, the best trainers in the country, the trips to Europe when those trainers think it's time to grab some international experience. Where would I be in my career if money wasn't a limiting factor?

As Erica Lewis trots towards me with a five-man T.V. crew in tow, I can't help but think that I definitely would NOT be wasting my time with a ridiculous equestrian princess reality T.V. show for some hack cable network.

I immediately regret leaving Margaret's side as Erica calls out, "Emily! I've been looking all over for you." Before I have a chance to run in the opposite direction as fast as I can, Erica grabs my arm with her perfectly-polished claws and pulls me towards the barn.

"Do you mind if we move into the tack room for a chat?" she screeches, "BOYS! Let's set up in the tack room!" Being trapped in a tack room with the likes of Erica Lewis is the last place I want to be right now. But her freakishly sharp fingernails are drawing blood from my bicep. I'm afraid that if I pull away, I might lose an arm.

Erica's tack room is lit up like a Barbara Walter's Christmas Special. Before I know what hits me, some "dude" wearing a Sundance Film Festival T-shirt shoves a release form with the title, *Erica Lewis, One Rider's Journey to the Olympic Gold*, under my nose.

"It's just a working title," Erica explains, "The production team will only use it if I actually make it to the Olympic Games of course. Listen to me being all humble! Hey, Brad, make sure to get my Hermes saddles in the shot. Middle America will love that!"

Against my better judgment, I scribble my name across the bottom of the paper. And just when I thought things could not get any weirder, Erica says, "Hey, Brad, let's shoot Emily only from the neck up. I don't want my viewers thinking I buy horses from stable hands."

Before I have a chance to ask the lunatic standing across from me what she's talking about, Brad yells, "Action!" Erica's voice suddenly gets ten octaves lower, carrying a dramatic-flare appropriate for a bad Mexican soap opera, as she recites, "Emily, I am so glad I ran into you. I would like to make an offer on that horse you are selling. I think he has the potential to take me all the way to the Olympics."

Is this some kind of joke? Off my confused/horrified/disgusted expression, Brad yells, "Cut!"

The lights are making Erica sweat like she's actually working, and I can tell by the look of growing irritation on her face that she doesn't enjoy the sensation. Her voice is back to its regular screech, as she demands that someone bring her a fresh polo shirt and a Gatorade. Margaret should be about done cooling out Chocolates. Even if she's not, I've had enough of this circus.

But Erica is not letting me out of her clutches that easily. "Emily!! Where are you going?!!! I'm trying

172

to buy your horse from you! Now, this time when I say action, say something nice about how exciting it is to sell your horse to a rider with so much potential and talent. Action!"

Erica's eyes get all dark and serious again. I dare not move a muscle. With a look that can only be described as "sexy Cruella De Vil", Erica says, "Emily, I am prepared to offer you sixty thousand dollars. Do you accept this generous offer?"

Generous offer? What the hell is she talking about? Erica throws her hands up in the air, yells CUT and starts screaming again about that fresh polo shirt. "I'm starting to get pit stains here!!!!" A wardrobe assistant appears from out of the blue with fifteen different white cotton polo shirts for Erica to choose from. A confused, crazed expression clouds Mommy Dearest's face as she says, "Why do these all have burgundy monograms???? I said I wanted a shirt monogrammed in every color BUT burgundy. NOT every shirt IN burgundy!!!! Someone better fix this!!!!"

Brad kills the lights and the room is instantly twenty degrees cooler. Four terrified little production assistants are sent into town in search of acceptable polo shirts and the crew breaks for lunch. Nobody here seems to realize that they're trapped in The Twilight Zone. OK. I'll just back away slowly.

But Erica grabs my arm again and squeezes as she says, "EMILY, I'm serious. Don't worry. I don't have any delusions of taking that skinny little horse of yours to the Olympics. The producers are worried that show isn't glamorous enough to attract the non-equestrian audience. So I talk about the Olympics a lot and make Brad shoot close-ups of anything with a Hermes logo."

I have never wanted out of a barn so much in my entire life. But Erica has me firmly in her clutches. So I ask, "Why do you want to buy him?"

This whole experience is almost worth enduring just to see the indignant look on her face as she snaps back, "I resent that! I don't want to buy Brad! Daddy is funding the project because as a businessman he knows a good opportunity when he sees one!"

I clarify that I meant to ask why she wants to buy CHOCOLATES.

"What can I say? I like buying Margaret's stuff. I loved buying every last one of Margaret's show horses after her family went broke. Oh, I didn't need the horses. I already had more than I could possibly ride. But who could resist an opportunity to twist the knife that was already stuck in Margaret's back?"

What a bitch. No wonder Margaret can't stand letting this woman get the best of her.

Erica takes out a checkbook and starts writing me one for sixty thousand dollars. I stand there, completely frozen with indecision. Half of sixty thousand dollars would get me to England for sure. I could leave tomorrow. I should be all over this, right? So why do I have a pit in my stomach?

I tell Erica that I need time to talk this over with Margaret. Chocolates is her horse, too, so I can't do anything without her OK.

Erica looks at me like I'm a fool and says, "Yeah, well, Margaret hates it when I buy her ponies. I'm counting on you to smooth things over. Maybe you could just tell her you sold him to one of your Pony Club buddies."

When I explain to Erica that I don't have any "Pony Club buddies" with sixty thousand dollars to spend on a horse, she laughs like I just said the funniest thing in the world. "You don't tell her you sold the horse for sixty thousand dollars, silly! I'll make the check directly to you. Give Margaret a couple grand and pocket the rest. I approached you directly, so you should get a bigger piece of the pie for, like, putting the deal together and everything."

And that's when I discover that Erica Lewis is, in fact, pure evil. There is no way I'm selling that horse to her now. My relationship with Margaret may not conform to the traditional definition of friendship. But I am not the kind of girl who screws over her almost-friend just to make a buck.

I take great pleasure in telling Erica that she can take her check for sixty thousand dollars and shove it.

She just shakes her head and says, "That's really sweet, Emily, but let me give you some advice. This is a tough business, especially for the plucky little girl living in her trailer. You can't be afraid to get your hands a little dirty."

That's rich coming from a girl who can't make it fifteen minutes wearing the same polo shirt.

* * *

I'm not going to tell Margaret about this whole unsavory conversation. The last thing I need is for her

175

to think that I plan to make a habit out of putting her needs before mine.

This was a one-time deal. From now on, I'm not going to let anything get in between me and that one-way ticket to England.

CHAPTER 17
~ Margaret forgets who she is ~

I'm still high off my weekend riding with Geoff. Seriously, could life get any better? Then I see Matty's name next to mine on the Boss's exercise chart. Yay! I've pretty much decided that Chocolates is my equine doppelganger, but Matty is my muse. I can't wait to get on him and feel all that wonderful horsey energy and excitement that he's got coursing through his veins.

The Boss meets me at the barn where Matty is waiting in the crossties. He's got his business face on as he instructs, "Remember, this one can be a handful. So do not let your guard down for one second." I don't know why the Boss is acting so uptight. It's as if he forgot that I'M the one that galloped the snot out of him the other day. I pat the Boss on his strong, well-developed shoulder and assure him, "It's OK, Boss. I think it's safe to say that I know what I'm doing here."

I stroke Matty's neck as I extract him from the crossties. *We had a good go the other day, didn't we? Now let's show the rest of these wannabes how it's done and tear up this track!* The Boss rolls his eyes. Once again leaving me with the creepy impression that he can read my mind. I think to myself, *"Take me now you handsome devil!"* Crickets. All I get from the Boss is a totally unnecessary leg up. I know I'm strong enough to catapult myself up onto this beautiful beast with that same graceful, sweeping motion that Emily loves to show off. But I let the Boss have his way. Anything to give him a chance to check out my well-toned derriere, right?

There is absolutely nothing playful about the way the Boss says, "All right, Princess. You're just jogging Matty today." It's a letdown for sure. No flirting. No galloping. I'm not sure why the Boss is so determined to make this just another boring day at the office.

But that doesn't stop me from winking atop my steed and saying, "You're the Boss, Boss." I can't believe how flirtatious that was. What can I say? This horse gives me courage. Besides, now that I know the Boss is a total Hunter Princess man-slut, I'm less concerned about looking like a floozy. Who is he to judge, right?

I mosey onto to the training track with complete confidence.

And immediately get run away with like I have never been run away with before.

All I can hear are Matty's hooves pounding, my heart racing and the Boss screaming. Matty is running hell-bent for leather and there is NOTHING I can do to stop him.

This is not exhilarating. This is terrifying. More terrifying than that moment when you realize you've outgrown your old custom boots and are forced to ask yourself if you're experiencing a normal growth spurt or an unacceptable weight gain. Time seems to have slowed down, giving me the chance to ask myself, "What the hell are you doing with your life, Princess?"

And with that, I'm catapulted into the air at forty miles an hour.

Smash. I bite the dust. Everything is blurry. I'm totally disoriented.

A wise old man with a fuzzy beard stands over me and says, "Kid, are you alright?" God? Is that God? Wait. Why does God's breath smell like a Denny's Grand Slam Special? The name Sam swirls around my scrambled brain. I wonder what happened to God. "I THINK SHE'S OK," God screams. "She's just needs a shot of whisky before she's good to ride another one!"

And then it hits me. I'm probably dead.

The silhouette of a hunky, Adonis-like creature approaches, and I know I've made it to heaven. "Princess, can you move?" he asks. Yes, my love. I'm not minding being dead so much if it means I get a hot new boyfriend.

But then the shrill sound of someone screaming, "Margaret!!! MARGARET!!! Is she OK?" takes me back to the living. Thanks, Emily. I always knew I could count on you to suck the fun right out of a good situation.

I look down at my body to make sure it's still in one piece. Something is very wrong here. I'm wearing jeans! Why am I wearing jeans! Who put these things on me? I look like some kind of farmworker. Nobody is taking my concerns seriously. They're just calling for a paramedic and yelling at me not to move. Where do these people think I am planning to go? I'm wearing jeans! I am certainly not going to go out in public dressed like this!

Ten minutes later, I'm still screaming, "Margaret Fletcher does not ride in jeans! Why do I look so poor and dirty?!"

Only now I'm screaming it at a hospital. Good news: I can walk and all my bones are in order. But it seems I have a concussion. At first, I think the doctors are being silly. Then it slowly dawns on me that not only does Margaret Fletcher ride in jeans, she is poor and dirty. I suppose my little outburst is proper cause for concern. So when the doctor agrees to release me from the hospital on the condition I spend the night at a friend's house, I accept his terms. I just wish my friend's "house" wasn't the living quarters of her rundown horse trailer.

I'm feeling better. But most of my day is still a blur. Luckily, Emily is here to play back most of embarrassing moments for me.

"You kept screaming, "Why am I wearing jeans?" until the Boss finally told you to shut up," Emily says,

"Then you got totally offended and punched him in the face. It wasn't a real punch. It was more like that punch you gave me when I tried to touch your hairnet. But the Boss was totally stunned, and I think a little turned on. Then, with NO warning at all, you accused him of looking at your butt. He turned bright red. But that didn't stop you. You just kept repeating "You have to stop looking at my butt!" over and over again. I swear you had everyone in the emergency room cracking up."

Emily has strict instructions to watch me for the next twenty-four hours in case I wake up vomiting or something. No big deal. I could use the company, even if I really wish she would stop replaying my greatest hits. And even if she has to wake up every four hours and cold hose a horse's leg for the Boss. One of the perks of living on the farm, I guess.

So I'm spending the night in Emily's trailer. Great. Emily encourages me to think of it as practice for when she makes me sleep in a stall at The New London Classic. Wonderful.

Emily invites Sara over to the party. Why not use up every inch of available horizontal space, right? Emily's Crock-Pot only makes dinner for one, so we order a pizza and gather around it like a campfire. I'm not reaching for a random analogy here. Emily's heater is broken. For the next fifteen minutes, that pizza is the only thing radiating any heat in this tin box.

Neither Sara nor Emily seem bothered by the uncomfortable accommodations. Nope, they're too busy reliving old concussions and riding injuries. At Emily's urging, I show Sara my tooth necklace. She's impressed. But compared to their laundry lists of dislocated shoulders, broken collarbones and torn ligaments, I feel that I have little to offer.

When Emily and Sara push for more stories, I come up empty. But Emily refuses to believe me. "Come on, Margaret. How many horses were you riding for how many years? You've got to have more than just a broken tooth to show for it." I guess riding well-schooled, even-tempered school masters isn't the same dangerous proposition Emily and Sara grew up with. Cue the supportive encouragement from the peanut gallery. *No way, you're a tough girl! It takes guts to sucker punch the Boss like that!*

But there is nothing disingenuous about my statement. I know how to ride. Hell, I've KNOWN how to ride my entire adolescent life. But it's only recently that I've been expected to do so in less-than-ideal circumstances on less-than-perfect mounts. Geoff Maurice accusing Erica of being a PASSenger and not a riDER was one of the great moments in equestrian history. But everyone in this "room" knows that I'm only just starting to make the transition myself. It's turning out to be a lot more difficult and humiliating than I would have ever expected. For the first time since Daddy lost his fortune, Margaret Fletcher has been shaken to the core.

"I've got to be honest, girls, I got really scared up there," I quietly admit. "Sure, I've jumped big fences and ridden in front of some of the toughest critics.

But I've never been out of control like that before, and I'm not a hundred percent sure that I'm going to have the guts to ride that horse again."

The girls exchange looks. Emily starts talking to me like she has just realized I sustained minor brain damage. "Margaret, you're not going to have to. The Boss has a mandatory one-week no-riding rule after a concussion. Besides, I overheard him say that he doubts he'll ever put you on that horse again."

I should be relieved, right? So why do I feel like I've just been told I'm being held back a grade? Emily tells me that she overheard the Boss scratching Matty from his first race, on account of him working too hard today. "As glad as he might be that you're not dead, nothing pisses him off more than having to scratch a horse because one of his exercise riders screwed up."

Screwed up! I didn't screw up. "I fell off!"

"No. First you let him run away with you and then you fell off," Emily says. Sarah nods her head in agreement and tells me that I'm lucky the Boss likes me so much. He has been known to fire riders for less. What?!!! How am I the fall guy here? It's not like I fell off because I'm slacking on the job. It's not like I didn't try my damndest to stop Matty from running away with me.

I can see that I'm not going to get any sympathy from my companions here. The walls of Emily's trailer are closing in on me and I want out. So when her egg timer alerts us that it's time to go cold hose that horse's leg, I struggle to my feet and offer to do the job.

Emily and Sara share another one of their looks. I bet they think I don't know how to cold hose a leg. Look at them, waiting for me to ask instructions like some kind of rube. Well, I've got news for you girls. Margaret Fletcher may not always be able to stay on her horse, but in the past few weeks, she's learned a thing or two. I've been reading those Pony Club manuals of yours ever since the Boss laughed at me for calling myself a horseman. I crawl out of that trailer with my head held high.

There's more to Margaret Fletcher than meets the eyes, girls. More than meets the eye.

* * *

Just as Emily promised, the Boss gives me a full week off without pay. He insists that my suspension is not a punishment. "It's for your own safety and the safety of my horses," he says. "Matty could have gotten seriously hurt galloping around the barn like that."

Why does everyone keep acting like I got dumped on purpose? I DID EVERYTHING I COULD TO STAY ON!!!!

I resist the urge to throw a temper tantrum and politely remind the Boss that getting dumped was Matty's idea, not mine. The Boss is unsympathetic. He doesn't even bother to look up from his work chart as he insists, "No, Princess, you were cocky and let your guard down."

Cocky? I was doing my BEST to ride a DIFFICULT horse. So I got dumped. Sounds like that kind of thing used to happen to Emily and Sara all the time. Why is it such a big deal when it happens to me?

I've never been one to turn down a week vacation. But I've got bills to pay now. Using my best damsel in distress voice I plead, "Have a little sympathy for a working girl, Boss. You wouldn't want me to go hungry would you?" The Boss plucks an apple out of his desk drawer and (with no regard for my poor reflexes) tosses it in my direction. It lands on the concrete floor with a thud, its juicy destruction providing an apt metaphor for the past twenty-four hours of my life. He still hasn't looked up from his paperwork. And I can't help but feel offended by his lack of concern for my situation. Against my better judgment I say, "Did Erica get pissed off at her mirror again and whip up a batch of poison apples?"

The Boss stops scribbling on his chart and looks at me squarely, "Watch it, Princess. You're walking on thin ice."

Thin ice? Isn't he the one who should be shaking in his boots? Undeterred by his authoritative tone, I snap back, "Fine. Suspend me. As soon as we negotiate whatever workman's comp I'm due for the pain and suffering YOUR horse caused ME, I'll be out of your hair."

But the Boss just laughs. "Princess, if you expect to get compensated every time you get hurt, you need to find another job. Maybe there's a tack shop somewhere that could benefit from all your years of experience shopping."

OK. That felt like an insult and this time I'm not taking it in stride. I pick the what's left of Erica's poison apple up off the floor, slam it on the Boss's desk (with no regard for the delicate mahogany finish) and say, "If the only thing I'm good at is racking up credit card debt and looking cute in fancy breeches, why am I galloping the toughest horse in the barn?"

The Boss snorts dismissively, "Don't flatter yourself, Princess."

I chuckle, "You think I'm flattering myself? Then tell me, who is going to gallop Matty while I'm out?"

All I need to do is take one look at his face to know he hasn't quite figured that part out yet. Watching the Boss slowly come to the realization that HE is going to have to ride the one horse in the barn that is strong enough to dump his best Gallop Girl at forty miles an hour ALMOST makes my suspension worth the cost to my bottom line. A better person would just claim victory and head home. But I wouldn't want to *flatter* myself into thinking that I'm a better person. Nope. Instead I just look at my panic-stricken boss and say, "What's a matter? All you have to do is make sure you don't get cocky and I'm sure the whole experience will be easy as pie."

He doesn't appreciate my sarcasm. But I think he likes the situation that I've put him in even less. I can see that every bone in his body is telling him to scold me for insubordination. But he doesn't. I bet if I stick around long enough, he'll cave and offer me a big fat bonus if I agree to exercise his horse during my "suspension." I'm not going to do that. Because I think somebody here could stand to learn some manners, and it's not the girl with road rash on her butt.

I just walk away with my head held high and my fancy ass swaying in the wind.

* * *

The painkillers I got at the hospital make me feel all warm and fuzzy inside. Temporarily disarmed by the delicious narcotic glow, I ask Mother to meet me at the only salon in town willing let her pay for her pedicures with designer labels ripped out of the seams of her once-fashionable wardrobe.

"In my heart, I will know that it's an Alexander McQueen even if I no longer have proof that it is, in fact, an Alexander McQueen." Mother pulls out two Christian Dior labels procured from the soles of a pair of well-loved stilettos. There is a tense moment as the beauty technician complains about residual foot odor. Fortunately, Mother has a couple Ralph Lauren Black Labels in her back pocket to smooth over the transaction.

Watching Mother trade worthless scraps of dirty fabric for actual goods and services inspires me to ask for her advice on my current financial situation. "Oh, don't worry honey," Mother comforts me, "You're not screwed until the I.R.S figures out how to garnish your PayPal account. Good luck trying to making money selling your old crap on eBay after that happens."

The mushy effects of my painkillers wear off the moment my feet hit the cold, soapy water bought and paid for by Mother's bizarre barter system. Suddenly, my mind becomes lucid enough to fully grasp the consequences of my actions. The Boss was going to relax the terms of my suspension. I could feel it. All I had to do was ask one more time. But there's no way he's going to do that now. Especially after I told him he could kiss my fancy ass and then waved it in front of him like a tasty little morsel he can never sample.

Full-blown panic sets in as I remember storming out of the Boss's office, proudly proclaiming that the riders in my Equestrian Barbie collection have a better shot at galloping Matty than he does. Oh dear. What if he fires me?

"You know, honey, maybe this is a sign that you should give up on this ridiculous horse obsession of yours," Mother says as she admires the blood red varnish on her nails.

In a weak moment, I almost agree. Then again, I don't see Mother giving up anything so easily herself. I see her getting the weekly pedicures that I'm sure Daddy's accountant told her she can no longer afford. Mother holds on to her old life with whatever white-knuckled grip she can maintain. So why can't I do the same?

Later that afternoon, I corner Emily in the tack room of Green Acres and ask her how much board money she earns in exchange for all the little chores she performs around the farm. Emily rolls her eyes and purses her lips as if she is preparing to deflect an insult.

I cut her off before she has a chance to get defensive. "It doesn't matter. Whatever the amount, it's more than I'm making at Winning Edge right now. Why don't I take your place so you can use the extra time to pick up my rides at Winning Edge? Chocolates' board will get paid, I will be covered in all kinds of unspeakable farm detritus and you can finally start pulling your weight in this partnership of ours."

That last sentence didn't go over too well. For the next seven minutes, I have to listen to Emily rant and rave about all the important ways in which she contributes to our partnership. "You know, Margaret, I would love to see you drive to the barn every night and wrap Chocolate's legs or clean his water bucket or keep on top of his hay order or do ANY of the many chores I handle in order to keep our horse alive!"

Emily eventually settles down and agrees that something has to be done about my temporary halt in income. Reluctantly, she admits that even I, Margaret Fletcher, have the skills to pick up her slack at Green Acres and we shake hands on the agreement before I have a chance to come to my senses. The problem is solved. But I have the nagging feeling that Mother would have managed to strike a better deal.

* * *

My duties at Green Acres are pretty simple. I am to muck stalls, feed lunch hay and bring horses in and out of pasture. So why is Emily acting like I'm being asked to negotiate peace in the Middle East? She's got her business face on as she squawks, "MAKE SURE you cross-reference the feed chart before throwing hay. DON'T just rely on memory. God forbid Susan Smith's Hanoverian gets alfalfa instead of timothy. You'll hear about it all week. I know it's an easy job and I'm sure you can handle it. I just want to make sure you take it seriously."

Et tu, Emily? Et tu? I don't understand why everyone suddenly has the idea that Margaret Fletcher is untrustworthy around their animals.

Emily rummages around in that plastic container she calls a "trunk" and produces a pair of crusty deerskin gloves. She gives me strict instructions to wear them whenever I handle hay. The gloves have the name of the tractor supply store where Emily purchased them stitched into the palm in bright green lettering. Yeah, I won't be wearing these. I smile and nod, doing my best to hide my irritation, and reassure her that I plan to follow instructions to the letter.

A clap of thunder fills the air and the heavens open up outside. Then I remember the four days of rainstorms in the forecast. Emily warns me that I better have a good pair of wellies if I hope to get through the next few days without contracting gangrene. Ugh, yes, I have a pair of pink rubber boots with little doggies holding umbrellas on them. Now leave me alone so I can find my painkillers and take a nap before I have to feed lunch.

DAY ONE

So, it turns out my pink rubber boots with the little doggies holding umbrellas on them are not waterproof. These things were all the rage on the Hunter/Jumper circuit three years ago. Everyone had a pair. I mean everyone. I don't care if was ninety degrees out without a cloud in the sky. Any self-respecting Hunter Princess hanging out in between classes had her pink rubber boots on. I can't believe no one ever figured out these things don't actually work in the rain!

Luckily, Sara is around to help me line my two hundred dollar decorative "rain boots" with plastic grocery bags, and I am able to muck thirty stalls without getting too much urine on my favorite pink socks with little cats holding fancy canes.

Halfway through lunch, I curse the decision to turn my nose down at Emily's deerskin gloves. My hands and arms are covered in tiny little scratches from the hay. When the scratches turn into puffy little welts, I bring them to Sara's attention. Knowing my luck, I'm probably infected with some kind of incurable barn skin fungus. She tells me that her skin does the same thing when she handles hay without gloves. Apparently, the welts are the product of a hay allergy. I'm allergic to hay? How is it that I've been around horses my whole life and it's only when I have an entire barn full of them to feed that I discover that I'm allergic to hay???!!!

I'm a sniffling, sneezing, puffy mess with urine-soaked trash bags on my feet. It can't get any worse, right? Oh, but it does. I've got three ponies in a muddy pasture that need to be brought in. Three EVIL little ponies who think it's absolutely hilarious to slowly trot just out of my reach. After watching this comedy routine for fifteen minutes, Sara takes pity and gives me three buckets of bran mash. Those fat little ponies get one whiff of that mash and descend on me like they haven't eaten in a week. I manage to avoid getting knocked down in the mud, but my shirt is completely covered in mash by the time I get each pony back in its stall. Wonderful.

Sara takes pity on my situation and encourages me to take the rest of the day off. I want to scoff at the suggestion that I take it easy. Haven't I just spent the past six weeks trying to prove that I'm tougher than I look? But the urine-soaked garbage bags on my feet are starting to smell and the bran mash crusted on my slicker looks like vomit. I'm out of here.

DAY TWO

Against my better judgment, I return to the scene of the crime. I couldn't bring myself to pick up a pair of ugly green rubber boots at the tractor supply, so

I'm wearing my ONLY pair of paddock boots. I used to have seven pairs of paddock boots: one for each day of the week. A lot of people don't realize that fine leather needs a full weeks rest after the good soaking of sweat that comes with a hard day's ride. Not that I ever actually rode in my paddock boots. Bunny insisted on field boots only. But they were good to have around in case my seven pairs of field boots all sprung a defect at once.

But I can no longer afford that luxury. I've got ONE pair of paddock boots at the precise moment in my history when I am actually required to ride in them seven days a week. These babies better hold it together 'til I get myself back on the payroll at Winning Edge.

It rains all morning. I'm hoping this means that I can forgo turning horses out in that swamp of a pasture. But Sara informs me that the mud in the pasture isn't sitting atop a slick, hard base of compacted stone dust like the barn aisles are. So I go ahead and throw Chocolates out, seeing as he's one of the horses in the barn smart enough not to run around like an idiot in pasture. I take one look at the deep mud of said pasture, however, and I KNOW my paddock boots won't survive even one step inside.

I make sure Sara is occupied sweeping out the tack room and grab a lunge whip from Emily's locker. The plan is to unhook the lead rope from Chocolate's halter and use the lunge whip to encourage him inside the pasture without actually setting foot inside myself.

I know Emily would absolutely NOT approve of my actions. But she is not here to offer me a better solution. So I go for it.

Everything is going swimmingly until Chocolates panics at the slight of the lunge whip and bolts in the exact opposite direction of the pasture. The ten minutes that Chocolates spends galloping loose around the barn at full speed are the longest of my life. Fortunately, he stops in front of the hayshed long enough for Sara to catch him. I tell Sara that Chocolates, one of the laziest horses in the barn, inexplicably took it upon himself to jump out of the pasture. It's a ridiculous story, and Sara knows it, but she decides not to press the issue any further.

I take Chocolates from Sara and walk him deep into the pasture until mud sucks the soles right off my precious paddock boots. I can feel the filthy pasture grime creep in between my toes and under my toenails. There isn't a pedicure this side of the Mississippi that could get the smell out anytime soon. It serves me right for putting the safety of a pair of replaceable boots ahead of my one-of-a-kind Chocolates.

DAY THREE

Emily is waiting for me in the feed room. Uh-oh, I'm in big trouble. Sara told her all about Chocolates jumping out of the pasture and my pristine paddock boots. Crap. I've never been a good liar. So, I break down in a sloppy, blubbering mess and confess my sins. I'm not even mad at Sara for busting me. I deserve whatever punishment Emily dishes out.

But she just stands there and stares at me with a look of pity. Is this some kind of Jedi mind trick designed to make me feel even worse than a good tongue lashing ever could? Because it's working. I repeat the story for Emily again. In case she missed any of my unforgivable behavior. But she just looks at me with a calm expression and says, "It's OK, Margaret. I'm sure you learned your lesson."

"No, Emily. It's not OK! I've been screwing up left and right all week. My negligent actions could have caused serious harm to my two most favorite horses in the world," I yell and scream and spit more mucus across the tack room.

But Emily is not biting. She continues to look at me with understanding and tells me that she is sure I have learned my lesson.

I snort in disbelief, "Come on, Emily, we both know that all it's going to take is one more lapse of judgment on my part and one or both of those horses will be dead!"

Nothing. Nada. Not even a slap on the wrist.

Fine. I really bring out the big guns and wail like a banshee, "I'm not cut out for this! My priorities are all screwed up. How could I be so concerned about a stupid pair of paddock boots? They're not even custom! What am I saying? That shouldn't even matter! Right? I should probably just give you

Chocolates, find myself an office job and never set foot in a barn until I can afford to have a team of trainers supervising my every move!"

My plan is backfiring. Emily is so uncomfortable with my dramatic self-flagellation, there's no way she's going to yell at me now and risk my further descent into madness. I end with, "I give up, Emily! I give up!" and hope that the humiliation of the last fifteen minutes is an adequate punishment for my totally unforgivable behavior.

But then Emily says, "You can't give up now, Margaret. You're too good at this." I'm beginning to think that the little trailer hermit over here is actually some kind of Machiavellian genius. I have never in my life been so desperate for someone to put me in my place as I am right now. I'm terrified to open my mouth. Anything that I say could be easily twisted into another unwelcomed compliment designed to make me feel like crap.

Emily breaks our uncomfortable silence with, "That's right, Margaret, you're a really good rider. Believe me, it's totally annoying how easy you make galloping look. Just when I thought I could handle you and all your natural confidence-building balance, you go and make a feral off-the-track thoroughbred look like a sixty thousand dollar hunter!"

Now Emily is sounding like the person who is about to go off the deep end. I finally open my mouth to snort, "Chocolates is nice, but he's no sixty thousand dollar hunter."

"Then why did Erica offer to buy Chocolates for exactly that after you kicked her butt in that Geoff Maurice clinic?" Emily challenges back.

WHAT?

Suddenly, the waterworks in my tear ducts shut off like somebody forgot to pay the bill. I'm no longer blubbering so much as mentally depositing thirty thousand dollars into my checking account.

Emily senses the instantaneous change in my mood and smiles. "Don't worry. I told Erica to take a hike. We're not selling this horse until you have a chance to make your triumphant Hunter Princess return at the Classic." I'm speechless. No wonder this girl lives in an unheated trailer. Emily isn't finished, though, and proudly proclaims, "Some things are more important than money. Some things are even more important than being a working student in England. So you don't have to worry about me selling your dream down the river, Margaret. I'm not that kind of friend."

Let me get this straight. Emily turned DOWN a sixty thousand offer on a horse that's barely worth a buck fifty?!!! I want to scream all kinds of horrible things at the top of my lungs. But then I remember that pain medication and an angry Margaret Fletcher isn't a pretty mix. I take a deep breath and ask dear Emily, "Do you honestly think that this is my dream? I spent three hours yesterday doing barn chores in shoes with NO SOLES! I don't like Erica Lewis any more than you. But it's not like her ponies aren't well-cared-for. Her farm has five equine Jacuzzis for Christ sake. Call her back and tell her we accept."

I can tell that my reaction isn't what Emily was expecting when she told me that she took it upon herself to turn down a ridiculous amount of money for a horse that we are both hoping to sell for a ridiculous amount of money. Don't get me wrong: selling yet another one of my ponies to the likes of Erica Lewis is not ideal. But the situation gets a lot more palatable in direct proportion to how much Erica Lewis is willing to overpay for said pony. Sure, I would be bummed to miss out on the Classic. But thirty thousand dollars could get me to the next big horse show in style. Or, I don't know, maybe buy me another pair of paddock boots!

When Emily tells me that she is pretty sure the offer is off the table, I suddenly feel a lot poorer than a barefooted barn lackey should. I patiently wait for her to apologize and promise to never do something so stupid again.

She doesn't. Instead, she says, "Wow, Margaret. I really thought you were different. But you're just like all the other rich girls who just use their horses to get what they want before moving on to the next one. Meanwhile, those of us who think of our horses before ourselves get left in your dust. No wonder I can't seem to get anywhere in this business no matter how hard I work."

"Emily, you can't get anywhere because you do stupid things like turn down a sale that could have afforded you the opportunity of a lifetime. You're the one who crapped all over that free ticket to England, not me."

Emily looks like I just punched her in the gut. Tears well up in the corners of her eyes as she tells me that I need to go back to the Boss and beg for my job back because I have done enough damage here.

That's it. Margaret Fletcher can only take so much self-righteous attitude in one day. I let those painkillers take over and scream, "Living in a trailer does not make you better than me!"

Now it's Emily's turn to act like a petulant child and stomp out of the feed room. I decide to wait five minutes for her to regret her actions and come back.

Fifteen minutes later, I'm still standing in the tack room wondering what to do next. The path isn't clear. But one thing is certain: I won't be begging Emily for forgiveness just so I can continue my indentured servitude here at Muddy Scratchy Farms.

Margaret Fletcher may have gotten her head scrambled like an omelette on the track at Winning Edge Farms. But she is most definitely not the one acting like she has a screw loose!

CHAPTER 18
~ *Emily is fed up* ~

Ever since the day Margaret crashed and burned on the track, I have done everything in my power to support her and make her feel good about herself. And how does she repay me? By nearly killing our horse, and then telling me that it's MY fault I can't afford to make my dreams come true. That Hunter Princess really is a piece of work. My first instinct is to call Uncle Sam and complain about how wronged I've been. But he's bound to come to Margaret's defense with a ridiculous analogy about her baking skills. I've got too much anger boiling up inside me. I have to let some of it spill out of the pot.

I call Sara. Who else could possibly understand what I'm dealing with? But Sara isn't cooperating. No, she thinks Princess Fancy Breeches has a point. I refuse to listen to whatever traitorous thing she has to say. Margaret Fletcher has done nothing but wreak havoc on my ego ever since she set foot on the grounds of Winning Edge Farms. I'm sick of it. She dresses better than me. Gallops better than me. And just when I think I've finally got her where I want her, she rides a green show horse better than me. Not that I was looking for her to fail. But come on! How on earth did she come out of that clinic looking like a hero?

When Sara asks why I turned down Erica's offer without consulting Margaret first, I don't know what to say. It felt right, OK? Never in a million years would I have expected such a grilling from the one girl in my life who understands what it's like to be the only poor girl in the room. I can't believe it. I'm ready to hang up now. But she is not letting me go. She starts blathering on about how I'm a really good rider, but I just don't give myself enough credit. What is Sara talking about? I'm always saying what a great rider I would be if I had more money. That doesn't sound like someone guilty of never giving herself enough credit.

I hear Sara sigh at the other end of the line. She is trying to tell me something and I'm just not getting it. So I change the subject to something I'm more comfortable with and say, "Did you know that you're supposed to color coordinate your jacket with your horse?"

Sara laughs and warns me to prepare to be introduced to a whole new world of crazy at The New London Classic. I hadn't thought of that. I've been so focused on Margaret's silly behavior, it never occurred to me that I'm about to travel into the eye of the storm.

"Any advice on how to blend in with the fancy natives? Should I get a pair of fake diamond earrings and call everyone Lovey?" I joke.

I can feel Sara rolling her eyes as she responds, "Emily, you're focused entirely too much on money. Just remember that no matter how much you have, in this sport there is always going to be someone richer than you. So if you want to have any kind of longevity as an equestrian, you've got to have more to offer than a fat bank account."

I think Sara has forgotten who she's on the phone with. Of course there is always going to be someone richer than me. I'm broke! That's the problem. That has always been the problem. Even if I sold Chocolates to Erica Lewis for sixty thousand dollars, that would still be the problem.

I make a big show of yawning and thank Sara for her totally useless advice before hanging up the phone. I'm still mad at Margaret. But in the quiet of my own company, I can admit to myself the real reason why. I asked the Boss to give me the ride on Matty while Margaret cooled her heels at Green Acres. And he said no. I didn't push for an explanation because deep down inside I was glad he wouldn't let me. I'm terrified of that horse, as is every other rider at Winning Edge. I was just the only one with the guts to pretend to want to gallop him.

But I know that come next week, Margaret is going to get right back up on Matty. When she does, I'm pretty sure it will be the final blow to whatever is left of my ego. And once again, Margaret Fletcher, Hunter Princess extraordinaire, will deliver the wallop without even realizing what she has done.

CHAPTER 19
~ *Margaret girds her loins* ~

Mother insists I bear witness to another one of her fake shopping sprees. I should say no. It's embarrassing to watch her try on clothes that she can't possibly afford. And I feel sorry for the salesgirl shuttling garments back and forth, believing that the crazy woman admiring herself in the dressing room mirror still lives in a world where a seven thousand dollar evening gown is a reasonable purchase. Poor thing is probably already calculating the commission on this star-spangled monstrosity of a dress.

"Margaret, honey," Mother screeches as she zips it up over her boney hips, "Allison is having another one of her fundraisers for poor children that want to ride horses. I don't know how I'm going to fit it into my schedule. But you know Allison! She'll be absolutely furious if I don't attend. I think this dress might just be the thing to wear. It's kind of got a rhinestone cowboy feeling to it, don't you think?"

Dr. Allison Swanson may have a habit of buying horses for talented young riders of modest means. But this fundraiser is a figment of Mother's overactive imagination. I know this because even if Dr. Swanson was inclined to throw a charity ball for otherwise-privileged juniors who can't *quite* afford the equestrian lifestyle, she would never in a million years invite Mother. Back in heyday of the Fletcher family fortune, Mother referred to Dr. Swanson as her personal white whale, on account of the fact that the good doctor was the one social connection she could quite never catch. "Mark my words, Margaret. One of these days, I'm going to find the right harpoon!"

I don't know why Mother put such a premium on obtaining Dr. Allison Swanson's friendship. But she sure did everything in her power to try and get that woman's attention. She even showed up at Dr. Swanson's hunt club unannounced, dressed to the nines and ready to Tally Ho. After being told that she couldn't ride to the hounds on the golf cart she stole from Daddy's country club, Mother finally gave up.

I can't help but notice that the poor salesgirl is working way too hard for her fictional commission, and I feel the need to make it stop. "Remind me Mother. Did they ever let you back in Daddy's club after the golf cart incident?"

Mother immediately starts looking a little green around the gills and quietly slips out of the dress that she never had any business trying on in the first place. "Why would you bring up a silly thing like that now," she says sheepishly, like a kid who just got caught with her hand in the cookie jar. I brought up the notorious golf cart incident up because it has always been the one thing in Mother's history guaranteed to take her down a peg. Besides, I've always been genuinely curious to know how she found the courage to face her peers after three quarters of the club demanded the Fletcher family produce a clean bill of mental health for her as a condition of Daddy's membership reinstatement.

After sending the salesgirl on a fool's errand to find the red, white and blue rhinestone nightmare in a size negative zero, Mother and I slink out of the boutique before anyone has a chance to ask us to leave.

Ten minutes later, we're sitting across from each other, staring at a giant plate of pancakes that neither one of us is touching. Mother isn't one for fluffy, gluten-filled breakfast treats. But the pancake house is the only place in town that serves white wine at ten AM.

"I don't know what possessed me to think that stealing a golf cart was a good idea," Mother admits, "Your father never forgave me. He said I humiliated him in front of all of his friends. Do you know how hard it is to hold your head up high when everyone in town thinks you're a lunatic? I lost all confidence in myself. It got to the point I couldn't even look at the social calendar without getting a pit in my stomach. Then your father lost all our money and the invitations stopped coming. You know, honey, life can turn on you so fast. One minute, you're the belle of the ball and the next, you're racing around on a stolen golf cart, completely oblivious to the brick wall that you're about to smash into head-on."

Kind of like how one minute, you're galloping a difficult horse and the next, you're lying on the ground wondering what your name is. And that's when the pit starts growing in my own stomach. Do I really have the courage to continue to risk life and limb for twenty dollars a head? Last week may have been the first time I fell off at forty miles an hour. But if I keep on galloping, it won't be the last. I would be crazy to ask for my job back, right?

Mother interrupts my introspection with a story about how she was unable to get out of bed after Mitzi Malone accused her of mixing one too many prescription medications with her afternoon cocktail. "Let's face it, Margaret, I've always been something of a loose cannon. It was only a matter of time before I did something to really embarrass myself. When it finally happened, I was paralyzed with the knowledge that, if left to my own devices, I would probably do it again. But what was I supposed to do? Stop being myself because the consequences of my behavior can be scary? What kind of life would that be?"

It would probably be a very dull life, spent sitting behind the reception desk at a veterinary clinic or some other uninspired office space with unflattering fluorescent lighting. I wouldn't have to worry about inconveniences like road rash, concussions or trips to the emergency room. But I also wouldn't get to feel the wind slapping me awake at five thirty in the morning as I gallop faster and freer than I ever thought possible. The muscles on my arms would shrink and the best years of my life wouldn't be spent smelling like horse sweat and bridle leather.

You know what, Mother? You're right. Some things are worth acting like a crazy person for. I take a heaping forkful of pancake, pouring extra syrup on top before shoving it in my mouth. Don't worry, I'll be galloping the calories off as soon as I convince the Boss to let me saddle up again.

* * *

Exactly two seconds after my feet touch Winning Edge soil again, I see the Boss limp towards me with Matty in hand. I'm still upset about the way things ended between us. But there's something about seeing him in this weakened state that tugs gently at my heartstrings, and I can't help but chuckle as the Boss hobbles towards me with the grace of a broken-down old man.

"Alright, Princess, you win. Nobody in this barn can gallop Matty like you can. Including me. You were right and I was wrong. I'm sorry." I think that might be the sexiest thing that man has said to me to date. My chest swells with pride as I bask in the glow of the Boss's unabashed admiration.

But when he begins handing over the reins of the equine firecracker that nobody in their right mind wants to gallop, I question if this is a challenge worth tackling. The part of me with a strong sense of self-preservation says no. But that pesky little voice inside my head, the one that always gets me into trouble, says it's time to show the rough-and-tumble riders here at Winning Edge Farms that Margaret Fletcher kicks ass.

I gingerly take the reins out of the Boss's hands, letting my fingertips graze the pleasing protrusions of his manly knuckles for one blissful moment, and consider my options. I know I should say no. But every bone in my body is telling me to ride that stallion.

Pull yourself together, Fletcher. Besides, he's a taken man, remember?

"What about Emily?" I say, "She's a bold and brave cross-country rider and I'm just a silly little Hunter Princess. Wouldn't she be a better choice for such a challenging horse?"

The Boss informs me that Sam won't let her risk her neck on the strongest horse in the barn. "So unless you can produce a concerned family member, you're up, kid."

Ouch. That hurt. It's not like I want some crusty old Uncle interfering in my affairs. But now that the Boss brings it up, it would be nice if someone sharing my DNA had an opinion about me risking my life for twenty bucks a head. Now that Daddy and I are finally getting to know each other, I'm sure he would have all kinds of protective things to say about the harrowing situation that I am about to put myself in.

Wait a minute! Uncle Sam LOVES me, probably even more than Daddy. At least he knows more about what is going on with my life right now.

"Sam is not going to let you jeopardize my safety any more than Emily's," I inform him with an imperious nod.

But the Boss just smiles and says, "Putting you back on Matty was his idea."

Et tu, Sam? I guess blood is thicker than water. I take a moment to wallow in a little self-pity when Emily bursts onto the scene, guns ablaze, screaming, "You're going to let Margaret do it and not me?!!!" Completely unconcerned about her appearance, the rant continues with Emily insisting that life is not fair and if a rube like Margaret Fletcher can ride that horse, she can ride it better.

Offended, I'm about to come to my own defense when the Boss looks Emily in the eye and quietly says, "You're a good rider. But you're not Margaret."

Silence.

Emily's voice shakes as she replies, "I know you think that puffed-up Princess with her custom socks and monogrammed shoelaces is a better rider than me. But you're wrong."

The Boss breathes a heavy sigh and with the gravity of someone about to crush a young girl's dream, he says, "You can't hesitate on a horse like that. You've got to believe in yourself because if you don't, he sure as hell won't. It takes grit to get something that cocky to listen to you. And that is just not the kind of rider you are, Emily."

The old Margaret Fletcher might have been offended by the association with such an inelegant word as "grit". But even though it sounds like something one would use to scrub a stubborn stain out of public men's room toilet, I'm beginning to understand that grit is something desirable in a horseman. Maybe even more desirable than a perfectly-polished pair of custom boots. And then it hits me: the Boss really does think of me as something bigger, something more than a puff pastry. My chest swells up with pride. Suddenly, I can't wait to get in the saddle and prove myself worthy of his admiration.

The sad look on Emily's face stops me in my tracks. With slumped shoulders, she trudges off in the direction of her hovel. Even though I'm still angry with her for turning down Erica's offer, I hand the reins back to the Boss and go after my friend.

It takes a lot of grit to ignore Emily's verbal assault as I push my way into her poorly barricaded trailer. Once inside, I let her temper tantrum run its course until she no longer has the energy to manufacture insults aimed my well-monogrammed wardrobe. It's a spectacular display that lasts much longer than I ever would have expected. I had no idea she was so offended by way I cover the tips of my ears with hairnet or my propensity to shift my belt buckle to the zipper side of my side-zip breeches. "And another thing, Princess Fancy Breeches, who wears diamond stud earrings gallop RACEHORSES!"

After twenty minutes of listening to Emily's jabs about my custom socks and monogrammed hairnets, I begin to wonder if she has any respect for me at all. Twenty-one minutes ago, I was merely angry with

Emily for throwing away what could have been a great opportunity for the both of us. But now that I know the ugly truth of what she really thinks of me, I'm hurt. I'm starting to wish that I had never set foot in this dingy old trailer to begin with.

"Say whatever you want about me, Emily. But when push comes to shove, Margaret Fletcher isn't afraid to put herself on the line," I say, becoming more confident with each word, "Even if it means that I might not look so perfectly-polished at the end of the day. Can you say the same?"

I wait for Emily to spit back a cruel, calculating response meant to belittle me for taking proper care of all my fine leather goods. But she just sits on the floor of her trailer, not moving a muscle or saying a word. I notice the terrified look on her face and realize that for the second time this week, I've hit a nerve.

And then it dawns on me. Emily isn't yelling at me because she thinks my only real contribution to the world is singlehandedly keeping the French leather industry afloat during my cash-rich teen years. She's yelling at me because she's frustrated with herself for not having the grit to grab life by the horns.

Suddenly, I'm awash in feelings of empathy. I get down on the floor with Emily, look her square in the eye and say, "I know putting yourself out there can be scary. Especially when failure means re-evaluating the life plan you started drawing up the day you were born. You might totally suck in England. But the only surefire way to fail in life is to never try."

I thought that was a pretty decent pep talk. So I'm not sure why Emily is laughing so hard all of a sudden. Are those tears rolling down her cheeks? Seriously. What did I say that was so funny?

"I'm sorry," Emily manages to wheeze out, "I don't know why I'm laughing. It's just sometimes you sound so much like my Uncle Sam. Go ahead: tell me that I'm afraid to get flour all over the kitchen. I can take it."

I know Emily has had a rough couple of days and that flour comment has me worried that she's suffering some kind of breakdown. Before I have a chance to call her next-of-kin she says, "You have no idea what it's like to spend your whole life believing you're one thing, only to wake up one day and suddenly find out that you're not."

"Oh please," I exhale, exasperated, "Of course I know what that feels like. Just look at me. I ride in jeans now."

Emily throws her hands up in frustration, like an exhausted parent losing the will to deal with her difficult child. "Margaret, you're an amazing rider, no matter what kind of pants you're wearing! That's the point. You're a better rider than me. I know it, the Boss knows it and, if I'm not careful, Turtle Cumberbund will know it, too!"

My feeling of empathy are waning. And nervous breakdown aside, I want to tell Emily to buck up and quit all the drama before it really gets out of hand. I know I should tread lightly. But I can't help myself.

"So go to England and stink up the joint so you can come back here and tell me you told me so," I say, "Think of all the fun you could have yelling at me for making you put the cart before the horse!"

Emily smirks, undone by my irresistible charm, "You know you're ridiculous, Margaret Fletcher."

I just smile and say, "True. But look at how much fun I'm having."

* * *

Remember, Margaret, you've got grit. At least that's what I keep telling myself as I watch Matty prance towards me at the end of the Boss's lead shank. Here comes Sam, my favorite cripple. I can't help but blame him for my situation. I never really paid much attention when he rattled on endlessly about the good old days at the track. But suddenly, I recall in vivid detail Sam's account of the last day he ever sat on a horse and the accident that forever changed his life. Forget the maxi pads taped to my shins. I'm going to need a diaper.

I've always been a pretty gutsy rider. But today, I'm petrified. Sam takes one look at my trembling hands and says, "Remember who has the bigger brain in this operation. You get up on that horse and let him know who is boss. Because today, you're bigger than him. You're stronger than him. And if he wants that bucket of grain waiting for him in his stall, he better listen to what you have to say."

I want to take comfort in Sam's words. But my knowledge of his traumatic brain injury prevents me. According to Emily, only half of what he says should be considered reliable information and the rest disregarded as complete gibberish. As good as that pep talk sounded, convincing a horse like Matty that I'm the stronger party isn't something that I can wrap my fully-functioning mind around.

I'm quaking in my boots. But there's no turning back. I give Sam my bravest smile and let the Boss hoist me up on Matty. The moment my butt hits the saddle, I bridge my reins, press my knuckles into his withers and put the sucker to work. *Matty, I am bigger than you. I am stronger than you. And if you want that bucket of grain waiting for you in your stall, you better listen to what I have to say.*

With that mantra repeating in my brain, I gallop that horse faster than the Boss would have liked, but not out of control. When I'm finished, I pull him up with strength I didn't know I had and hop out of the saddle like it's giving me a bad case of hemorrhoids.

The Boss congratulates me on a job well done. Before I have a chance to mutter "You're welcome," I promptly throw up all over his paddock boots. The old Margaret Fletcher would have been horrified. The new Margaret Fletcher is grateful that today someone else's footwear played sacrificial lamb.

Forgiving me for the unfortunate spillage, the Boss smiles that boyishly handsome smile I have grown to adore. I melt like regurgitated English muffins on a hot summer day. "Princess, Matty is running his first stakes race a week from Monday. I found a good jockey. But I want you to be his exercise rider."

Between the adrenaline of my morning gallop and the pheromones wildly swirling around in the space in between me and the Boss, I'm almost seduced into saying yes. But that's the week of my triumphant return to the show world at The New London Classic. And I'm still not sure how I am going to manage to show a horse without a groom, professional braider or proper trainer by my side. Trying to do that AND waking up extra early in the morning to gallop that lunatic of a racehorse is certain Hunter Princess professional suicide.

Sensing that I am about to say no, the Boss looks into my eyes with a grave expression of genuine concern. He gently places his strong, manly hand on my welcoming shoulder and says, "Nobody at this farm can gallop that horse like you can. I need you."

I'm speechless. Which is probably a good thing. Because right now, I'm pretty sure I would agree to anything. Be strong, Margaret. You're going to need every ounce of energy and focus you have for The Classic. Even if the show grounds are only twenty minutes away from Winning Edge Farms and nothing would be more romantic than clandestine pre-dawn meetings with the Boss, privately enjoying a vigorous gallop, just the two of us.

Moments before I submit to the Boss's romantic request, I remember everyone at The New London

Classic who can't wait to watch POOR Margaret Fletcher make a fool of herself in the ring.

"Sorry, Boss. I already made a commitment to myself and my horse. And we're both going need one hundred percent of my focus that week."

The Boss offers to give me twice the normal rate for the week, but I remain unmoved. He still isn't giving up easily. We're talking about a man who spent his youth catering to the whims of countless nubile Hunter Princesses long before we ever met. He goes straight for the jugular. "What would you say to a new pair of breeches, Princess?"

I am immediately reminded of Erica's super fancy German breeches with magical air conditioning crystals and added slimming properties. Those really would help me look the part. Especially if I could pair it with the matching show coat made of one hundred percent breathable elastic that looks exactly like Italian wool but stretches perfectly with your every move.

The Boss is surprised to learn such a coat exists — and that it costs twelve hundred dollars. He makes a face like he's finally smelling the English muffins on his shoes, but reluctantly agrees to my pricey terms.

I should say no to this deal we're negotiating. No jacket, no matter how exclusive, will save me when I am alone in that arena with Chocolates. But when the Boss say, "Just promise me you'll keep your lips sealed about our arrangement. Erica can get kind of jealous. And I can't imagine she'd be too thrilled to hear that I'm spending extra time with you," we shake hands.

The thought of being dressed head to toe in clothes secretly purchased by Erica Lewis's boyfriend is JUST too tasty a proposition to pass up.

THE NEW LONDON CLASSIC

I wake up at four AM to the sound of driving rain. The weather clears up soon enough. But by the time I make it to Winning Edge, the track is one big muddy mess. I've been around long enough to know that I am going to be expected to gallop in these sloppy conditions and to come to work dressed in the proper undergarments. My poor paddock boots have no hope of surviving the morning. But I'm not the same person I was just a few short weeks ago. I emerge from the comfort of my car and slosh my way to the barn, where I find the Boss grooming the elegant grey filly standing by Matty's side in the cross-ties.

"Hey, Princess, meet Rosa. She's not the speediest horse in the barn. But her ass is nice enough to encourage even the fastest young stud to slow down and enjoy the view. So I'm going to gallop her ahead of you guys to help you keep pace. I bet you won't even have to touch the reins."

Using a young filly's hindquarters as a training aide doesn't sound like classical horsemanship to me. But as I watch the Boss bridling Rosa, my eyes wander to a well-muscled bottom that certainly has the power to stop me in my tracks. Maybe this plan isn't such a bad idea after all. Visions of the Boss's gorgeous gluteus maximus waving softly in my sightline as I gallop Matty behind Rosa dance in my head.

The Boss hands me eight pairs of goggles. "You're going to get a face full of mud galloping behind Rosa. Put them on top of your helmet. When you want to see, pull the old goggles down around your neck and grab a fresh pair from your helmet."

Trying to coordinate extra equipment in the saddle has never been my strong suit. Just the thought of riding with two reins in a Pelham bridle sends me into a cold sweat. But I don't want anything to get in the way of my view of the Boss. So I grab the goggles with gusto and prepare to enjoy the show.

I don't know if anything in life can fully prepare you for the sensation of being pelted the face by mud at galloping speed. Chunks of track dirt mixed with flecks of horse feces are flying off Rosa's hooves with every stride, costing me my sight way too early in the game. Desperate to get back to admiring the perfect fanny dangling in front of my face, I pull down my soiled goggles as instructed. And in that brief moment of vulnerability, a not-so-tiny mud bomb hits me square in the eye. I'm blinded and not one of the seven pairs of fresh goggles perched on top of my head has any chance of saving me now.

I can hear the sound of Matty's hoof beats. I can feel the sharp sting of mud and manure slapping me in the face with painful regularity. But I can't see where I am going or what might be on the verge of crashing into me. This is a very dangerous situation.

219

Suddenly, the sound of the Boss warning me that he is about to pull up pierces through my mud-caked ear canals. Fortunately, the sight of Rosa's beautiful booty shifting to a lower gear does the work of pulling Matty up for me.

I hop off at the first opportunity, demand that the Boss take over my charge and bolt off to the nearest ladies room to fix my face. Several splashes of water directly onto my appreciative eyeballs restores my vision. I look at myself in the mirror and scream at the sight of my recently-abused visage. The mud is gone. But the puffy, little, mildly infected welts on my face are not.

When I finally find the courage to emerge from the ladies room, the Boss gasps in horror at the sight of the creature standing in front of him.

"Knock 'em dead," he manages to say with all the confidence of someone sending a lamb out to battle a lion. I know it's not a good idea for me to attempt any kind of triumphant return to the Hunter world looking like this. But I don't have much of a choice, do I? So I accept the garment bag filled with incredibly expensive show clothes the Boss hands me.

The look on his face says it all. I'm screwed.

* * *

Emily thinks I'm an idiot for sacrificing sleep for the sake of a pair of breeches. She said she's not cutting me any slack when it comes to chores. I am expected to meet her at the barn to help pack the trailer. When I arrive, she has water hoses, plastic buckets and pitchforks strewn about the barn. Fortunately, she's too busy messing with all that crap to notice my mud rash. Two hours later, we've got the trailer filled with all kinds of things I had NO IDEA one had to take to a horse show.

Off we go. Emily pulling her trailer/apartment with that dirty old truck of hers and me following closely behind in my well-maintained Honda. I'm happy to have a little time to myself to focus on what lies ahead. My first warm up class is at eleven-thirty AM. That should give me just enough time to get dressed and polished for my big debut.

A pit starts to grow in my stomach. I pull over on the side of the road and throw up. Oh dear, I wonder if the bacteria stuck to my face has migrated to my stomach. Not that Margaret Fletcher hasn't been known to fall victim to the occasional show nerves. But that won't hit me until the Ring Steward calls my name, and should be gone after I jump my first fence.

I've thrown up three times since Emily and I started this short journey. I'm all out of breakfast, so the unpleasant vomiting should be over. But the sick feeling pulsing through my entire body just won't go away. I would turn myself in at the nearest hospital. But I'm certain that one look at my crusty face and I would be immediately shipped off to the CDC for further examination. Besides, I'm not entirely sure that the little shop of horrors on my skin is entirely to blame. *Margaret Fletcher get a hold of yourself! You're going to a horse show! You're going back to where you belong and you've got the breeches to prove it!*

I pull over one last time and somehow find the last bit of breakfast waiting to expel itself from my stomach. Oh dear.

I follow Emily's trailer as we pull onto the show grounds, and I thank my lucky stars that I didn't give into the urge to have a second English muffin this morning. The place is full of well-heeled Hunter Princesses and their perfectly-muscled horseflesh. Everyone looks so polished and prepared. Luxurious curtains drape the stall doors, fresh sod blankets the V.I.P areas and signs announcing the top barns on the East Coast are proudly displayed beside rows of matching tack trunks. Everything is just as I remember. Not a hair out of place. As a rumble quakes inside my empty belly, I realize that I am no longer in my comfort zone.

CHAPTER 20
~ *Emily sees how the*
other half lives ~

The New London Classic looks like one big freak show to a girl raised on Pony Club rallies and local horse trails. Sara warned me that these people spare no expense when it comes to their personal comfort. But I wasn't prepared for the landscape architects barking orders to construction crews building private gardens at the end of each barn aisle. I'm not talking about a few houseplants and a couple strips of sod. At the end of EVERY barn aisle on these show grounds is a magical fairy garden, complete with a little cabana housing silk couches and flat screen TVs. Silk couches at a horse show? Who has time to lounge on a silk couch at a horse show? There is so much work that needs to get done!

Chocolates is just as unsettled by the aggressively monogramed surroundings as I am. He gingerly backs out of the trailer, takes one look at a giant air conditioned tent filled with massage tables and bolts in the opposite direction. Chocolates spends the next fifteen minutes running around the barns at full speed, screaming at the top of his lungs, knocking down any unsuspecting Hunter Princess caught in his wake. I can't say that I blame him. I wish I could do the same. I've never seen so much hunter green, navy and burgundy all at once in my entire life. It's a little hard to take. Fortunately, Chocolates eventually realizes that this temper tantrum is about as much work as running an actual race and lets me catch him.

Margaret is horrified by the impression that we're making. She seems to have spontaneously broken out in some kind of horrible rash. I swear this woman keeps finding new ways to overreact and I just don't have time for this nonsense. I instruct Princess that she needs to get into the warm-up arena as soon as she can. She nods in queasy agreement and immediately disappears. I deposit Chocolates in his stall, lay down bedding and fill his water bucket. I'm too busy throwing down bales of hay from the roof of my trailer to notice that Margaret isn't lifting a finger to groom Chocolates. Twenty minutes later, I've got Chocolates pretty well situated in his new home. But the only thing Margaret has accomplished is dressing herself up in some overpriced, highly-elasticized show outfit that is going to get really dirty really soon.

"Emily, why is Chocolates such a mess? You said you were going to take care of him. What have you been doing with yourself all this time?"

I don't have time to explain to Margaret that horses need things like water and hay to survive. I shove a bucket filled with a sponge and a bottle of shampoo in her hands and tell her to get to work. Before she has a chance to open her mouth in protest, I give her a look that says "Shut it, Princess." Stunned, she ambles towards the wash racks about to give what I am sure is the first horsey bath of her life.

Fifteen minutes later, Margaret Fletcher returns with Chocolates. The horse is clean from head to toe. Margaret, on the other hand, looks like something the cat dragged in. She is still dressed in that ridiculous show outfit of hers. Only now it's covered in dirt and soapsuds. When I suggest she take the jacket off and run a lint brush over it, she bursts into tears and tells me that she can't. Apparently, the whole get-up is made of super-powered German elastic. It's got her in a vice grip and she's worried that if she tries to remove it, she might dislocate a shoulder.

Twenty minutes later, we've got Chocolates looking presentable. But Margaret is still a lost cause. I encourage her to focus on the positive. She's mere moments away from returning to the one place where she always felt she belonged. "Soon you'll be jumping eight perfect fences in front of a real judge. You're at The New London Classic! And everyone who matters is here to watch you perform."

I thought my little speech would get Margaret excited for what's ahead. Referring to the lunatics strolling around these show grounds as "everyone who matters" didn't exactly come naturally. But she just turns bright green and runs towards the nearest porta potty. I don't know why I even try to understand that woman.

From there, the afternoon only gets weirder. Margaret returns with a skinny little drunk woman dressed like some kind of slutty sailor by her side. I hear her squeal, "Margaret! Honieeee! WHAT'S WRONG WITH YOUR FACE?!!!" She retrieves a small aerosol can from her purse and immediately starts spraying a fine mist in Margaret's direction. "It's ionized spring water from France. It will soothe your pores. Quick, let's get you to the V.I.P. tent. I want to make sure everyone important sees you looking useless before your class so they think we have a full staff doing all the dirty work for you."

I am in the presence of the infamous Mrs. Fletcher.

Margaret doesn't like to talk about her family. All I know is her father is having some kind of yoga-inspired nervous breakdown and her mother has a minor drinking/shopping/being obnoxious problem.

"Mother, I'm already covered in all the dirty work! We're not going to fool anyone!" Margaret spits out.

Mrs. Fletcher ignores Margaret and screams to no one in particular, "Bunny! Is that you, Bunny? Bunny! I'll see you in the V.I.P. tent. I just have to straighten some things out with Margaret's grooms first. It's so nice to find one that speaks English. Of course you have to pay extra for that!"

Wow. Next to her mother, Margaret Fletcher actually looks like a sane, reasonable person. I can't hear what Margaret is saying to her mother. But neither Fletcher appears to be very happy. Fletcher Senior eventually throws her chicken arms up in frustration and runs off in the direction of the air conditioned massage tables.

Margaret's face is now covered in dirt, soap, tiny welts and pure frustration. I don't think I've ever seen her look so disheveled. I find myself experiencing genuine feelings of sympathy for the Princess.

So I just smile, pick up the cleanest rag I can find and say, "Let's get this show on the road."

CHAPTER 21
~ *Margaret finds herself caught in a sticky situation* ~

I'm still shell-shocked from the last horrifying hour of my life. I don't feel like someone who is about to amaze a crowd with my triumphant return to the Hunter ring. I feel like someone who just finished a morning of hard labor dressed in a sweaty tuxedo jacket that is trying to kill her. I can't present myself in front of a judge like this! I want to go back to Winning Edge Farms and gallop Matty. Because that would be A LOT less terrifying than what everybody is expecting me to do right now.

Emily doesn't look like she is prepared to listen to reason. So I let her molest me with a dirty rag meant for cleaning the slobber out of Chocolates' nostrils. I know she is trying to be helpful. However, the only thing she accomplishes is grinding more dirt and soapsuds deeper into the elastic of my jacket. I'm guessing there is a fifty/fifty chance that the judge will dismiss me the moment I walk into his arena dressed like a dirty trailer hobbit. But I mount Chocolates anyway. As I swing my leg over his back, my tooth necklace rubs against my chest. I am reminded of the McClay Finals and that blood-splattered jacket. Looking like a murder victim didn't stop me from laying down the trip of a lifetime. So why should today be any different? All right, Chocolates. Like the girl said: let's do this thing!

I do my best to hold my head high as Chocolates and I make our way to the warm-up arena. Perfectly-presented Hunter Princesses look on in horror as the disheveled Margaret Fletcher passes by. I can hear whispers of "Is that who I think it is?" mixed in with cheap shots aimed at my outdated tack. I should be coming unglued right about now. But I'm not. Chocolates doesn't understand any of the snide comments aimed in his direction. All he knows is that everyone is looking at him. I can feel the pride welling up inside him as he marches through the crowd of adoring fans, his head held high and the sway of his tail emphasizing the swagger in his step. How could I feel like anything but a Princess sitting atop such a wonderful animal?

The warm-up arena is crowded with Hunter Princesses on horses cantering, trotting and jumping in all different directions. Chocolates takes one look at the commotion and immediately dissolves into a puddle of anxiety. We make tentative steps towards the chaos. I scratch Chocolates on his withers, letting him know that everything is OK. Eventually, I work up the nerve to ask for a trot. Chocolates is tense, unfocused and moving way too fast. I am terrified to ask for a canter. I see Emily ringside, watching us with that look of horrifying uncertainty she wears so often. She doesn't think we can do this and neither does the trembling mound of horseflesh quaking beneath me.

Well, somebody is going to have to believe in us, starting right now. And if it's not going to be Emily and it's not going to be Chocolates, then it has to be me. I take a deep breath and pick up the canter. It's way too fast and almost out of control. Every Hunter Princess around me stops riding to watch the trainwreck unfolding before their eyes, terrified to share the arena with such a wild pair. Perfect, that means I've got all the jumps to myself.

Mere seconds before I am about to take my first fence, a familiar high-pitched whine shatters my concentration. Mother is standing at the far end of the arena, polishing off her second or third cocktail and squealing at the top of her lungs, "Margaret! What horse are you riding? You know I can never keep track. YOU HAVE SO MANY!" Mother isn't actually talking to me. She's just making loud proclamations in the hopes that someone will overhear her and think that we're rich again.

I've still got ten minutes to survive before it's my turn to go. I do everything in my power to expel the sound of Mother from my universe and focus on the task of getting warmed up. Once again, I pick up the canter and the Hunter Princesses scatter to safer shores. I aim Chocolates at a small cross rail and he leaps over it like it might eat him alive. I can feel him unraveling under the pressure. So I forget about the jumping and do a couple of walk/trot transitions in hopes of settling him down. It's working. I've finally got Chocolates moving like a good hunter. Until a gentle breeze claims the absurd sailor hat perched atop my mother's head and sends it flying in our direction.

At the sight of Mother's hat coming towards him, Chocolates leaps in the air, bucking and farting all at the same time. Any hope I had of a quiet, calm hunter round is gone. I try to do more of those magical, horse-calming walk/trot transitions. But this time, they're not working. Then I realize that Mother has reclaimed her hat and is in the middle of the now nearly-empty arena, vigorously shaking it in an obnoxious attempt to make it clean. Chocolates is horrified by the spectacle. He stands completely still, frozen in fear of the offending object and the crazy woman threatening to kill him with it.

Emily screams across the arena, "Margaret, you have to go in now! I can't make them hold the gate any longer!" But I've only jumped one warm-up fence and it was a disaster. And my horse refuses to move. My mother, too self-absorbed to notice the trouble she is causing, continues to wave that hat around like it's the only thing that matters.

I beg Mother to stop her destructive behavior. But she doesn't hear me. Her pretty little hat is dirty, the rest of the world be damned. Sam always says that you can't make cookies without breaking some eggs. Well, Chocolates, it's time to mess up the kitchen.

I bridge my reins and smack Chocolates on the flank with my crop as hard as I can. I gallop into the show arena like no Hunter Princess before me ever has. I'm sure everyone watching us is bracing herself for a disastrous performance.

Instead, magic happens. The kind of thrilling, improbable movie magic that seemed impossible mere minutes before.

Chocolates takes one look at the carefully-decorated jumps, the judge's stand and the unusually large audience that has gathered to watched him perform, and breathes a sigh of relief. As the tension leaves his body, I can also feel it also melt away from mine. I pick up a nice quiet hunter canter and point Chocolates towards the first jump, not sure what to expect. I hear the crowd gasp as Chocolates jumps the snot out of that fence and lands in the perfect hunter lope.

I have ridden plenty of hunter rounds in my lifetime. But it has NEVER felt this good. Each jump is more brilliant than the next, and I can feel Chocolates becoming more comfortable with himself as the course goes on. Tears of joy and relief stream down my cheeks as we walk out of the arena. All that hard work and humiliation was worth every miserable second. I have no idea if the judge will look past my homeless equestrian appearance and give us a ribbon. Honestly, it doesn't even matter. I have never been prouder of a horse or the eight fences that we jumped together than I am right now.

Everyone around the arena watches in stunned silence as Chocolates and I strut out. Everyone except for my mother. No, she is still trying to clean that ridiculous hat of hers using whatever is left of her fourth or fifth gin and tonic. I walk right past her, prepared to just ignore the whole situation. But something makes Mother look up and really see me for the first time since she set foot on the show grounds. I try to contain my anger as I hear her say, "Honey, why do you look so sweaty and dirty? You're at a horse show. You should know better."

I just put in the performance of a lifetime on a horse that cost several thousand dollars less than this absurd outfit that I am wearing. I did it in front of a crowd of over-privileged, spoiled brats who were rooting for me to fail spectacularly. And all this woman has to say to me is *You should know better?* I want to rip Mother's unmoving, Botoxed face off. Then I remember the people watching me right now don't need another reason to think I've gone off the deep end.

Instead, I calmly ask Mother why she is even here. She gives me a confused look and says, "Oh, honey, I'm here to support you no matter how poorly you do."

"POORLY," I involuntarily scream at the top of my lungs. The crowd gasps in unison. Margaret Fletcher has gone off the deep end and now everyone within earshot knows.

"Honey, I was a little distracted while you were riding and I didn't actually get to watch. I may not know a whole lot about the horses that you're so obsessed with. But no judge is going to give any kind of award to someone so disheveled!"

Screw it. Margaret Fletcher is going to cause a scene and she doesn't care who is gathered around to watch. Let's give the crowd a show. I hop off Chocolates, hand the reins to Emily and say, "Well, it's too bad. If you were here to actually support me instead of just fluffing up your social connections, you would have seen me kick ass."

The crowd, not even pretending not to listen to the once-proud Margaret Fletcher scream at her mother, instantly doubles in size. This little sideshow just became the main event. Now it's Mother's turn to be horrified. She has the nerve to say, "It's a good thing your father isn't here to witness this temper tantrum!"

"That's rich. Bring up Daddy," I say, "Would this be the same father I'm not allowed to share my life with, thanks to you, Mother?"

A shadow casts over my mother's face as she suddenly goes quiet. She seems to want to give up the fight as quickly as she started it. The drama is over and the crowd starts to dissipate. Then, as if sensing she's about to lose her audience and whatever last bit of relevance she had in this A-Circuit crowd, Mother screams, "Your father is not here BECAUSE HE LOST EVERY PENNY WE HAD BETTING ON HORSES! So I WON'T allow him near them!"

A collective gasp from the audience encourages her to continue, "That's right. Daddy has a gambling problem. That's why I hate this whole Gallop Girl thing and that's why I would never allow your father to come to your horse shows. I'm sorry, Margaret. I truly am. I hope one day you can understand why I didn't want to expose my precious little princess to the seedy underbelly of our family."

The crowd stands in silence, mouths agape in frozen expressions of shock that only a rainstorm of carbohydrates could close. Mother bursts into tears and storms off. A gust of wind blows that ridiculous hat off her head once again. This time, she leaves it behind. It sits in the arena dirt for a few seconds before getting trampled flat by the next rider.

Day One at The New London Classic horse show is complete and true to form, Margaret Fletcher made a splash.

* * *

Fighting with Mother is something of a horse show tradition. Over the years, we've had some real doozies. But yesterday was unusually spectacular and I'm still exhausted from it all.

I arrive at Winning Edge Farms at the prescribed three o'clock hour to find Matty waiting for me in the crossties. He looks so innocent. Harmless even. It's hard to believe that his kind are responsible for bankrupting my father. I suppose I am being unfair. Matty never met my father. But it's horses like you, Matty, the strong, beautiful ones, that seduce us into making the kind of decisions that change our lives forever.

The Boss finds me slowly stroking Matty's mane, rubbing tears from my eyes. I have no confirmation that he heard about what happened yesterday. But knowing Erica, he has.

Without acknowledging my tears, he looks at me and says, "Princess, I lost my shirt buying Chocolates. I thought I was the one trainer who could unlock his potential. But that trainer is you. I heard you brought the house down yesterday. Congratulations."

The Boss then strokes Matty's mane and says, "I only took this guy on because I couldn't afford anything else after Chocolates cleaned my clock. I never expected he'd amount to much of anything. But when I watch you gallop him, I start to believe I have something here. He might even be good enough to take me all the way to the Kentucky Derby. If I was smarter, I would probably sell him right now and make a nice profit. But I think I'm going leave my chips on the table and see how far he can take me. And if that makes me a gambler, so be it."

I'm not exactly sure what just happened. But it feels like the Boss exposed himself to me in a pretty intense way. I meet his smoldering gaze with an equally provocative look, daring him to flinch. Instead, he tucks a stray lock of hair behind my ear and says, "What are you doing showing up at my barn without your hairnet, Princess?"

I need a moment to gather my thoughts. This feels a lot more serious than casual flirting and I'm not sure that I'm ready to become part of a love triangle that involves Erica Lewis. But the Boss isn't looking away, and I'm not either. I smile softly, cocking my head to one side like a girl that wants to be kissed and say, "Sometimes an uptight princess like me has to throw caution to the wind and take a gamble."

The Boss pushes his fingers deeper into my unsecured locks, gently cradling the back of my head with his big, strong Johnny Racetrack hands and says, "I guess gambling is in our blood. Probably not much we can do about it now." I part my lips and breathe a sigh of agreement, the sensation of the Boss's breath on mine is making it impossible to think or speak clearly. And then, it happens. He leans in for the kiss I've been hoping for since the first day I saw those beautiful baby blue eyes crinkle.

It's a long, slow, thorough kiss. The kind that fills a girl's brain with wonderfully disorienting natural chemicals leaving her too incapacitated to fully appreciate the consequences of her actions.

But just as I am about to slide my hand down the small of the Boss's back and onto firmer ground, he pulls away. His face wears a look of regret and I can feel the perfection of this moment slipping out of my grasp. "Sorry, Princess," he says before scurrying away.

I stand there frozen for a few beats, trying to wrap my mind around what just happened. I'm attracted to the Boss and he's attracted to me. If that kiss proved anything, it's that. So why do I have the feeling that somehow none of this is going to work out in my favor?

Matty breaks my reverie with a loud clearing of his nostrils. I look into his soft liquid brown eyes and I can almost hear him say *remember, you've got bigger fish to fry.* Bigger fish, indeed.

* * *

I'm still thinking about the Boss as I drive onto the show grounds. My first priority is to find Emily and tell her everything that happened in totally sordid detail so she can help me decide what I should do about it all.

But I'm thrown off my purpose by the sight of Erica Lewis standing outside Chocolates' stall with her weedy little arms crossed in front of her chest. A smile spreads across her thin lips as she says, "Margaret. You showed up today! How incredibly plucky of you! I am so sorry to hear about your family tragedy. I honestly had no idea. Totally surprising considering that MY father runs a successful thoroughbred racing barn, I know. Wow, is it just me? Or are you also struck by how ironic this whole situation is? Maybe "ironic" isn't the right word. Is it "coincidence"? Whatever. I just want to point out that my dad makes A LOT of money with our racehorses and your father lost ALL of his money betting on them. Now you're forced to risk life and limb riding them for like five dollars a pop just so you can afford your rent! Hey, is it true that you slept under Bunny Beale's trailer last night? Hmmm, maybe the right word is "KARMA"!"

I have to hand it to Erica. She's in rare form today. But I have an ace up my sleeve. I'm smug with the memory of kissing her boyfriend. You want a fight, Erica? I'll give you a fight. I let a greedy smile spread across my luscious, recently-kissed lips and say, "Oh, I was planning on sleeping under someone's trailer. No money for a hotel room and all. But your boyfriend's been keeping me up all kinds of outrageous hours this week. So I haven't really had that much time for sleep." Wink.

The look on Erica's face tells me she had NO idea that her man's been partaking in private early morning gallop sessions with my fancy ass. Perfect. I make like I'm using every available muscle to appear innocent as I say, "Well, don't tell me you don't know what we've been up to." It's cruel. I know. But the joy I get from watching Erica struggle to maintain her composure while I insinuate all kinds of inappropriate behavior is priceless. So I'm not going to stop. I mean, would you? I didn't think so.

Erica is not too keen on looking like a fool in public. She makes a big show of rolling her eyes and telling me not to worry. She doesn't keep secrets with the Boss. But I can't help but notice that her lips are getting tighter and tighter as she insists that she knows exactly what is going on.

239

I should back down. Instead, I ask her to assure me that she is OK with everything that is going on and I mean "everything". I know that I am winning this tete-a-tete the moment Erica starts jerking her head back and forth in a spastic attempt at nodding. It looks like it's about to fall off her neck. I should probably show some mercy and put this baby to bed.

I breathe a fake sigh of relief and say, "That's so cool. You must be really secure in your relationship. Anyway, I'm so glad we got everything out in the open. You know how it is with guys. They tell you that they've cleared "everything" with their girlfriend and half the time they're lying through their teeth. Anyway, I am exhausted, as I'm sure you can imagine. So I'm going to go see if I can find a quiet place to grab some shut-eye before my class. Toodles."

I do my best to kick up a little dirt as I make my exit. Well, look at that. Dirt sticks to Erica's over-priced German breeches, too.

CHAPTER 22
~ *Emily makes a scene* ~

Despite the drama yesterday, I've got a handful of trainers ready to buy Chocolates for one of their over-privileged clients. I've never been good at the negotiating part of selling horses. But Margaret insists I do all the dirty work. She says she doesn't want to "wheel and deal like some kind of pushy middle management functionary". But I know deep down inside, Margaret is afraid that when push comes to shove, she won't have the heart to let Chocolates go.

I'm not sure that she is fully aware of the depth of her feelings for the horse that brought her back to the A-Circuit. But I can see it in the glow on her face every time a crowd gathers to ohh and ahh at Box of Chocolates' amazing jump. And that is exactly what everyone is doing right now. Ohhing, ahhhing and gossiping like a bunch of green-eyed, over-privileged hens.

I heard Margaret Fletcher gallops thoroughbreds to pay off her dad's gambling debts.

Margaret Fletcher galloping thoroughbreds? Please, that girl can't ride anything that doesn't run on autopilot.

That has to be one nice horse to cart her butt around the pre-greens like that. Who knew that racehorses are so easy to ride!

How hilarious is it that her Daddy is nothing but a lowlife deadbeat gambler!

I used to assume Margaret could never make friends on the A-Circuit because she was such a pain in the ass. But I'm not even sure these girls are human, let alone friendship material. I know I should mind my own business and walk away. But I can't help but stick my nose into these very smelly waters.

So I elbow my way into the center of the witches den, look the tallest, prettiest one right in the eye and say, "Excuse me, I just have to say that I totally understand your need to belittle Margaret Fletcher. It used to drive me nuts to watch her ride the pants off EVERYTHING she sits on. How can someone who appears to care more about the brand of breeches she's wearing than the act of actually riding be SO MUCH BETTER THAN ME. My life was much easier when I believed that girls like Margaret Fletcher only won because they have money. But that's not the case here. She's a better rider than me. So I can guarantee you that she's a better rider than any of you."

That's the second time I've said those words out loud. *Margaret Fletcher is a better rider than me.* But it's the first time they haven't made my stomach turn. Because Margaret Fletcher, the girl who puts more thought into adjusting her hairnet than what she's doing in the saddle, IS a better rider than me. Sure, my riding career would have benefitted if I had more money and opportunity to throw at horses. But money alone may not have been enough to put me among the best. And yes, I am terrified to go to England and learn the limits of my own talent. Because even with the best trainer, I still might not be as good as Margaret Fletcher. But you know what? I'm going to do it anyway. Because if I don't, I won't be any different than these horrible girls sitting on the sidelines squawking about all the things they could be if only they had what girls like Margaret Fletcher have.

I take a moment to be super proud of myself for all these grownup revelations. The moment passes, and I'm pretty sure a good five minutes have gone by. So why is this large crowd of people still staring at me? A matronly woman dressed in a perfectly-pressed pair of breeches and impossibly shiny custom field boots breaks the silence with, "Are you saying that horse is not a packer?"

And then I realize what's going on here. I just told every trainer in earshot that their clients have no hope of doing as well on Chocolates as Margaret. And nobody wants to be responsible for training a horse when all that five-figure potential fizzles under their inferior rider.

A good saleswoman would start backpedaling. I should undersell Margaret's riding ability and insist that any idiot can pilot that beast in style. But I can't bring myself to give Margaret's haters the satisfaction. So I tell everyone in earshot that Chocolates might be a packer one day. Maybe. But right now he's a five year old off-the-track thoroughbred. Three months ago, his skills included galloping in a straight line and stopping. So no, he's not a packer, even if Margaret makes him look like one.

My little speech is met with predictable silence. But if you listen really close, you can hear the sound of a nail being driven into the coffin of my hope to sell this horse in time to pay for that trip to England as all those trainers with rich clients slowly back away.

Instinctively sensing that her "fan club" is no longer watching her ride, Margaret stops jumping and trots on over. If I tell her what I just did, she is sure to be furious and accuse me of self-sabotage again. Even though I'm pretty sure that is NOT what I was doing, the evidence suggests otherwise. So I tell Margaret that word got out about a big Hermes belt sale and everyone went running. But Margaret's not buying one second of my story. Apparently Hermes belts never go on sale. Not even in the worst of economic times. I'm about to make a big show of acting all offended by Margaret's suggestion that I'm lying. I'm sure if I yell, scream and cry enough, I can confuse her into changing the topic of conversation.

But then Erica Lewis trots up to my rescue. She's got a look on her face that could kill a basket of puppies. "Fletcher, do you have a bill of sale for that horse of yours?"

Margaret's mouth is wide open, but no words are coming out. Oh, I am definitely off the hook here.

On Margaret's silence, Erica screams louder, "FLETCHER! Do you have a bill of sale proving that you actually bought that horse of yours?"

Margaret looks at me like she's expecting me to bail her out. That's not going to happen. I'm guessing that not only does Margaret NOT have a bill of sale, she has no idea what such a document is for. I suppose it's a good thing I chose Margaret's honor over Chocolates' marketability. Because without a bill of sale we don't legally own a horse to market.

Margaret stammers something about none of this being any of Erica's business. She bought Chocolates from the Boss for one dollar, paid in full.

A chill runs down my spine as Erica treats us to her evil grin and says, "It's my business because my EX-boyfriend had no right to sell you that horse. Per his contract with my father, he is not allowed to sell ANY horse of his without offering it to Daddy first. I just got off the phone with Daddy and he doesn't remember hearing anything about this Box of Chocolates. Honestly, I'm not sure a bill of sale would even be of help in this situation, since legally the slimeball had NO right to sell you that horse in the first place."

Wow, I'm not going to England and it's totally not my fault. I am immediately overwhelmed by a sense of relief. Not the right feeling, I know. But I'll deal with my confused psyche later. Right now, the look on Margaret's face says that she knows she screwed up. Big time. I'm not sure what she did to invite Erica's persistent wrath. I don't really care. I know I should be upset about all the time and money I've invested in this horse for nothing. But I don't see the benefit of making poor Margaret suffer the humiliation of this exchange any longer.

So I step in and tell Erica that regardless of whether we have a bill of sale or not, Chocolates isn't her horse. As far as we're concerned, Margaret purchased Chocolates from the Boss fair and square. Any beef Erica has is with him.

Erica trots away, cackling like a nefarious cartoon character, promising to have the last word. Moments later, I start receiving texts from trainers canceling appointment to show Chocolates to their clients. I know the real reason for these cancellations has nothing to do with the dispute in ownership. But the morally complicated, self-sabotaging, chicken-hearted side of me lets Margaret think otherwise. I do my best to don a stern expression and sound disappointed as I insist that Margaret needs to call the Boss to straighten this situation out. She tells me not to worry. Chocolates is our horse. Erica is just being a brat because she can't stand to see Margaret in the spotlight again.

When Margaret says, "I'll fix this, I promise," I believe her. Because I've learned when Margaret Fletcher sets her mind to do something, she gets it done. So I'm probably going to England, whether I like it or not.

CHAPTER 23
~ *Margaret meets her*
father for the first time ~

Erica Lewis is NOT getting away with highway robbery! I've left the Boss several messages insisting he set his woman straight immediately. No response. He's ignoring me. I'm guessing he's embarrassed to be associated with such a horrible, soulless wretch. Or more likely, he's still confused by our successfully steamy interlude the other day and doesn't know what to say. Whatever it is, I don't care. I'm going to Winning Edge to confront this problem head on.

I show up at the farm perfectly on time and ready to gallop Matty. But I'm greeted with a hearty, "Go home, Princess" from the Boss. I believe I'M the injured party here. So why is HE acting all upset? "INJURED PARTY?" he bellows at the top of his lungs like an angry lumberjack with a dull axe. "Erica broke up with me, thanks to you!"

Wait. What did he just say? I knew Erica and the Boss are no longer a couple (never before has the word EX-boyfriend sound so sweet as it did coming out of Erica Lewis's mouth.) But she broke up with him? Shouldn't it be the other way around? And then there is the whole matter of the Boss still yelling and screaming things like, "It was a mistake, Margaret. I said I was sorry. So why did you have to tell her?" Mistake? Margaret?! And more importantly, what the hell does he think I told her? On my confused expression, he lowers his voice several octaves and says, "You told her about the kiss... right?"

"Of course I didn't," I say with complete and utter honesty. I DID insinuate that we are having mysteriously torrid affair in the wee galloping hours of the morning. But I decide to keep that part to myself. I feel bad about my role in this whole situation. But as far as I'm concerned, the Boss is still responsible for Erica's behavior. With the look of a technically innocent person on my face, I tell him about the bill of sale that I don't have and Erica's claim that he didn't legally have the right to sell me Chocolates in the first place. The Boss looks like he's still pretty annoyed with me. So I remind him that Emily is the real victim here. Selling Chocolates is the only way she is going to scrape together the funds to get to England anytime soon. And she is the only person in this whole situation who hasn't behaved poorly.

The Boss is compelled by my argument on Emily's behalf. I'm waiting for him to apologize for yelling at ME when he didn't need to, but he's not budging. I consider reminding him that I only IMPLIED to Erica we were having a torrid affair in the early morning hours. He's the one that SPILLED the actual beans about that harmless little (or was it?) kiss. But I take the higher ground and don't mention that this is pretty much all his fault. Poor Boss. He's got the weight of the world on those handsome, defined shoulders, doesn't he? Between managing a vengeful ex-girlfriend and pinning his entire career on a horse he can't gallop without the help of a love interest he's too afraid to pursue, you've got to feel sorry for the guy.

"Look, Princess, I don't know what the solution to your problem is yet. But I promise to find one." Then, he sheepishly asks me if I'll gallop Matty for him after all. I could use the time alone to clear my head, so I say yes and let him give me a totally asexual leg up.

As Matty and I make our way out to the track alone, my thoughts wander to the morning of that kiss. I'm having a hard time believing that it didn't mean anything to the Boss. Now that Erica has been elbowed out of the picture, I don't see any reason why we couldn't/shouldn't move our intimate little negotiation up to the privacy of the hayloft. But the Boss said pretty much everything he needed to when he grabbed my calf like some old boarding school buddy and hoisted me up on Matty without so much as a pat on my ass.

That kiss was a one-time deal. It's back to business as usual.

All right, Matty, let's get this show on the road. I slowly raise my body up out of the stirrups and Matty responds by rocketing forward with enough power to light up New York City. I'm having a really hard time holding him without Rosa around to serve as a distraction. I do my best to keep Matty from working too hard, but today my best just isn't going to be enough.

By the time I manage to pull up, the Boss is bright red and yelling at the top of his lungs all over again. The man really needs to find a tension tamer. Maybe Daddy can give him some free yoga lessons. Soothe his aura until he's behaving like a reasonable person again.

"Princess," the Boss bellows, "If you keep working that horse too hard, I'm not going to have anything left to win the race with!" The ranting and raving continues for a good ten minutes before he finally gives up and says, "Why am I bothering to yell at you? You couldn't possibly understand everything I have riding on this horse."

I'm pretty sure that was some kind of poor little rich girl dig. The old Margaret would have taken it without saying a thing. But that's because THE OLD MARGARET WAS RICH! "Excuse me," I politely remind him, "But I'm pretty sure that you don't have any right to be upset with me when I just lost an amazing opportunity to turn a nice profit on a HORSE THAT YOU HAD NO RIGHT TO SELL ME!"

The Boss is startled by my outburst. But I am not the slightest bit deterred. "Sorry, Boss, but I am not like the Erica Lewises of the world anymore. I am just as poor and in over my head as everyone that has no business playing around with horses." Then I look him in those beautiful blue eyes of his and say, "If you don't think I'm good enough to gallop Matty, fire me. But don't give some crock of shit about not understanding what it's like to be under pressure."

The Boss returns my gaze with the kind of respect and admiration his type usually reserves for real horsemen. All my anger melts away and I feel that we are on the verge of sharing another moment. Maybe another kiss? "Listen, Princess, I screwed up with Chocolates. I'm sorry. I just didn't think Mr. Lewis would have any interest in buying a proven loser."

It's always a mistake to underestimate Erica Lewis's desire to kick Margaret Fletcher when she's down. The Boss rolls his eyes and tries to pretend that his evil ex is not that bad. But we both know I'm right. There's no reasoning with that woman. And as long as she has the legal upper hand, we're screwed.

"Princess, even if I can't legally sell Chocolates to you, I'm not going to sell him to her. So just keep showing him and have fun. I won't pull the rug out from under you. I promise."

Wow. My knight in shining armor, right? But what about Emily? Part of me can't believe that I actually feel that way. Don't get me wrong. I'm a charitable person. I was always the girl handing down last year's breeches to whatever working student deserved them the most. But when it comes to passing on opportunities to ride and show, I've never been one to share. I love this sport more than anyone could love anything. And Chocolates is one hell of a show horse. I know we could go far together. So really, this whole not being able to sell Chocolates works out well for me.

It's times like this when not having any friends would come in handy. But that's not my life anymore. Emily is my friend, and it turns out I care more about her chance to go to England than my own shot at returning to A-Circuit glory.

I decide that I can't afford to sit around and wait for the Boss to solve this problem. It's time to take matters into my own hands. It's a good thing that I can FINALLY ask for advice from the one person in my life clever enough to outsmart the likes of Erica Lewis.

* * *

Mother and I make a deal: I'll forgive her for her idiotic behavior at The Classic. In exchange, she allows me to tell Daddy all about my new Gallop Girl lifestyle.

Excited to finally begin a meaningful relationship with the man who helped bring me into this world, I tell Daddy everything about my new job, my friends and all the ways in which Erica Lewis is trying to mess things up. But I'm pretty sure Daddy stopped listening to me the moment I first said the word "thoroughbred". His eyes are filled with the kind of lusty expression Mother probably hasn't seen since their wedding night. Drool dribbles out from the corner of his mouth as he says, "You own a racehorse?"

I start all over again and explain that I USED to own a former racehorse that isn't worth anything to anybody interested in winning races. Daddy slowly comes back to earth as I encourage him to accept that this racehorse of mine isn't worth falling off the wagon for.

All right, ONE more time from the top. Daddy, I need help. I'm in a rough situation here. Mother doesn't understand problems that involve helping other people. I need your sharp tactical mind on this one.

I'm about to give up on Daddy offering any helpful advice when, out of the blue, he looks at me with clear eyes and says, "You know, Cookie, Martin Lewis is a gambler. Anybody who owns racehorses is a gambler. He just hasn't had occasion to let himself get carried away like I did. Gamblers don't like to get stuck holding onto losers. It sounds like that Chocolates of yours is a loser, at least on the racetrack. You know what guys like Martin Lewis like? They like winners. They're addicted to winners. You find yourself a winner and I bet you could get him to trade that loser of his for your winner."

Daddy is wearing his hemp sweatpants and the room is filled with the scent of those awful peace and harmony candles. But for the first time in a long time, I can see a glimpse of the captain of industry I once longed to get to know. The more Daddy talks about winners and losers, the more frantic he becomes. I can feel his heart beating faster and his breath getting quicker. My eyes dart around the room in a fruitless search for a gluten-free hemp treat to calm him down. Sweat starts to bead on Daddy's forehead and he says, "A winner, Cookie, a winner. That boss of yours is not a winner. He's a gambler. Anyone that works in his line of work is a gambler and gamblers are always losers. Trust me, Cookie, I know."

I am beginning to realize that the whole Zen Daddy persona is totally an act that goes poof! the second you mention racehorses. OK, Mother. You're right. You were not trying to sabotage my chance at finally having a close relationship with Daddy. You were protecting me from the monster that comes out at the mere smell of an opportunity to put a couple bucks on a nice pony.

I should shut my mouth and slowly walk away, right? But amazingly, Daddy's not-entirely coherent advice sparks an idea. Without thinking, I blurt out, "Matty is a winner."

Daddy instantly goes into overdrive, demanding to know, "Who's Matty? Is he really fast? How is he working? Do you think he has what it takes to be a grade-A stakes winner? Do you own this horse, Cookie? COOKIE. COOKIE, DO YOU OWN THIS HORSE?!"

I'm starting to worry that Daddy would push me into oncoming traffic if that's what it took to get more information on Matty.

And that's when it hits me. Daddy and I don't have a close relationship because Daddy and I are never going to have a close relationship. And it's not because he's too busy or Mother is in the way. It's because Daddy is an addict. He always has been an addict and he's always going to be an addict. If it's not work, it's a racehorses or yoga and gluten-free hemp cookies. But whatever it is that has Daddy's attention, it's probably not good for him and it's definitely not me.

Daddy is completely covered in sweat. He's extinguishing the peace and harmony candles and whispering like he's convinced the room is bugged. He tells me that all I have to do is convince the Boss to sell Matty to Mr. Lewis on the condition that Mr. Lewis gives up all claims to Chocolates. It's actually a pretty good plan. I'm starting to feel guilty for giving up on Daddy so quickly.

But then Daddy starts insisting that he come to Winning Edge the next time I'm scheduled to work Matty. He mumbles something about buttering up the Boss. But I know he's just looking for an excuse to get within smelling distance of a racehorse. I turn the offer down.

Daddy is not giving up easily here, though. He looks at me with way too much intensity, lowering his voice until it's almost impossible to hear and says, "Your boss is a gambler, Cookie. No gambler is going to want to give up his winning horse without some serious coaxing. You're going to need my help."

That's it. I'm not even pretending to take Daddy seriously anymore. The Boss isn't a gambler. He's a horseman! I want out of this room before I start to suffocate. All of a sudden, Daddy looks really small and ashamed. He revealed a side of himself that he hoped to always keep hidden, and I can see the regret spread across his face. He takes one last look at me and say, "Cookie, do yourself a favor. Don't ever ask a gambler to help you with your problems. We'll just disappoint you in the end."

Well, there you have it. After twenty-two years twisting in the wind, I'm finally getting some fatherly advice that might actually help me out in the world. I never thought of the Boss as a gambler. But if Daddy is right, he's the last man I should be trying to attract.

I leave my father alone in his peace and harmony room. The younger, innocent Margaret Fletcher might have fallen for Daddy's song and dance about wanting to come to the track to help me out. But real life has a way of making it harder to fall for the same crap you believed before your fairytale lifestyle came crashing down around you, leaving you with only a tiny apartment and a closet full of last year's breeches.

For all our dysfunction, I guess Mother really has been a pretty decent parent to me. Even though every piece of the advice that she has given me has been completely inappropriate, she was always there. And you know what they say: ninety-nine percent of life is about showing up.

I find Mother in the kitchenette baking a tiny Quiche Lorraine in the toaster oven (Mother has always been too intimidated to bake in the full size model). I wait until she finishes setting the timer and give her a hug. The experience leaves her a little startled, and I leave before she can figure out how to hug me back.

That's OK, Mom. I know you love me too.

CHAPTER 24
~ Emily meets her spirit guide ~

To: Turtle Cumberbund (Turtle@CBFarms.com)
From: Emily Morris (eventer4life@ghostmail.com)
Re: With Regrets

First let me express my gratitude for the opportunity that you so generously offered me. Unfortunately, the funding I was relying on to get to me England has suddenly fallen through. So it is with my deepest regret that I must decline what is probably the opportunity of a lifetime.

* * *

From: Turtle Cumberbund (Turtle@CBFarms.com)
To: Emily Morris (eventer4life@ghostmail.com)
Re: With Regrets

Why on earth would you let a silly detail like funding get in the way of living the high life in grand old

England mucking stalls and dishing out bran mash in the pouring rain?

* * *

To: Turtle Cumberbund (Turtle@CBFarms.com)
From: Emily Morris (eventer4life@ghostmail.com)
Re: With Regrets

Maybe my previous email came across as a little flip. Let me assure you that "funding falling through" is not code for "bought one too many custom frock coats this season and need to tighten the Hermes belt before the fall helmet fashions hit the tack shops". Unlike many of my peers, I have been begging, borrowing and sometimes stealing my way through the horse world my whole life, waiting for my big break. Three weeks ago, I was sure I'd won the equine lottery. But it turns out the ticket is counterfeit.

* * *

To: Emily Morris (eventer4life@ghostmail.com)
From: Turtle Cumberbund (Turtle@CBFarms.com)
Re: With Regrets

You're broke. So what? All that proves is that you're foolish enough to try and make a living in the horse world. Sounds exactly like the kind of person who need to beg, borrow and steal her way to England to come work for me.

To: Turtle Cumberbund (Turtle@CBFarms.com)
From: Emily Morris (eventer4life@ghostmail.com)
Re: With Regrets

I can't believe that I am in a situation where someone of your caliber is trying to persuade me to come to England and work for her. I'm touched. Really. But in addition to my insufficient funds, there are bigger concerns keeping me on my side of the pond.

* * *

To: Emily Morris (eventer4life@ghostmail.com)
From: Turtle Cumberbund (Turtle@CBFarms.com)
Re: With Regrets

Please elaborate.

* * *

To: Turtle Cumberbund (Turtle@CBFarms.com)
From: Emily Morris (eventer4life@ghostmail.com)
Re: With Regrets

I think I might suck as a rider.

* * *

To: Emily Morris (eventer4life@ghostmail.com)
From: Turtle Cumberbund (Turtle@CBFarms.com)
Re: With Regrets

Of course you suck. I haven't started teaching you yet. All the more reason to beg, borrow and steal your way to England so you can stop sucking post haste.

* * *

To: Turtle Cumberbund (Turtle@CBFarms.com)
From: Emily Morris (eventer4life@ghostmail.com)
Re: With Regrets

Well, there is still the issue of funding.

* * *

To: Emily Morris (eventer4life@ghostmail.com)
From: Turtle Cumberbund (Turtle@CBFarms.com)
Re: With Regrets

Figure it out. Get yourself to England and learn how to stop sucking. Simple, but not easy, right? Just like riding.

* * *

Simple, but not easy. I never thought of it that way. Sounds like the kind of self-contradictory statement Uncle Sam would make. So I turn to him for decoding. But all I get is, "That woman is right. Life is simple, but not easy. The solution to your problem, simple. Just sell that horse of yours for enough money to get to England. Getting around the fact that you don't legally have the right to sell him? Well, that's not going to be easy."

Uncle Sam doesn't need to know that I single-handedly wiped out all interest in Chocolates before Erica pulled the rug out from under the operation. As far as I'm concerned, the only "facts" that matter involve Margaret's ridiculous high school rivalry and how her reckless behavior put me in this difficult situation. Margaret claims to have some foolproof plan that will fix this whole mess. Do I dare trust her again?

Uncle Sam puts his arm around me, signaling that he's about to give me some fatherly advice, so I better hurry up and listen. He says, "Kid, you're right. That Margaret Fletcher is totally bonkers and any reasonable person wouldn't trust her as far as they could throw one of those Hermes belt buckles of hers. But here's the thing: it's the crazy people who have the courage to lead extraordinary lives. You're the dirt poor daughter of a single waitress and you want to ride horses in the Olympics. Sounds pretty extraordinary to me."

My first thought is: I could actually throw one of those Hermes belt buckles pretty far. So I don't think Uncle Sam has a firm grasp of how that analogy is supposed to work. But as much as I hate to admit it, the rest of what he said is spot-on. Margaret Fletcher is totally bonkers and no reasonable person would be stupid enough to put their fate in her perfectly-manicured hands. So if I want to think of myself as reasonable, I should say sayonara before Princess has a chance to entangle me in whatever crazy plan is brewing under that cubic zirconium tiara of hers.

But if I want to be the fearless eventer that I have always imagined myself to be, brave enough to tame the wildest beast and insane enough to boldly tackle cross-country, I'll need to be brave enough to hitch my cart onto Margaret Fletcher's horse.

So what's it going to be, Morris? I think to myself. *Are you in or are you out?*

* * *

As it turns out, Margaret's plan is just plain crazy. Convince the Boss to sell the best horse he's ever owned in exchange for a clear title on Chocolates?

Sure, Mr. Lewis would love to get his hands on a horse like Matty. But the Boss isn't going to hand that one over. He's been trying for years to find something that can finally put him on the map. I bet he thought he would never own a horse like Matty. And now that he does, I can't imagine that anyone could convince him to give that up. Not even Margaret Fletcher.

I try my darnedest to convince Margaret that her plan is ridiculous. But, surprise, surprise, she refuses to listen to reason. Take a deep breath, Emily. It's the crazy ones that have the courage to lead extraordinary lives, remember?

Margaret feels confident that she can trick Erica into demanding her Daddy buy Matty. "All YOU have to do is convince the Boss to take the deal on the condition that we get to keep Chocolates. Don't look at me like I'm asking you to do the impossible. You're a poor girl with a big dream. It's a compelling story. Just sell it."

I probably shouldn't be rolling my eyes right now. But I can't help myself. "Margaret, do you have any clue how important a horse like Matty is to a guy like the Boss? There is no way that he would ever let him go."

The cheery expression vanishes from Margaret's face as she reminds me that no one knows more than her how difficult it is to sell a nice horse. "But sometimes you don't have a choice because it's the only thing that will keep your family from drowning. So you kiss them on the nose, say "I love you" and let them go. And years later when you find out it was all because the man you used to admire has an uncontrollable urge to behave irresponsibly, you try not to hate him for destroying everything you loved."

I have a feeling that we're not talking about the Boss and Matty anymore. I give Margaret a moment to wipe the stray tear from the corner of her eye, and then I cautiously break the news that I just don't think this plan is going to work.

But Margaret isn't in the mood for my negativity. "Oh, Emily, it's time for you to start taking responsibility for your own life." Off my raised eyebrow, Margaret concedes that I can always be relied upon to do grunt work and act like a martyr about it. However, when it comes time to do the heavy lifting of making sure that I have the funds necessary to make my big dream happen, the responsibility has been falling squarely on her shoulders alone. Before I have a chance to open my mouth in protest, she reminds me, "I found Chocolates. I came up with the idea to flip him. And now that we find ourselves in what appears to be an impossible situation, I've come up with the brilliant plan on how to solve our problem. It's time for YOU to start fighting for yourself, Emily. I can't be your Spirit Guide forever!"

Spirit Guide?! Wow, this girl really has some ego. The problem with Margaret's plan isn't that I don't want to fight for myself. No, the problem is THE PLAN IS STUPID.

But Margaret refuses to listen to reason and accuses me of sounding like my Mother. Since when does Margaret Fletcher know anything about my Mother? Seriously. I demand to know.

"Uncle Sam and I talk about your mother all the time," Margaret casually says, like it's not big deal, "He says you're just like her, totally capable of amazing things, but too afraid to actually try."

I'm hurt, horrified and flabbergasted all at once.

"Emily," Margaret sighs, patting me on the shoulder in a patronizing manner, "Sam and I actually talk about all kinds of things. We're friends. I didn't really have any friends growing up, and finally taking the time to make some has been a positive change in my life. Aside from me and Sara, you don't seem to have many friends, either. So you might want to start working on that."

I'm still fuming with the knowledge of Uncle Sam and Margaret's character assassination and I'm ready to storm out of the room in a fit of anger. But then Margaret says, "Just a little hint. When a friend — and just so we're both on the same page here, I'm referring to ME — goes through something traumatic like finding out that her father is deadbeat gambler, you should check in and ask how she's doing."

Ninety-nine percent of what Margaret Fletcher has said in the past fifteen minutes is complete crap. But I have to admit that she's got a point with that last bit about me coming up short as a friend. Despite the unlikely situation, Margaret Fletcher and I have become friends.

I'm not sure what to do here. Do I offer a hug? Say something mean about her dad? Or lie and insist that this whole gambling thing is just a phase? I guess I really am pretty bad at this whole friend thing.

Sensing my discomfort, Margaret asks if I'm up for a drink. I nod my head and we call Sara.

I get the feeling I'm going to need a stiff one tonight.

CHAPTER 25
~ *Margaret trades in her crown* ~

Emily and Sara make it clear that I get ONE drink tonight. If I start slurring my words, it gets taken away from me. I order a Grand Marnier and make a toast to Mother. Here's to you! You may be a total lunatic, but at least you never led a secret double life that ended with the demise of our family fortune. Bottoms up!

Everyone takes a sip of their drink. But no one knows what to say.

Not one to enjoy getting woozy off the toxic fumes of a pity party, I break the silence, "It's fine, ladies. Everything is fine. Sure, it's kind of a bummer that just when I started to appreciate my father's yoga, hemp, Zen Daddy persona, I learn that he's actually a lowlife gambling narcissist with zero self-control." I down another gulp of Grand Marnier and continue, "I guess my father is not as strong of a person as I always imagined. Is it sad that I had to imagine WHO my dad is and I got it wrong?"

Nobody answers my question. They simply look at me with the concerned expressions usually reserved for someone about to go over the edge.

I polish off my glass and order another. Anyone feel like trying to stop me? "You know what, girls? Men suck. Across the board. Doesn't matter if he's your absentee father or your tease of a boss. I finally reached a point in my life where I was starting to feel like I had some clarity. I've got a job I like. I'm riding horses again. And I'm FINALLY coming to terms with the limits of my wardrobe. But now, without warning, everything is suddenly back in the crapper."

Yes, girls. Margaret Fletcher just used the word "crapper". I down my second Grand Marnier like it's a cup of refreshing marathon water and signal for another before Emily can stop me. "I have a confession to make. I made out with the Boss. Erica found out and that's why she's being such an ass. Emily, I screwed up your plans and I wouldn't blame you if you hated me."

Emily should be ripping my head off right about now. Instead, she slyly signals the bartender to speed up the arrival of my next Grand Marnier, hoping the extra lubrication will coax me into dishing like a tipsy teenager at a slumber party.

Something that sounds vaguely like, "I ammmthh not an adultererthh" stumbles out of my mouth. Two and a half drinks, and I'm already slurring my words. How can Mother possibly stand up after one of her "lunches?"

Sensing that I am rapidly losing my ability to participate in the conversation, Sara jumps in with a story about her own experience sleeping with a boss. The room is spinning and I'm having trouble focusing. But I'm able to digest the main thesis of her argument, which is that having an affair with one's boss is a BAD idea. At least if one has any desire to keep one's job.

Sara points out that I can probably ditch the whole scruffy Gallop Girl lifestyle anyway. I'm about to make big money selling Chocolates. I've got all the skills and connections to repeat the process as many times as I see fit. There's a whole living to be made buying failed racehorses and turning them around for profit.

I should be all over this, right? So why is my first instinct to resist? "I'm not selling Chocolatesthh. I screwed that up. Remember? Emilyth, you should be really pished. Why aren't you pished?"

I may be drunk. But I recognize the panicked look on Emily's face. We all know that she would rather stay home and blame her problems on ME than pack her bags and find out what SHE'S made of.

But instead of acknowledging her guilty conscience, Emily accuses me of berating her for being too understanding. "Margaret, listen to yourself. Twenty minutes ago, you were saying that I'm not a good friend. Now you're giving me a hard time because I'm not angry enough with you over one little screw up. Do you hear how ridiculous that sounds?"

Sara reminds Emily that *one little screw up* might just cost her an opportunity of a lifetime. "Just last week I had to listen to you complain about Margaret for forty five minutes —"

Wait. What?

"—because she refused to load hay nets on account of not wanting to risk getting orchard grass caught in her hairnet. You threatened to refuse to speak to her until she was ready to put Chocolates' nutritional needs above her own neurotic grooming habits. I'm pretty sure destroying your chances of going to England because of some silly crush is a much bigger offense."

I'll admit that my perception of the situation is clouded by one, two, three too many cocktails. But it appears that Emily's lower lip is trembling and, yep, I'm pretty sure I see pools of liquid forming in the corner of her eyes. Without further warning, she bursts into tears. "I've always thought of myself as such a brave person. What's wrong with me? Why am I so afraid?!"

Seeing Emily bare her soul for everyone to see is like a shot of adrenaline to my Grand Marnier-addled brain. I regain the lucidity I'd lost with too much old lady liqueur and tell Emily, "It's OK. You can be brave and terrified at the same time. That's what bravery is: being scared of something, but doing it anyway. It's hard, I know. But some of the most exhilarating moments of my life happened only moments after I was almost paralyzed by fear. It didn't matter that I was scared as long as I kept on moving."

The tears dry up and Emily looks at me as if she is truly seeing me for the first time. "Thank you, Margaret."

"You're welcome," I kindly say. I feel a warm glow spreading in my chest and I'm pretty sure it's not the Grand Marnier. My sea legs are slowly coming back and I'm ready to enjoy the rest of the evening with my girls.

But then, out of the blue, Emily slams her beer on the table and starts acting like she's all irritated with me again. "Margaret, how could you screw up my lifelong DREAM for a boy?"

I want to point out that sixty seconds ago, Emily's lifelong dream was to find a suitable excuse to stay home and blame her problems on everyone else. But as a friend, I am here to support her moment of personal growth, so I take the beating. "What were you thinking, anyway? He's your boss, MARGARET! Is having an affair with somebody else's boyfriend really worth throwing you job away for?"

Emily is making the situation sound pretty trashy. I inform her that HE kissed me. And yes, he WAS a taken man. But Erica has been taking things away from me for years and it was MY turn to have a little fun at her expense. OK. That didn't sound as classy as I thought it would. Emily gives me one of those disapproving looks that she usually reserves for when I've inadvertently made an inappropriate comment about someone's plastic helmet or brightly-colored rubber reins.

I am suddenly overwhelmed with the urge to clear my good name. I concede that kissing the Boss was a huge mistake. Not only did I put a chink in the armor of my own integrity, I jeopardized the partnership that I care for very much. Once again, I promise Emily that I will make things right. Chocolates will be ours to sell and I'm putting Emily on a plane to England if it's the last thing I do!

Just when I think Emily and I are turning a positive corner in this conversation, she reminds me that she thinks my plan is stupid. I'm still too flustered from allowing myself to sound like a floozy to argue effectively. Deep in my heart, I know she's wrong. My plan is going to work and we are going to sell Chocolates for more money than Little Orphan Emily has ever seen in her entire life. And I'm going to embark on a new career, selling Hunters for big profit. Screw this scruffy Gallop Girl life. Margaret Fletcher is back and the Hunter Princesses of the world better watch out!

I'm feeling pretty good about the whole situation when I am suddenly struck with a queasy sensation and it's not the Grand Marnier. Just when I feel like I am about to throw up, I scream, "I LOVE BEING A GALLOP GIRL! AND I WON'T LET ANYONE TAKE THAT AWAY FROM ME."

Sara and Emily are confused by my outburst. But for me, nothing has ever been more obvious. I am a Gallop Girl. Not because I have to be, but because it is who I am. I can't imagine a life that doesn't include waking up before dawn to gallop hard and fast until every muscle in my body is sore with satisfaction. Having an affair with the Boss would have been the most stupid thing I could have possibly done. Sure, I'm attracted to him. But I love this life. And I'm not willing give that up so I can be some guy's girlfriend.

I could return to the Hunter world fulltime. I still love the challenge of trying to nail eight perfect fences. But now that I know the thrill of running fast, free, and completely oblivious to the condition of my quaff, I don't think I could ever go back. Even if it means that I never get to ride in a proper pair of breeches again.

* * *

Despite Emily's negativity, I have full confidence in my plan to get Chocolates back. Time to execute.

Word on the street is Erica Lewis gets fitted for a new pair of custom field boots every Tuesday to accommodate any micro changes in her weight. So I spend most of my Tuesday morning at Mary's trying on every pair of breeches she has in stock. Eventually, Erica walks in the front door, announcing her arrival by loudly proclaiming to no one in particular, "You know what they say: everyone needs at least three pairs of custom boots. A pair of Italian boots, a pair of German boots and a pair of American boots to help remind one just how lucky one is to be able to afford the Italian and German boots. MARY! GET THE MEASURING TA…"

Erica pauses in her tracks when she sees me standing in the middle of the store, dressed in a pair of fancy German breeches with aromatic massage oils woven into the fabric around the buttocks and thighs. She looks me up and down with a smirk on her face. I can't tell if her joy is from the knowledge that I can't afford the breeches, or the fact that the massage oils meant to soothe sore muscles have instead formed a sticky film around my most intimate of areas. She chuckles to herself, puts on a fake smile and says, "Hey, Margaret, that's your old saying. Too bad that doesn't apply to you anymore. You probably only have ONE pair of AMERICAN boots now! And I bet they're OFF THE RACK!"

I have no idea what Erica is talking about. I would NEVER say something so ridiculous. But then she reminds me that junior year at Nationals the zippers broke on my good old Konigs. My Tuccis were already in the shop, so I had no choice but to wear my Vogals. Bunny mentioned that she thought they looked a little coarse and I said, "Everyone needs at least three pairs of custom boots" and all the obnoxious crap that came after that.

I am completely disgusted with myself. That doesn't stop Erica from driving the knife in deeper, "It must be difficult to be reminded of the good old days, huh? I bet you blocked all those memories out, like some kind of trauma victim. Poor thing, you probably don't remember much about what it's like to be a part of top sport. You don't even have that crappy excuse of a hunter anymore. Sorry about that. WAIT, NO, I'M NOT!"

Oh, you can wipe that smug look off your face, Erica. I've got you right where I want you and you're too self-involved to even realize it. I lean in and say, "I wouldn't say that's one hundred percent true, Erica. I've been galloping a horse that is sure to be the next Kentucky Derby winner. I would say that's top sport. Wouldn't you?"

Erica lights up with predictable glee and starts blabbing about how she OWNS me now. One call to her father and I'll never sit on that horse again!

She thinks she's got me sweating in my splotchy breeches. Well, I've got news for you, Lewis. That's not sweat. That's German engineering!

I take a moment to savor the taste of revenge before flashing my own evil grin, "Erica, your daddy doesn't own this horse. Your EX-BOYFRIEND does. And I'm pretty sure, he's happy to let me gallop that baby as LLLLOOOONG as I want."

I know I vowed to never again engage in sexual innuendo. It's not very classy. But watching Erica's face scrunch up into a little prune of rage is worth temporarily debasing myself. I wait for one of her cackling comebacks. But nothing is coming. In fact, Erica is pulsing so hard with anger, Mary can't get a reliable measurement on her right calf.

I'm pretty sure my job here is done. I disappear into the dressing room to change out of these sticky breeches and wait three, two, one...

On cue, the entire tack shop shakes with the eruption of Erica's temper, "Margaret Fletcher, you

THINK you have the upper hand here. But I have the UPPER HAND. I've always had THE UPPER HAND!"

Three hours later, word of Mr. Lewis's obscene offer to buy Matty is spreading around Winning Edge.

Erica, you are so predictable that manipulating you is hardly any fun anymore. To be honest, it was almost boring.

CHAPTER 26
~ *Emily Meets her Spirit Guide* ~

Margaret is proud of herself for playing Erica like a cheap violin. I'm impressed, but I don't let on. The last thing that girl needs is a bigger head. She already sent the Boss a sternly-worded email demanding that he promise to ONLY sell Matty on the condition that Chocolates is part of the deal.

We both know that Margaret and her feminine charms are better equipped to convince the Boss of anything right now. But she insists that her days of using sex as a weapon are over. So it's up to me to take charge of my own destiny and persuade the Boss to let go of the most valuable thing he has ever owned.

The workday at Winning Edge is over and everyone's gone home, but the Boss's truck is still in the driveway. I find him in Matty's stall, stroking the colt's neck with a faraway look on his face. It feels like I am intruding on a private moment. I want to tiptoe away before the Boss sees me.

Before I can move a muscle, he looks up at me and says, "I'm not selling him, Emily. I'm sorry. I know this is your big shot and I'm partly to blame for screwing it up. But I just can't sell him."

I can't say that I'm surprised. The Boss is just as hungry to prove himself in his sport as I am in mine. In the equestrian world, it doesn't matter how talented you think you are if you don't have a good horse to help you show everyone else. I can't fault the Boss for wanting to hold onto Matty with every appendage on his body.

I didn't come to this fight empty-handed. I've got a pretty strong argument in favor of selling Matty up my sleeve. But I would be a hypocrite if I tried to convince the Boss to give up on his dream. So I tell him that I understand. There is nothing money can buy that's better than a good horse. I can almost hear Margaret screaming in my ear right now, *"Emily, I simply CANNOT help you if you refuse to help yourself!"* However, I can't bring myself to try to convince the Boss to give up his one opportunity to grab the brass ring. I'll get my chance one day and it won't be at the expense of someone else's.

The Boss is clearly surprised by my behavior. He reminds me of everything I have at stake here.

I let him know I appreciate his concern, but "I can't be responsible for you making the biggest mistake of your life. This could be it, Boss. This could be your chance to make a real name for yourself in this business. You can't give that up just because it's a little risky."

He flinches at the word "risky". I'm not sure why. The Boss isn't new to this game. I can't imagine he hasn't thought of all the money he's going to have to lay down on the table to try to get this horse to The Derby. Last I checked, the entry fee is two hundred thousand dollars. That has to be keeping the Boss up at night. Seriously. How is a guy like him going come up with two hundred thousand dollars? The only thing he has of any real value is that horse. And he can't sell him AND run him in The Derby at the same time. What a mess. I'm glad it's not my problem.

The Boss gives me a look that suggests he forgot about that entry fee and all the other big dollar entry fees he'll need to pay in order to get Matty qualified for The Derby. I'm sensing that he's starting to panic. I can't say I blame him. It's really an impossible situation. But now that I'm learning how to believe in myself in the face of certain failure, I feel the need to share my newfound courageous outlook on life.

"Sure, it's a gamble, Boss. But that's what this business is all about. Right?"

I thought that was harmless encouragement. But he looks even more upset than when I said the word "risky". His brow is sweating and his eyes are getting a little buggy. I'm definitely not doing a very good job of teaching him how to have a courageous outlook on life. In all fairness, this is all new to me, too. All right, Emily, focus! Believe in your ability to turn this thing around.

"Don't worry, Boss. I'm not saying that you're a gambler like Margaret's dad or anything. I'm just pointing out that if you want to win big, you've got to be comfortable putting all your cards on the table. It's not that I think you're a heartbeat away from throwing it all away like Mr. Fletcher. It's just that one has to be prepared to take chances in life. Sometimes, you just have to dive into the deep end — even when you're not entirely sure that you can swim."

Wow. I can't believe a speech like that just flowed effortlessly out of me, Emily Morris, the girl always looking for an excuse to play it safe. I take a moment to reflect on how much I've grown in the past few months. It feels good to be such a strong confident woman.

On the other hand, the Boss looks like he couldn't find the confidence to ride a tricycle, much less train a world champion racehorse. He wipes his sweaty brow, mumbling to himself that he knows what he's doing. But the tone in his voice sounds more like *Crap, I'm in over my head and I'm probably going to end up living under a bridge*. I know exactly how he feels right now. He's caught in the churning riptide of self-doubt, and I need to dive into those familiar waters and save him before he drowns.

I put on my best "stiff upper lip" face and gently tell him, "I know what it's like to believe that you have what it takes to be competitive even when you don't have that ONE good horse to prove it. I KNOW you can do this. That whole sink-or-swim thing is just about the financials and you'll totally figure those out. I can't tell you how many times I thought to myself, "What is the daughter of a single waitress doing trying to make it in the horse business? It's the Sport of Kings."

The Boss gives me the saddest puppy dog face and asks me to assure him that despite my hardships, I've always figured it out.

I put my hand on his shoulder and remind him that if we had sold Chocolates, I would have finally figured how to get the world-class training I can't otherwise afford. And that would have been a real fairytale ending to my Cinderella story. I was just a photo finish away from my impossible dream coming true. So if the poor daughter of a single waitress can almost come up with the cash to move to England and train with one of the top riders in the world, the Boss can overcome the seemingly-insurmountable obstacle of finding a two hundred thousand dollar entry fee and winning the Kentucky Derby.

Even though I believe with all my newly-courageous heart that the Boss can make this happen, it sounds pretty ridiculous coming out of my mouth. Looking at his pale face, I'm beginning to think I might have a secret superpower… the ability to implant self-doubt in anyone or anything that comes near me.

And then he says, "Almost accomplishing something is the same as failing, Emily. If you really want to go to England, you need to actually try to convince me to sell Matty."

What? Clearly, the Boss doesn't realize that I'm a totally different person now. Sure, the old Emily would have encouraged him to hang onto Matty in some sick expression of self-sabotage. But Margaret really set me straight last night. I WANT to go to England now. It's not like before, when I said I wanted to go but secretly did everything in my power to prevent it from actually happening. Sure, all that stuff about helping the Boss grab his personal brass ring doesn't really hold up to scrutiny. Yes, I realize that there is no way he could possibly afford to campaign Matty all the way to the Kentucky Derby on his own dime. I'm not blind to the fact that the money he would make selling Matty would go a long way towards building his business. Obviously, the ONLY sane thing to do here is to sell the horse and give me back Chocolates so I can make my dreams come true! I'm only trying to convince the Boss to do otherwise because...

I'm doing it again, aren't I? At least Margaret wasn't around to witness my relapse and there is still time to clean up this catastrophe before word gets back to Her Highness. Before I have a chance, the Boss slumps off into his office and locks the door.

I stand frozen in indecision. I know I did something really bad here. But I have absolutely no idea how to make it right. I should probably do something. But what if what I do only makes things worse? Maybe not doing anything and letting the chips fall where they may is the best course of action. Where is Margaret when I need her? It figures that she wouldn't be here at the exact moment when I need her guidance the most.

And then it hits me like a ton of golden Hermes bricks: Margaret Fletcher IS my Spirit Guide! I may think she is nothing more than a silly little once-upon-a-time rich girl with no practical hands-on experience. But for the past two months, she has been the only person making anything happen in my sad little life. I didn't want to believe it when she accused me of refusing to take responsibility for my life. But the irrefutable evidence is staring me in the face right now.

Still in shock from the realization that self-sabotage is only my second most-debilitating character flaw, I don't move a muscle when the Boss emerges from his office and heads in the direction of the Winning Edge parking lot. I don't need Margaret to tell me that I need to do something right now. Emily, you need to DO something. Right now!

Like a rocket blasting into space, I spring into action, chasing the Boss all the way to the parking lot. I'm waving my arms wildly and screaming at the top of my lungs, "Boss, wait! Stop! Don't get in that car!" My behavior may be a little over-the-top. But I don't care. I'm drunk with the power of positive action and I can't wait to see what happens next.

I take a moment to catch my breath, look the Boss square in the face and say, "Uncle Sam always told me success in horse sports is all about the long game. For those of us not blessed with money, it will look impossible for most of our career. But if we keep at it, opportunities will present themselves. This offer on Matty is your opportunity. Selling Chocolates and going to England is mine. So don't screw it up for both of us."

I don't think I've ever been so persuasive in my entire life. I have no idea if the Boss is moved by my argument. But it almost doesn't matter. I just grabbed life by the horns for the first time in twenty-one years. No matter what happens next, I am never letting go.

The Boss looks like he has no idea how to handle the strange new creature standing before him. He furrows his brow, trying to formulate a rebuttal. But he can't. He knows I'm right.

He's selling Matty and I'm going to England.

I have a feeling today might be the first day of a whole new life for Emily Morris.

CHAPTER 27
~ Margaret's plan comes full circle ~

Emily convinced the Boss to sell Matty all on her own. I'm shocked. I was all set to run damage control on this one. But she wrapped it up in a neat little bow without any help from me. I think she's finally learning. And like a young colt trying to feel his way around the start gate for the first time, Emily appears to be on the verge of finding the confidence to break away all on her own. I can't help but take a little pride in her transformation myself.

Of course, Emily did leave one last mess for me to clean up. Oh, I heard all about her misguided attempt to defend my riding abilities to all the A-Circuit trainers interested in Chocolates. What was she thinking? No Hunter Princess wants a horse that is still rough around the edges. A Hunter Princess is looking for a mount whose temperament will aid in her lifelong pursuit of effortless elegance. Not some racetrack reject that requires a damn good rider to look good. So by telling every Hunter trainer in a thirty-mile radius of The New London Classic that Chocolates isn't the packer that Margaret Fletcher makes him appear to be, Emily rendered him pretty much worthless.

Fortunately, Margaret Fletcher has a brilliant plan up her sleeve, as usual. Chocolates may still be too much of a challenge for the average Hunter Princess, but I know one pony collector who isn't afraid of a difficult ride.

Remember Dr. Allison Swanson? Mother's own personal white whale? Reputed to love animals far more than she could ever love a human, Dr. Swanson has been purchasing hunters for ambitious riders to show ever since she hung up her spurs in 1997. And if you want to ride for the good doctor, you better not be afraid of a challenge. I once overheard her tell Geoff Maurice that she likes to buy the kind of horses that demand to be ridden with skill and tact.

"Any kid that's going to get a free ride on my dime better be prepared to work hard if she doesn't want to hit the dust."

Well, Dr. Swanson, I think I have just the horse to add to your collection.

* * *

Mother has never been afraid of a challenge. I remember when the I.R.S repossessed her prized collection of fur coats. Most people would have accepted their fate and stocked up on fleece pullovers.

But Mother got herself a hunting license, a sewing machine and never looked back. By the time the next winter rolled around, that woman had a full closet of politically incorrect outerwear for every occasion.

So I'm a bit taken aback when Mother balks at my sincere request to invite Dr. Swanson to lunch. "Margaret, honey, that is just not going to happen. I don't think I could face her again after that whole golf cart incident. She told me that the only way she would ever participate in a foxhunt with a silly woman like me was if I dressed up in a red fur suit and let her chase me around on horseback! Besides, everyone knows that unless you're a horse or a destitute African child in need of a mosquito net, you have NO hope getting Her Highness's attention."

Destitute African child in need of a mosquito net? I'm intrigued. According to Mother, everyone knows that if you want to spend time with Dr. Allison Swanson, fill a suitcase up with mosquito nets and prepare to spend a miserable summer distributing them all over Africa with her charity group. I had no idea that Dr. Swanson had another passion besides horses.

Mother rolls her eyes at the sound of the word "passion". "Oh, Margaret, please. Fine wine is a passion. Shoes are a passion! Poor kids who can't get it together to apply a decent insect repellant sound like a problem to me."

"Look at me, Margaret. I'M destitute. But has Dr. Swanson bothered to put together a fundraiser to help me? NO! I bet she doesn't even realize I've left the social scene. She probably thinks I'm still rich and happy. She's probably pissed off, wondering why it's been so long since I've written her a check."

Mother continues to host an exclusive pity party for one while I put the finishing touches on the genius plan percolating in my head. "Mother, do you think Dr. Swanson would return your call if you offered to donate half the Fletcher family fortune to whatever charity she saw fit?"

Precious gin flies out of Mother's nostrils as she snorts dismissively at the suggestion. I concede that the Fletcher family no longer has half of a fortune to donate. But as Mother already pointed out, Dr. Swanson is too busy worrying about the flea-bitten to notice that we've gone broke.

"All you have to do is call her up," I push, "Tell her you want to talk about giving her half of everything you have over lunch. What have you got to lose besides a couple of possum fur coats?"

The suggestion immediately stops Mother in her tracks. As her cheeks regain the soft glow of normal human flesh, I can see her mentally weighing the pros and cons of my proposal.

"I promised myself years ago that I would never let Dr. Allison Swanson humiliate me again," she muses, "But I've also spent most of my adult life desperate to have lunch with the elusive Dr. Swanson. It's a dream I gave up long ago. Could it be possible that it is now, when I am at my most destitute, that I finally have the right harpoon?"

She's in. Signed, sealed, delivered. And if my calculations are correct, Emily will soon have enough money to get to England.

Let's just hope I don't regret weaponizing the one woman in town who has already proven herself dangerous around heavy machinery.

* * *

Less than twenty-four hours after Mother leaves a message with Dr. Swanson's social secretary, the Fletcher girls receive an invitation to lunch at the good Doctor's home. Panic-stricken at the thought of not being dressed properly for the lunch of lifetime, Mother pours through her outdated, cannibalized wardrobe, desperate for an outfit worthy of Dr. Allison Swanson. When she comes up empty, she insists on wearing my very best breeches, boots and hunt coat.

"Mother, you don't ride. Even if you did, why would you show up to a lunch dressed in your best breeches?"

With desperation in her voice, Mother reminds me that this lunch could be her LAST chance to return to society. Dr. Allison Swanson isn't like every other socialite. She CARES about things. "Margaret, honey, I need to let her know that I care about the same things that she cares about and I am NOT wearing some kind of fishnet headdress!"

Who am I to argue with crazy? So I knock the dirt off my magic crystal breeches and run a lint brush over that elastic wool torture device the Germans call a hunt coat.

Mother insists we park my Honda just outside Dr. Swanson's estate and take the long walk down the endless gravel driveway. My heart skips a beat as we pass the pristine barn, lush pastures and the regal horseflesh contained within them. I haven't been in the presence of such pricey perfection in a long time. It feels good.

I think all this luxury is having a similar effect on Mother. "Oh, Margaret, I can't tell you how much I miss being around rich people and all their nice things. Let's pretend that this is our house and we're just out for a little afternoon stroll."

So I take her hand in mine, improve my posture and point my finger in the direction of one of Dr. Swanson's perfect pastures. "We really should talk to the groundskeeper about reseeding in the spring. I want to make sure everything is positively green when our imports from Germany get out of quarantine."

Mother's face displays an expression of sheer bliss at the sound of the words "groundskeeper". I haven't seen her look so relaxed and happy in a long time.

Dropping to a lower social class has been a difficult transition for Mother. There have been times when I have found her inability to accept the new limits of her purchasing power disturbing. Times like this. When she is inexplicably dressed up in breeches and an elastic hunt coat. But now that I know the truth, the whole truth and nothing but the truth about

Daddy's little problem, I'm amazed she hasn't gone completely off the rails.

"Do you ever think about leaving Daddy now that you know what kind of man he is?"

She doesn't skip a beat before answering my controversial question. "Margaret, I have always known exactly who I married. He is a sensitive man who is prone to self-absorption and irresponsible impulses. He's not strong like you. He never was, even when he wore a suit to work every day. Honestly, I have no idea where you got that will of yours. But I've always done my best to encourage that quality in you. I think that's why you're the only member of this family who hasn't fallen apart."

A small lump forms in my throat and tears creep into the corners of my eyes. I don't think I've ever given my Mother enough credit for what a good parent she has been all these years. Sure, she's ridiculous and humiliating to be around. But she has always been there straightening my collar and making sure every strand is tucked into my hairnet. I can't help myself. I give my mother the second hug in our recorded history.

"Careful, dear. I don't need you kicking up dust and making my breeches dirty."

* * *

Moments later, we arrive at our destination. Dr. Swanson answers the door dressed casually in khakis and a light cotton shirt. Mother's costume looks even more ridiculous in comparison and the doctor makes no attempt to hide her disgust.

"Oh, Lester," Dr. Swanson says to the room, "Bring me a scotch on the rocks. I have a feeling this is going to be a long afternoon. Anything for you, ladies?"

Thankfully, Mother is too starstruck to place a cocktail order. I can see the sweat seeping out of her elastic coated armpits. By the time we finish winding through the complex labyrinth of Dr. Swanson's richly-appointed home and make our way out to the garden, Mother is hyperventilating from the stress of feeling so much social pressure while simultaneously wearing such a confining outfit.

Dr. Swanson gestures for us to sit down. However, I'm not sure Mother actually can. So the three of us stand awkwardly while she tries to discretely fan her décolletage with the back of her hand.

Dr. Swanson turns her attention to me and says, "You know, Margaret, I have been following your riding career for some time. You beat more than a few of my ponies in your heyday. I was always very impressed by your trainer's ability to find you nice horses to ride. But I never thought that much of you as a rider, I'll be honest. When your father lost all his money, I thought for sure a girl like you would just lie down and die. So I nearly spit my thirty year old Glenfiddich all over my eighteenth century Afghan rug when I heard that you are galloping the Lewis thoroughbreds. Good for you."

Mother's rigid posture softens. The jig is up. We are flat broke and her most coveted social connection knows. For the first time since this lunch of a lifetime started, Mother opens her mouth. "I'll have a gin and tonic, thank you."

Dr. Swanson chuckles to herself and says, "I suppose I could use a little afternoon entertainment. Lester! Bring this woman a gin and tonic. Oh, and tell Juan to hide the keys to the Kubota. We wouldn't want you racing around the grounds pretending you're a fox, now would we, dear?"

With that, Mother releases a hearty guffaw worthy of her blue collar upbringing and begins the agonizing process of trying to remove her persistent jacket. "I don't know why I ever bothered with you, Allison. No matter how hard I tried to fit in, you just treat me like a clown!"

Mother struggles out of the German elastic nightmare until all that is left of her ensemble is a dusty pair of breeches and a sweat-soaked silk blouse. When Lester arrives with the gin and tonic, Mother collapses into her chair like a woman with no intention of leaving anytime soon and says, "Go on, Margaret, sell that horse of yours. Let's see if you can get the old hag to take a bite." And with that, Mother welcomes her cocktail like a long lost relative.

On the other hand, Dr. Swanson is amused by the situation. "You have a horse to sell, Margaret? How lovely. I'm assuming that we're talking about the skinny little thoroughbred I saw you parading around The New London Classic."

I'll admit to feeling a little hot around the collar in this moment. But if there is one thing that showing unpredictable flight animals in front of uptight judges will teach a girl, it's poise under pressure.

"Dr. Swanson," I begin, "Chocolates may be a little rough around the edges. But he is the best damn horse I've ever sat on. I don't say that because I think I could win a bunch of blue ribbons on him. I say that because in the past six weeks, he's taught me more than any of the overpriced warmbloods I rode back in the old days ever did. The old days when the Fletchers were the type of people you might have use for."

Dr. Swanson takes a sip of her scotch before gracing me with her iciest expression, "That horse of yours is all right. But I wouldn't say he's fantastic. Everyone says thoroughbreds are making a comeback in the Hunters. But I don't see that happening."

Sorry, Emily. I tried. For once, my special brand of Margaret Fletcher charm has fallen flat. I should have seen it coming. I was once a girl who could sell ice to a frozen Eskimo. But like Chocolates, Margaret Fletcher is no longer fashionable in this parts.

Just as I'm plotting exactly when and how to slink out of the estate in shame, Dr. Swanson puts her hand on my shoulder and draws me closer, "You, Margaret Fletcher, on the other hand, are fantastic."

A smile spreads across Mother's lips and I can see her take pride in the compliment. "That's right, Doctor. I may be a nut. But my daughter is fantastic!"

Two more gulps of scotch and Dr. Swanson is sounding more and more like family. I'm beginning to think that the flask of whiskey hidden in the breast pocket of her hunting jacket might have more to do with her love of chasing foxes than the hounds or the horses or anything else for that matter.

"Margaret, I've always had money and I've always had horses. I've been incredibly lucky. I enjoy spreading that luck to young women who haven't been as fortunate as I have. Deserving young women. Not spoiled little brats who can't be bothered to actually work for what they have."

Mother nods her head in agreement, as if she shares the same aversion to spoiled brats, "I'm sick of spoiled brats. They're always giving you a hard time when you commit some kind of social faux pas and things get messy."

There's no hiding the truth: Mother is drunk. Fortunately, Dr. Swanson isn't as steady on her feet as one of the medical profession should be at twelve o'clock in the afternoon, either. "Oh, darling," she says to Mother, "I've never taken you for someone who gives a rat's ass what anyone thinks of her. It's what I've always like about you. I just give you a hard time because how else am I going to entertain myself at those crappy luncheons?"

I don't think I've seen Mother beam so proudly since the year The New York Times featured one of her possum fur coats in the Style section. As Dr. Swanson and Mother share a laugh at the expense of every socialite on the Eastern seaboard, I feel my chances of selling Chocolates slipping away.

Twenty minutes later, I'm still dreading having to carry Mother on that long walk back to the car when

Dr. Swanson suddenly says, "Margaret, I think I will buy that horse of yours. Does forty grand sound good? What am I saying? Of course it sounds good. You're broke! I'm pretty sure I won't be able to find someone who can ride him, either. He looks pretty feral. So plan on showing him for me this winter."

Before I have a chance to answer, Dr. Swanson returns to her gossiping with Mother, leaving me alone with my thoughts. Showing in Florida with the likes of Dr. Swanson would put me right back where I was just before Daddy bet the farm away. And I can't think of a horse I would rather return to that lifestyle with more than Chocolates.

But signing up for this deal would mean giving up my new Gallop Girl lifestyle. And I AM a Gallop Girl, remember? Not being a Gallop Girl would mean that I'd give up wearing through at least one pair of jeans in a week and waking up a five AM to teach a young colt just how fast he can go.

"Dr. Swanson, I can't believe I'm saying this. But I don't think I can accept your generous offer. For the longest time, I didn't think I could ever be complete again until I found a way to get back on the show circuit. But I think I've found something I love even more. I'm a Gallop Girl now. It's my identity and I'm just not ready to give that up."

Mother looks me with a mouth full of sandwich wide open in shock. But Dr. Swanson just smiles knowingly and with a loving expression, she says, "Margaret, darling, don't make the mistake of reducing yourself to some two word catchphrase. You can gallop horses and show Hunters. You'll still be Margaret Fletcher regardless of how you choose to wear your hair. They have tracks in Florida. I'm sure someone will let you race around one of them for the winter."

I don't know what to say. Mother steps in for me. "We're wintering in Florida! I can hardly wait to break out my bikinis!" Her enthusiasm is surprisingly infectious. I tell Dr. Swanson to make room for my tack trunk on her trailer.

It's all settled. Margaret Fletcher's transformation is complete. I'm not exactly sure what I've become. No Hunter Princess worth her salt would be caught dead taping maxi pads to her shins to prevent chafing. And I have never met a Gallop Girl willing to coordinate her jacket with the color of her horse's coat.

But like Dr. Swanson said, I am more than just some snappy catchphrase. Who knows what rules now apply to my wardrobe now? More importantly, who cares?

I making up my own rules as I go along.

* * *

I feel good about the major life choices I've made the past twenty four hours. But that doesn't mean I'll take pleasure in giving notice to the Boss. Sure, things got a little weird at the end. But he's been an excellent mentor and I will forever appreciate the patience with which he introduced me to my new trade.

I arrive at Winning Edge Monday morning with a resignation letter in my hand and heavy heart in my chest. I gallop ten horses for the Boss, giving each animal one hundred and ten percent. At the end of the day, as I officially hand the Boss my resignation, part of me hopes that he will refuse to accept.

The Boss gives my letter a quick glance and says, "If this is because of my inappropriate behavior the other morning, I can promise you that it will never happen again."

I assure him that it's not and I tell him all about the amazing opportunity that just fell into my lap. The Boss gives me a big congratulatory hug and doesn't let go. I've never been comfortable with being hugged for too long. I tactfully wiggle out of the Boss's embrace and finish the gesture with a hearty pat on the back. He looks surprised by my rebuff and honestly, so am I. Erica is out of the picture. The Boss is no longer my boss. So what's stopping me from dragging him into an empty stall and having my way with him? Come on, Fletcher, you're finally getting what you want. So go ahead and grab him.

"You know, Princess, I've been thinking of making a move myself. Maybe it's time to start my own business, now that I've got all this money burning a hole in my pocket. I hear they have a lot of nice thoroughbreds in Florida."

Staying at Winning Edge just to be around the Boss feels like the kind of compromise my newly-re-imagined self would never make. But I don't see anything wrong with encouraging the Boss to follow me South for the winter. I could gallop his thoroughbreds in the morning and he could polish my boots in the afternoon. Sounds perfect, right? Then why do I suddenly feel more suffocated than I did the last time I put on the awful German straightjacket?

I look at the Boss's handsome angular face and know that I'm still attracted to him. What's the problem, Fletcher? Is it because Daddy called him a gambler? Or am I really that offended by the thought of sampling Erica's sloppy seconds?

I can't put a finger on exactly what gives me pause. All I know is my life has changed a lot in the past few months and I'm not sure that I should throw a new relationship into the mix.

"You know, Boss, I would love to gallop for you if you end up in Florida. Just make sure you fly South for the right reasons." Off the Boss's quizzical look, I remind him that Wellington, Florida has the highest concentration of Hunter Princesses on the entire Eastern seaboard. "Are you sure your libido can handle it?"

My heart skips a beat as he cracks a knowing smile and says, "OK Princess, I'll try to control myself. But that doesn't mean I won't try to convince you to go for a ride on the beach late some night."

I suddenly feel an unexpected tingle. And despite all my reservations, I know in my heart that this story isn't over yet.

CHAPTER 28
~ *Emily is on*
her way ~

Margaret Fletcher shows up at my front door with a check in her hands and a big Mylar balloon that reads: "You're going to England!"

That's right. I'm going to England.

I booked my ticket five minutes after Margaret told me about Dr. Swanson's offer. Turtle has a bed waiting for me in her working student quarters and long list of chores for me to tackle the moment I get off the plane. By this time next week, poor little Emily Morris is going to start receiving the best riding instruction that her money could never afford to buy. And I have one person to thank: Margaret Fletcher.

I look down at the check in my hand and realize… it's made out for forty thousand dollars. Margaret just shrugs, "I got more out of this deal than I could ever imagine. So take the money to England and find out how the other half lives."

Tears immediately well up in my eyes and I wrap my arms around her in a good old-fashioned bear hug. I don't know what to say. I've never been so grateful to a single person all at once.

Margaret is taken aback by my sudden display of affection. She wiggles out of my embrace and says, "Emily, forty thousand dollars might seem like a lot of money to someone like you, but it's really not. So don't do anything crazy like blowing it all at once on something silly." Like a German elastic hunt coat?

Of course, I don't actually say that out loud. I wouldn't even be going to England if it weren't for Margaret Fletcher. And it's not just because of the money. If that puffed-up Princess with her custom hairnet and tack oiling addiction hadn't been around to show me what real courage looks like, I'm not sure I'd have ever summoned the guts to finally display some myself.

It's funny how life works out. I always thought courage was about jumping high and galloping fast. But it's not the willingness to do things that might break your bones that separates the strong from the weak. It's about not being afraid to make mistakes in front of a crowd. And it's those who try — even when they know that they might come up short — who have the real guts.

I look at the woman standing before me in a salmon-pink and lime-green nightmare of a dress. She doesn't look like the same girl who showed up at Winning Edge Farms a few months ago and punched me for touching her hairnet. Sure, she still dresses like she's late for lunch at the county club. But beneath all that sherbet-flavored linen is a body strong enough to gallop the toughest horse in the barn.

Margaret takes a long look at the trailer where her amazing transformation began and says, "I change my mind. I want my share of the sale. But I want to use it to buy this trailer of yours and that awful truck you use to haul it around. I'll be traveling the circuit with Dr. Swanson and I'll need a place to live."

Of course my, first instinct is to point out that Margaret has never driven a truck and trailer before. Does she have any idea how to back it into a tight spot? Or even hook it up?

But then I remember who I'm dealing with.

So I hand her the keys, knowing that it's in very good hands.

ABOUT THE AUTHOR

Genevieve Dutil learned to ride as an adult and has been picking up the pieces of her shattered ego ever since. Horses have made her laugh, cry, drain her bank account and question her priorities. Like the characters in her book, she would be lost without them.
<u>Margaret Fletcher: Gallop Girl</u> is her first novel.